P9-EGM-718

#6

SEEKERS

SPIRITS IN THE STARS

SEEKERS

Book One: The Quest Begins
Book Two: Great Bear Lake
Book Three: Smoke Mountain
Book Four: The Last Wilderness
Book Five: Fire in the Sky

MANGA

Toklo's Story
Kallik's Adventure

Also by Erin Hunter

WARRIORS

Book One: Into the Wild
Book Two: Fire and Ice
Book Three: Forest of Secrets
Book Four: Rising Storm
Book Five: A Dangerous Path
Book Six: The Darkest Hour

THE NEW PROPHECY

Book One: Midnight
Book Two: Moonrise
Book Three: Dawn
Book Four: Starlight
Book Five: Twilight
Book Six: Sunset

POWER OF THREE
Book One: The Sight

Book Two: Dark River

Book Three: Outcast

Book Four: Eclipse

Book Five: Long Shadows

Book Six: Sunrise

OMEN OF THE STARS
Book One: The Fourth Apprentice

Book Two: Fading Echoes

Book Three: Night Whispers

EXPLORE THE WARRIORS WORLD

Warriors Super Edition: Firestar's Quest

Warriors Super Edition: Bluestar's Prophecy

Warriors Super Edition: SkyClan's Destiny

Warriors Field Guide: Secrets of the Clans

Warriors: Cats of the Clans

Warriors: Code of the Clans

Warriors: Battles of the Clans

MANGA
The Lost Warrior

Warrior's Refuge

Warrior's Return

The Rise of Scourge

Tigerstar and Sasha #1: Into the Woods

Tigerstar and Sasha #2: Escape from the Forest

Tigerstar and Sasha #3: Return to the Clans

Ravenpaw's Path #1: Shattered Peace

Ravenpaw's Path #2: A Clan in Need

Ravenpaw's Path #3: The Heart of a Warrior

SPIRITS IN THE STARS

ERIN
HUNTER

HARPER

AN IMPRINT OF HARPERCOLLINSPUBLISHERS

Spirits in the Stars

Copyright © 2011 by Working Partners Limited

Series created by Working Partners Limited

Library of Congress Cataloging-in-Publication Data

Hunter, Erin.

   Spirits in the stars/Erin Hunter.—1st ed.

     p.   cm.—(Seekers;[6])

   Summary: At the edge of the Endless Ice, the four bears Ujurak,
Toklo, Lusa, and Kallik reach Star Island, where a large group of bears
is in trouble but believes Lusa is destined to help bring back the favor of
the spirits.

   ISBN 978-0-06-087140-6 (trade bdg.)

   ISBN 978-0-06-087141-3 (lib. bdg.)

   [1. Bears—Fiction. 2. Fate and fatalism—Fiction. 3. Fantasy.]

1. Title.

PZ7.H916625See 2011   2010021975

[Fic]—dc22   CIP

                                        AC

Typography by Hilary Zarycky

11 12 13 14 15   LP/RRDB   10 9 8 7 6 5 4 3 2 1

❖

First Edition

Special thanks to Cherith Baldry

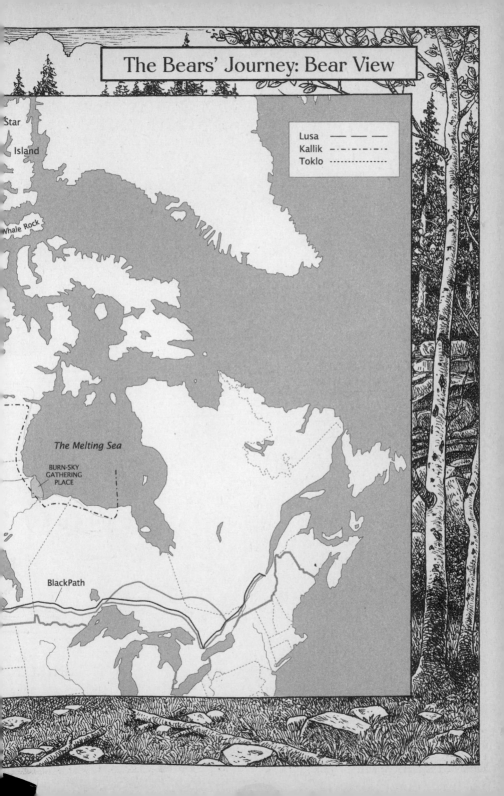

The Bears' Journey: Bear View

Star

Island

Whale Rock

Lusa — — —
Kallik —·—·—·—
Toklo ··········

The Melting Sea

BURN-SKY
GATHERING
PLACE

BlackPath

The Bears' Journey: Human View

GREENLAND

ESMERE

SLAND

Godthab

BAFFIN ISLAND

Iqaluit

Atlantic

Ocean

cle

Hudson Bay

St. John's

urchill

WAPUSK
NATIONAL
PARK

Lake
Winnipeg

Quebec

Trans-Canada   Highway   Montreal

nipeg

Ottawa   Boston

STATES   St. Paul

Toronto

Minneapolis

New York

CHAPTER ONE

Ujurak

Ujurak's legs ached as he tried to concentrate on just putting one paw in front of another. He and his friends seemed to have been trudging across the Endless Ice forever, though he knew that only a few sunrises had passed since they'd escaped from the flat-faces near the oil rig.

Glancing over his shoulder, he could see that his three companions looked just as tired as he felt. Toklo, the big brown bear, shambled along with his head down. Lusa stumbled after him as if she hardly knew where she was anymore, her small shape a black dot against the endless white; Ujurak knew they would have to keep a close eye on her, for fear that she would sink back into the longsleep. Even Kallik, who was more at home on the ice than any of them, padded along with a grim expression.

All around them the ice had been carved and twisted by the wind into strange shapes, which sometimes stretched over their heads into the sky. At first they had played hide-and-seek among them; Ujurak let out a small huff of amusement

1

as he remembered how good Lusa was at hiding, in spite of her black pelt. Sometimes they would slide down the frozen drifts, or look for shapes that reminded them of animals. Toklo had growled at an ice pillar that he thought looked like Shoteka, the grizzly who had attacked him at Great Bear Lake.

But we're too tired for games now, Ujurak thought. *Too tired for anything except this endless slog.*

His heart sank farther as he made out a frozen ridge across their path, a wall of ice that disappeared into the distance on either side.

"Now what?" Toklo grumbled, trudging up as Ujurak slowed to a halt. "Don't tell me we have to climb that."

"We do," Ujurak replied. He could feel that they were drawing closer and closer to the spirit of his mother, and the tugging on his paws was too strong to be ignored. "This is the way we must go."

Once the big grizzly would have argued with him. Now he just let out a snort of disgust. "I was afraid you were going to say that."

"But how?" Lusa asked, stifling a yawn. She and Kallik had plodded up next to them. "It's so high and smooth!"

Ujurak glanced at Kallik for advice, but the white bear only shook her head in confusion. "There were no ridges like this where I lived with Nisa and Taqqiq."

"I'll go first," Toklo announced. "I'll try to scrape some pawholds in the ice for the rest of you."

Without waiting for the others to respond, he began clawing his way up the slippery slope. Ice splinters showered down as he dug his claws into the surface; Lusa crouched and wrapped her paws over her head. "Hey, that stings!" she protested.

"Come on, you'll be fine." Kallik nudged the small black bear to her paws again. "You go next, and I'll give you a boost."

Working her shoulders underneath Lusa, the white bear heaved her upward. Lusa scrambled up the slope in Toklo's wake, struggling to thrust her paws into the holes the bigger bear had made. She let out a startled yelp as she lost her grip and began to slide down again, her forepaws splaying out against the ice while her hindpaws scrabbled frantically. Ujurak let out a sigh of relief as he saw her drive her claws into a gap in the surface and start climbing again.

"You next," Kallik suggested. "I'll keep watch for danger."

Ujurak agreed, though he wasn't sure they had much to fear in this desolate landscape. He almost felt that they were the only living creatures left in the world.

By now Toklo had reached the crest of the ridge and turned to call back to his companions. "Come on! It's easier on the other side!"

Ujurak climbed quickly, his paws strengthened by the feeling that his mother was watching over them, and reached the top of the ridge just behind Lusa.

The small black bear flopped down, panting. "I thought we might be able to see land from up here," she said. "But it's just more ice."

Gazing ahead, Ujurak saw that the ridge on this side sloped down gradually to an ice plain with a broken, choppy surface, like a frozen sea. The sky was covered with clouds, brightening to a milky radiance where the sun was trying to break through, and it was impossible to tell where the land ended and the sky began.

"We just have to keep going," Ujurak said.

As soon as Kallik arrived, shaking ice chips from her fur, they set off down the slope.

"I'm so tired my paws are falling off," Toklo grumbled, padding at Ujurak's side. "And my belly thinks my throat's been clawed out."

Ujurak pushed his snout into his friend's shoulder fur. "We'll stop to eat soon," he responded, trying to sound encouraging. "Kallik will hunt for us."

"She is good at that now," Toklo admitted. "Hey, Kallik, what about a nice fat seal?"

"Sure." Kallik raised her head, looking proud that Toklo was relying on her to provide for them. "Why don't you three rest, while I go and look for a seal hole?"

She paused, swinging her head around and sniffing—Ujurak guessed she was trying to sense the best place to start searching—then she plodded off across the ice.

Ujurak led the way to a twisted mass of snow that would give them some shelter against the wind that scoured the frozen plain. Lusa curled up in a hollow, wrapped one paw over her nose, and closed her eyes.

Toklo crouched beside her, scanning her anxiously. "I hope she's not falling into the longsleep," he muttered.

Ujurak nodded. Though Lusa had been more cheerful and

active since they'd escaped from the flat-faces, he couldn't help worrying just as Toklo did. *She needs to reach land. We all do.*

The two brown bears huddled closer to Lusa, sharing their warmth, while they waited for Kallik.

"She'd better get a move on," Toklo remarked, shifting uneasily. "I'm starving!"

"Me too," Ujurak agreed.

"I'm sick of seal, though," the big grizzly went on. "What I wouldn't give for a fresh salmon or a hare!"

Ujurak felt his mouth beginning to water, and his stomach rumbled at the thought. "I've heard Lusa muttering about grubs and berries in her dreams," he told his friend. "It won't be long now."

Toklo's only reply was a disbelieving grunt.

Ujurak couldn't help feeling optimistic. Awareness of his mother's presence tingled through him from his nose to his paws. But he didn't expect his companions to share his conviction. *They'll see,* he thought. *We must be near the end of our journey.*

Time dragged on, and Kallik did not return. Drowsily Ujurak let his mind drift back to the flat-face camp and to Sally, the young flat-face female who had been his friend. He remembered her dark hair and the laughter in her eyes, and the compassion she had shown when she was helping the animals who had been trapped in the oil. He remembered how shocked she had been when she'd seen him change back into a bear.

I wonder what she told the others about how Lusa and I disappeared. And will she try to find us again?

A pang of regret throbbed through Ujurak. It was weird to be missing a flat-face, and he knew it was best for them not to meet again. But he did miss Sally's cheerfulness and her kindness.

I'm not a flat-face; I'm a bear . . . aren't I? Not long ago he had almost lost the sense of who he really was when he had spent too long in whale shape. He didn't want to risk that ever again. *I'm a bear. And how would I explain myself to Sally if we met again?*

"Uh . . . Sally, you see I'm mostly a bear, but sometimes I'm a flat-face, or a bird, or . . ." he muttered out loud.

"Hey!" Toklo prodded him in his side, bringing Ujurak fully awake again. "Are you talking to yourself?"

"No, I was talking to Sally," Ujurak replied, not thinking how this might sound to Toklo.

"What do you want to talk to her for?" There was a tinge of jealousy in Toklo's voice. "She's not even here. And she's a flat-face."

"She's a good flat-face," Ujurak protested. When Toklo huffed angrily, the smaller bear stretched out a paw to touch his friend's shoulder. "But you're right," he murmured reassuringly, even though he couldn't understand why Toklo was getting so worked up over a flat-face they would never see again. "There's no point in talking to her."

Never again . . . he thought wistfully. *She was so good and kind, but we don't walk the same pathways.*

The sun had begun to slide down the sky by the time Kallik returned, dragging a seal behind her. Ujurak nudged Lusa awake, and the friends clustered eagerly around the catch.

"That's . . . er . . . great, Kallik," Ujurak said, trying to hide his dismay. The seal was the smallest he'd ever seen, not even fully grown. There wasn't nearly enough meat to feed all four of them.

"Yeah . . . brilliant catch!" Lusa added, but her voice sounded hollow.

Toklo just let out a growl as he tore off a chunk of meat.

"Don't say thanks or anything," Kallik muttered to him as they all crouched down to share the catch. "I waited *ages* for this!"

Lusa swallowed a mouthful of the seal meat. "We know you did your best—"

"It doesn't sound like it," Kallik interrupted, her voice rising in frustration. "If this isn't good enough for you, why don't you go and find some berries or hares?"

"You know we can't." Toklo rose to his paws, glowering at the white bear. "There's nothing here but seals! And ice! And more seals and more ice!"

He gave the remains of the seal a contemptuous prod with one paw and started to lumber away.

"Wait," Lusa cried, springing to her paws and scampering after him. "Come back! You're wrong!"

Toklo swung around and loomed over the little black bear. "Wrong, am I?" he challenged her. "If you're so clever, then show me these other things."

Lusa stretched out her muzzle toward him, a sudden intensity in her eyes. "*Listen . . .*" she breathed out.

Ujurak and Kallik exchanged a mystified glance. All the bears fell silent. Ujurak hardly dared to breathe. Then, far in the distance, he heard a faint barking.

"There!" Lusa exclaimed triumphantly.

"I suppose you've made your point," Toklo grumbled as he plodded back to his friends, with Lusa bouncing alongside. "But what is it? And can we eat it?"

They all listened again to the faint barking. Ujurak thought he should remember what animal sounded like that, but the memory escaped him. "Is it seals?" he asked Kallik.

The white bear shook her head, looking puzzled. Then suddenly her eyes brightened. "Walruses!" she exclaimed.

"What?" Lusa's eyes stretched wide with alarm. "They're scary!"

Ujurak's belly lurched, remembering the time that he and Kallik had been attacked by a walrus. Even with two of them to fight back, it had taken all their courage and strength to kill the fearsome creature.

"I know," Kallik responded. "We'll have to make sure we don't get too near them. But walruses never go far out onto the Endless Ice. Hearing them means we must be near land."

New energy flooded through Ujurak. With his friends hard on his paws, he scrambled and scampered over the ice in the direction of the noise. But however fast they ran, the sound didn't seem to grow any nearer.

"It's much farther away than I hoped," Kallik said.

"The air is so still," Lusa panted as she struggled to keep up with her bigger companions. "Sound travels a long way."

Twilight gathered as the sun sank down and the short day came to an end. But the clouds were breaking up, and the full moon soon appeared, floating high in the sky. The ice glimmered silver under its pale light.

"Let's keep going," Toklo growled. "I don't care where, just so long as we get off this stupid ice."

"Ujurak, can you see any signs?" Lusa asked.

Ujurak halted briefly and scanned the sky, but there was no sign that the spirits were present, only a few faint streaks on the horizon.

"We've hardly seen the spirits since we left the oil rig," he said, half to himself. "Have they given up on us because we've taken too long?" He felt as if a stone were in his belly, pulling him down. "Are we too late?"

"Don't think that!" Lusa encouraged him, pushing her snout into his shoulder. "You can still feel your mother urging you on, can't you? And now we've found a whole new place to explore!"

She bounded off again, her short legs pumping determinedly, and Ujurak followed, catching up to Toklo and Kallik. But their days of journeying and lack of food were sapping their strength. They couldn't keep running for long.

Ujurak thought that the barking of the walruses was a little clearer, but they were still a long way off when he realized that the bears were all too exhausted to carry on. Lusa had started to lag behind, blinking and shaking her head now and then as if she was trying to keep awake. Kallik was limping after treading on a sharp piece of ice, and even Toklo looked strained.

"We have to rest," Ujurak announced, coming to a halt. "The walruses won't go away."

His friends were too weary to argue. They found a sheltered spot at the foot of another ice ridge and curled up to sleep. As Ujurak closed his eyes, the barking of the walruses continued to echo in his ears, but the land still felt a long way off.

The whining of the wind and a raw chill in the depths of his fur woke Ujurak before the sun rose. Snowflakes whirled in front of his nose; the blizzard lashed his pelt and tore at his body with icy claws.

Beside him Toklo was crouching, with Lusa peering over his shoulder into the eddying snow. "Just what we need," Toklo grunted.

"We can't freeze to death now!" Lusa protested. "Not when we're so close to land. The spirits wouldn't be so cruel."

"We should dig into the snow," Kallik said, from Ujurak's other side. "That way we can keep warm."

For a moment Ujurak thought he was too exhausted to make a single scrape. But desperation gave strength to his paws. Together the four of them began to burrow into the snow at the bottom of the ridge, hollowing out a den.

"Stupid blizzard!" Lusa exclaimed as her paws worked vigorously. "If it weren't for that, we could be on our way toward the walruses again."

She dug even deeper, her hindpaws throwing up a bank of snow behind her, while her head disappeared into the bottom of the hollow. Suddenly she stopped, letting out a startled yelp.

"What's the matter?" Ujurak asked anxiously, afraid that his friend had hurt herself.

Lusa's head popped up again. "Stones!" she squeaked. "Earth!"

For a moment Ujurak gaped at her in disbelief; then he crowded around with Toklo and Kallik to see what the small black bear had found.

Lusa was right. Instead of water, or snow, or more ice, at the bottom of the hole was a layer of gritty pebbles. Ujurak reached down and touched the rough surface, feeling it solid beneath his paw. Thankfulness flooded through him.

We've made it!

As the four bears stood together, too overwhelmed to speak, the bellowing of walruses broke through the sounds of the storm.

"I name this Walrus Rock," Lusa announced solemnly. Scrambling into the hole, she pushed forward her snout to snuff up the smell of the land. Ujurak and Toklo squeezed in beside her; Ujurak closed his eyes and drew the warm scent of stones and earth deep into himself.

"Well," Kallik's voice came cheerfully from the rim of the hollow, "maybe now you'll all stop complaining about eating seals."

Ujurak looked up again, seeing the white bear as a dim

shape amid the whirling snow. As he clambered out of the hollow, he could see nothing in all directions except for the same snow-covered landscape they had journeyed over for what seemed like endless days.

Where are all the plants and animals? he asked himself. *How much farther do we have to go?*

Together they enlarged the hollow and huddled inside it while the storm screamed overhead. Two sunrises came and went while the wind whipped over the icy plain, driving the snow along with it.

Ujurak felt the pangs of hunger griping deeper in his belly with every day that passed, and he knew that his companions were suffering, too.

"It wouldn't be so bad if we couldn't hear the walruses," Toklo grumbled as the wind carried another gust of bellowing cries toward them. "I can smell them, too. I can't think of anything except for sinking my teeth into one of them."

Ujurak muttered agreement; he was hungry enough to risk attacking one of the savage creatures for the chance of gorging on the meat.

Kallik groaned and buried her snout deeper into Lusa's fur. All they could do was endure, and hope to sleep away the time until they could carry on.

At last Ujurak woke to silence. Raising his head, he realized that the wind had dropped. The sun was shining; light reflected from the undisturbed covering of snow that blanketed the ice in every direction.

"Wake up!" Ujurak prodded Toklo, then Kallik and Lusa. "The storm is over."

He hauled himself out of the hollow as his companions woke up, blinking in the bright light and unfolding stiff limbs to follow Ujurak.

Lusa scooped up snow in her paws and rubbed it over her face to wake herself up. "Come on!" she called, bounding enthusiastically away from the den. "It's this way! Let's—" She broke off suddenly as the snowy surface gave way and her small black shape vanished into a drift.

"Oh, for the spirits' sake . . ." Toklo muttered.

He plodded over to where Lusa had disappeared, wading through the fresh, powdery snow. Ujurak watched, half amused and half anxious, as the grizzly plunged his snout into the drift and reared back with Lusa's tail gripped between his jaws.

"Hey, that hurts!" Lusa protested, paws flailing as she emerged with snow clotted all over her black pelt.

Toklo hauled her to the edge of the drift and let go. "Watch where you're putting your paws."

"And don't go running off," Ujurak added as Lusa shook snow from her pelt, scattering it around her in a wide circle. "We're not sure exactly where we are."

"How are we going to find out?" Kallik asked.

Ujurak concentrated, but he couldn't hear or smell the walruses anymore. *Just when it would be useful . . .* And the spirits were still not sending him any signs.

There's one way, he thought, but fear stabbed his heart, colder and harder than sharp splinters of ice. *But I might lose myself forever.*

As the silence dragged out, his fear was thrust aside by guilt. *I can't let my friends down,* he decided. *Not when there's something I can do to help.*

"I'll turn into a bird and fly," he said reluctantly.

"But you don't like changing anymore," Lusa objected.

"That's not the point," Ujurak replied. "It's something I can do, and maybe that makes it my duty." *And if I don't stay in that shape for long, I should be able to remember who I really am.*

Lusa padded over to him and touched her snout to his. "Thanks, Ujurak."

Warmed by the way that his friend understood his hesitation, Ujurak spotted the tiny shape of a seabird in the distance and focused on it. Moments later he felt himself shrinking, and he saw his brown fur vanish to be replaced by the sleek black feathers of a cormorant. His forelegs fanned out into wings, and his hind legs grew bare and skinny. Before his hooked feet could sink into the snow, he took to the air with a mighty flap and soared upward. He let out a harsh cry of triumph as the land fell away beneath him. In spite of his fear he felt the exhilaration of powerful wings bearing him up and the cold air streaming through his feathers.

But I'm a bear. I'm a bear, I'm a bear. I must never forget what I really am.

His friends shrank to three tiny shapes at the foot of Walrus Rock. Higher still, and Ujurak could see that they were on an island, surrounded by the frozen sea. He couldn't tell exactly where the land ended and the ocean began, but he spotted exposed cliffs, and places where it looked as if the snow had been blown to a thin layer. There were no trees, but a few scrawny bushes clung to the cliff face.

Ujurak circled the whole island; at the far side he spotted the walruses, a whole mass of them on a plain near the sea, packed tighter together than grubs under a rock. Swooping down, Ujurak let his gaze travel over their glistening brown bodies, their whiskered faces and curving fangs. He went so low that some of them jerked back their heads and snapped at him.

Oh, no, Ujurak thought, gaining height again with a single flap of his wings. *You're not going to eat cormorant today!*

The walruses' smell gusted over him; he looked down in disgust as they slithered fatly over one another like huge slugs. The babies never stopped squawking, and the bellowing of the full-grown males filled the air like thunder.

Yuck! I'll make sure I never turn into a walrus!

As Ujurak flew back over the cliffs, another cormorant dove at him, her wings folded back as she let out a loud alarm call.

"All right! All right, I'm going!" Ujurak called back, guessing that she had a nest somewhere close by.

Swiftly he flew back inland, pushing down panic for a moment as he wasn't sure of the way back to Walrus Rock. Then he spotted the familiar twisted shape, with his three friends waiting patiently beside it.

The sun was setting as Ujurak landed in the lee of the rock and let himself change back into bear shape. At first he felt heavy and clumsy, and he missed the soaring freedom of flight, until the comfort of his brown bear shape flowed over him: This was the body he belonged in.

The other bears clustered around him excitedly.

"What did you see?" Lusa demanded.

Ujurak noticed that snow was sifted in her black pelt again. "What have you been doing, rolling in it?" he asked.

Lusa looked shamefaced, not meeting his gaze. "I fell into another drift," she admitted.

"Never mind that." Kallik pushed forward eagerly. "Tell us what you saw."

Ujurak described the island and the cliffs, and the stinking pack of walruses. "Far too many for us to think of hunting them," he said.

Toklo looked disappointed, but he didn't argue. "What do you think we should do, then?"

"Make for the center of the island, the highest part," Ujurak replied, jerking his head in that direction. "We might find some bushes there and be able to scrape down to the ground. But it's getting dark. Maybe we should stay here tonight and set off in the morning."

"I'm sick of that den," Toklo growled. "Let's get going now."

"Yes!" Lusa added with an excited little bounce. "We'll be okay traveling by night."

Ujurak glanced at Kallik, then nodded. Toklo charged off in the lead as they set out for the middle of the island. Privately

Ujurak felt that his friends were more confident about journeying in darkness because there was ground beneath the snow now, not ice or water.

"They feel they've come home," Kallik remarked as she fell in beside him.

But they haven't. Ujurak couldn't shake off his misgivings. *None of us has. Maybe we don't even know where home is anymore.*

CHAPTER TWO

Toklo

Toklo felt new energy tingling in his legs as he bounded up the slope toward the middle of the island with Lusa panting along beside him. There was still deep snow under his paws, and nothing broke the unrelieved white of the landscape, but it felt different, knowing there was land beneath the snow.

No more of that endless salt water with seals and whales floating around, he told himself with satisfaction. *There's firm, solid ground that we can dig into dens. There'll be prey for the taking. I can feel it, even through all this snow. I—*

His thoughts were cut off by a startled yelp from Lusa. The black bear fell through the surface of the snow and vanished; a moment later her head popped up, and she shook snow out of her ears.

"Not *another* drift!" Toklo exclaimed. "Honestly, Lusa, I think you're doing this on purpose."

"Oh, yes, because I *love* the snow!" Lusa replied crossly. "Get me out of here, Toklo."

The big grizzly waded through the snow and gave his

friend a push so she could scramble onto firmer ground on the far side of the drift. *She's doing her best,* he thought, *but she's still fighting off the longsleep.*

The short delay had given Ujurak and Kallik time to catch up, trotting in Toklo's footsteps. Toklo headed off again, toward the top of the hill at the center of the island, as Ujurak had suggested. He pictured again how the cormorant's glossy black feathers had shrunk away as his friend's body swelled and took on the familiar shape of a brown bear.

Funny, Toklo mused. *I'm so used to Ujurak changing shape now, I can hardly remember how shocked I was when he first did it.*

Abruptly he halted. A new smell had drifted into his nose; it had been so long since Toklo had smelled it that he felt stunned for a moment.

Prey!

It wasn't fish, or seal, but warm, furry prey—and it was just ahead.

"Stay back!" Toklo hissed with a glance at his companions. Crouching low, he crept forward, guided by the tantalizing scent. But however carefully he scanned the snow-covered hill ahead of him, he could see nothing. The moon had appeared, washing the slope with silver light, and nothing disturbed the smooth sweep of snow.

Where is it?

The scent grew stronger as Toklo advanced, pawstep by careful pawstep, but there was still no sign of the animal. His gaze swept across two small black dots, and he focused on them sharply as the dots twitched.

Yes!

Now that Toklo realized what he was looking at, he could make out the shape of an Arctic hare. Its pelt was completely white, hardly visible against the snow-covered hill, except for the black tips of its ears. It had been burrowing into the snow, but as Toklo bounded forward, it fled, its paws skimming across the frosty surface.

With a growl of hunger Toklo pounded after it, forcing his legs to pump faster and faster. For a few frustrated moments he thought the hare would outrun him, but then he forced himself into a final, massive leap, and let out a triumphant bellow as he felt his claws sink into the hare's fur. He dispatched it with a swift blow to the neck.

"Great catch, Toklo!" Kallik exclaimed as she and Ujurak ran up to join him.

Toklo's pride was warring with disappointment: The hare's fur was thick, but the body underneath was small and skinny. *At least it's real prey at last,* he told himself.

"Come and share," he invited the others.

Kallik and Ujurak settled down beside the prey, but there was no sign of Lusa.

"Where's Lusa off to now?" Toklo demanded, looking around, hiding his worry with a show of irritation. "If she's disappeared into another snowdrift, she can find her own way out!"

Gazing down the slope, he spotted Lusa snuffling around excitedly in the snow where he had first seen the hare.

"Hey, Lusa!" he called. "Don't you want your share?"

"I'm looking for my share," Lusa replied. "The hare dug down through the snow, and I can smell leaves!"

She scraped vigorously, and Toklo saw a sparse, small bush emerge from the powdery snowbank. Lusa bit off a whole twig and chewed happily.

"Delicious!" she exclaimed, her voice muffled by the mouthful. "You are clever, Toklo!"

Toklo snorted. "How in the world can you prefer eating sticks to warm hare?" he demanded.

Busy chewing, Lusa didn't reply. Toklo shrugged. *At least she's pleased.*

When they had finished eating, they set out again toward the top of the hill. As they climbed higher, the slope grew steeper, and Toklo felt his claws scrape on stone. The snow that covered it was loose, sliding away as he clambered upward to reveal the bare rock beneath.

As he hauled himself to the top of a huge boulder, Toklo heard a yelp behind him. Glancing over his shoulder, he saw Ujurak trying to cling to a crack in the rock, his claws slipping on the smooth, wet surface.

Before Toklo could scramble down to him, Ujurak lost his grip and fell back with a bellow of alarm. Lusa, climbing just behind Ujurak, scrabbled frantically to get out of his way, but she was too late. Ujurak crashed into her, and they both rolled back down the slope in a flurry of waving paws.

Toklo began climbing down, but Kallik was the first to reach the two bears, who were sitting up and looking dazed.

"Are you hurt?" she asked anxiously.

Ujurak rose to his paws, followed a moment later by Lusa. They both took a few tottering steps, while Kallik gave them a careful sniff.

"I think they're fine," she told Toklo as he plodded down to them.

"Sorry, Lusa." Ujurak gave his friend a guilty look. "I just slipped."

"It's okay," Lusa replied cheerfully, touching his ear with her snout. "There's no harm done."

"But we all need to be more careful," Kallik pointed out. "Let's not climb so close together, so if one of us falls, no other bear will be hurt. And it helps if you can keep to the edges of the rock where the snow is firmer. Follow me, and I'll show you."

Toklo let the white bear take the lead as they started to climb again. *She understands snow best,* he thought. Toklo wanted an enemy he could attack; he didn't know how he could defeat the snow.

At last the four bears trudged up the final slope and stood at the top of the hill. Gazing at the island spread out beneath him, Toklo felt a strong sense of achievement. Although everything was white, and he couldn't tell where the land ended and the sea began, a tingle in his paws told him that they were almost at the end of their journey. The exhausting trek across the Endless Ice lay behind them.

The far side of the hill fell away in front of his paws, leading to the beach where the walruses were crowded. There were masses of them like big brown, lumpy stars. The strong wind carried their noise and smell, powerful even at that distance. His belly rumbled, and he felt the gush of water between his jaws.

"No, Toklo," Kallik said sharply, as if she guessed what he was thinking. "Ujurak was right; we can't hunt them. There are too many, and they can fight as well as any bear."

She exchanged a glance with Ujurak as she spoke, and Toklo remembered that the two of them had fought and killed a walrus when they were alone on the ice. The story had scared him; he had to admit that even he didn't want to be attacked by a whole horde of them.

"All right, all right," he grumbled. "I just hope we can find some decent prey soon."

"We'll think about that in the morning," Kallik decided. "Right now I think that if a seal bobbed up in front of me, I'd be too tired to catch it."

There was a murmur of agreement from Ujurak and Lusa.

"We'd better dig a den down there," Toklo said, jerking his head toward the bottom of the slope.

He took the lead as the bears all climbed down again to a sheltered spot just below the ridge and dug holes in the snow to make dens where they could curl up for the night.

As soon as he closed his eyes, Toklo thought that he woke in a den of earth. Tangled roots stretched above his head, and in the distance he could hear the faint sound of rustling trees. He was pressed up against a mound of fur, and his mother's scent was strong in his nostrils. Blinking, he saw that his brother,

Tobi, was curled up between Oka's forepaws, his eyes closed and his breathing strong and steady.

A powerful sense of safety surged over Toklo. "Is this home?" he whispered.

"No." Oka's voice was a warm rumble. "But we are with you."

When Toklo woke, he could see the first pale flush of dawn, a line on the distant horizon. His friends were stirring around him, climbing out of their snow-dens.

In spite of his short sleep Toklo felt invigorated as they set out again down the shallower side of the ridge. His paws itched to be moving. Picking up speed, he found that he was running as if he were a carefree cub again, with the wind in his face and tugging at his fur.

His companions kept pace with him on either side, until they all lost their footing as the ground leveled out, and they tumbled to a stop in the snow.

"That was fun!" Lusa exclaimed, beginning to scrape down beneath the surface. "Oh, I want to smell the grass and earth again!"

Toklo set to work beside her, throwing the snow aside with powerful sweeps of his paws. But when he reached the earth, it felt cold and lifeless: bare ground with a few flattened stems of grass and scraps of lichen.

Oka was right; this isn't my home, he thought, disappointed.

Rising and shaking the snow from their pelts, they trekked on toward the edge of the island, avoiding the beach where the walruses lay packed together.

"Listen!" Kallik said, raising her snout as a sign for the others to halt. "Can you hear that?"

Toklo strained his ears; beyond the bellowing of the walruses he caught the creaking sound of the ice shifting. Though the covering of snow continued undisturbed ahead of him, he realized they were standing at the edge of the sea.

"I wish we could stay here," Lusa said, casting a wistful glance over her shoulder.

Toklo was annoyed to catch himself doing the same. He knew that they hadn't reached the end of their journey, but it had felt so good to have land under his paws again.

"We have to go on now," Ujurak urged them. "There's nothing here for us."

"What's the matter?" Toklo asked, disturbed by the note of anxiety in his friend's voice. "Why are you worried?"

"Look at the sky," Ujurak replied.

Toklo glanced up. The warm flush on the horizon was spreading; the moon had disappeared, and the stars were growing pale. "Nothing up there," he grunted.

"Exactly!" Ujurak retorted. "Where are the spirits? They were showing us the way to go, but now they've vanished."

"Why would they do that?" Lusa asked. "Does it mean we've arrived at where we're supposed to be?" But the doubt in her voice told Toklo that she too knew the end of their journey still lay ahead of them.

Kallik shifted uneasily, glancing around as if she expected to see something that would guide them.

Is she looking for her mother to show us the way? Toklo wondered. "We have to keep going," he said firmly. "We can't stay on this island forever."

To his relief his three companions nodded without any more protest or hesitation. Kallik led the way out onto the frozen sea. Toklo brought up the rear, and for all his determination he couldn't resist a final glance back. He had to force his last paw to leave the solid ground.

CHAPTER THREE

Kallik

A glimmer of satisfaction crept through Kallik as she and her friends returned to her familiar territory. Her pleasure at being back on the ice was joined by a wave of protectiveness toward her companions.

They don't understand this place. I have to look after them.

After so long on the ice, their stay on the island had felt strange to her, even though the land was covered with snow. She had grown used to being the leader—the one who took charge of hunting and finding good places to sleep—and handing back the power to Toklo had thrown her off balance.

Now she was focused again, intent on keeping their little group together as she scanned the sky for the lights that showed the presence of the spirits. But there were no lights. She thought that with the end of their journey so close, she would have seen her mother dancing in the sky with all the other bear spirits. Their absence was a pain clawing deep into Kallik's heart.

Where are you, Nisa? Have you abandoned us?

"I'm so hungry!" Lusa exclaimed, with a glance back at the island, now no more than a hump on the horizon behind them. "It's been ages since I ate those leaves."

"I'm starving, too," Toklo grumbled.

"Kallik, can you find a seal hole?" Ujurak asked. His tone was edgy, and his claws scraped impatiently on the ice.

"I'll do my best," Kallik replied.

The other three kept heading away from the island, while Kallik cast back and forth. Eventually she spotted the dark patch of a seal's breathing hole.

"Found one!" she called to her friends. "You wait there; I'll do the catching."

Kallik crouched down at the edge of the hole, making sure that her shadow didn't fall across it, and made herself comfortable for the long wait. She was hardly settled when she sensed there was something strange about this hole, though it took a few moments for her to realize what it was.

There's no fresh scent!

The only scent of seal was faint and stale, as if no seal had been there for a long time.

That's odd.

The moments dragged by as Kallik waited beside the seal hole. There was no sign of movement in the water. Now and again she cast a glance toward her friends, who were clustered a few bearlengths away. Lusa and Toklo were talking together quietly, and Kallik could read impatience in the twitching of their ears and the scrape of their claws on the ice.

Ujurak sat a little ways away from them, his muzzle raised,

his gaze scanning the sky. It was full daylight now, and the sun shone down, gleaming on the surface of the ice. Kallik longed for the night, when she would be able to see the Pathway Star, and maybe the spirits would return to guide them.

She made herself concentrate on the seal hole again, ready for the first swirling of the water that would herald the appearance of a seal. But everything was quiet. At last, in growing desperation, she peered down into the hole to see if she could spot any moving shapes. But she saw nothing except the shadows of the ocean.

"Kallik!" Ujurak's voice cut through her concentration. "We have to keep moving."

Kallik's first instinct was to protest, to beg for a little more time. But she had to admit to herself that however long she waited, there wouldn't be a seal for her to catch from this hole.

"Okay, coming," she replied, heaving herself to her paws and flexing stiff muscles.

Returning to her friends, she saw how anxious Ujurak looked, though he said nothing, allowing her to take the lead as they set off once more across the ice.

"We could go back to the island if we can't find food out here," Lusa suggested longingly.

"No." Ujurak's voice was uncharacteristically sharp. "You know that's no good. We have to go on. Besides," he added, "there's more land up ahead."

He angled his ears toward a smudge on the distant horizon. Kallik felt more hopeful at the sight. In fact all the bears seemed to have found new energy. Their pace quickened.

As she bounded along, Kallik could hear sounds that she hadn't heard for a long time: lapping water and the high-pitched creak of thin ice.

We're getting close to land again! Or . . . is the ice melting? A sharp pang of foreboding stabbed through her like a walrus tusk at the thought of being cut off from land, balancing on a diminishing ice floe as she tried to reach the safety of the shore.

Picking up Ujurak's urgency, she ran even faster. A low ice ridge blocked their path, but she pushed upward with powerful hind legs, springing easily to the top.

"Stop!" Kallik froze as she barked out the warning. "Danger!"

Only a few pawlengths ahead the ice had vanished. A wide channel about the width of one of the no-claws' waterbeasts had been gouged through it. The stink of burning oil fumes still hung around it, making Kallik gag.

Her friends scampered toward her, bounding up to the very edge of the channel and peering curiously into the water. Kallik stayed where she was, her paws turned to stone. The channel reminded her too much of the place where she and Taqqiq had needed to cross, where Nisa had given up her life to save her from the orca.

Toklo was balanced on the very edge of the ice. "We'll have to swim," he said. "It's not as wide as the Big River we crossed before Smoke Mountain. It won't take long."

"No!" Kallik choked out the word. "We can't. It's not safe."

Toklo narrowed his eyes at her. "Not safe how?"

Kallik swallowed, the terrible day when she lost Nisa

coming back to her all too vividly. "Orca," she whispered at last.

She stared down at her paws, struggling with terror, and realized that Lusa had padded over to her. She felt the comforting warmth of the black bear's pelt pressed up against her own.

"That's how your mother died, isn't it?" Lusa murmured.

Kallik couldn't speak, but she managed to nod.

"I know how you feel," Lusa went on, her voice warm and sympathetic. "But it will be different this time. Everything will be okay. It's not far, and we'll swim fast. Besides, we're much bigger than you and Taqqiq were back then."

You're not, Kallik thought. *And maybe the seal hole was empty because there are too many orca here.*

Lusa gave her a gentle nudge, and Kallik allowed herself to be coaxed as far as the water. Peering into it, she saw that the edge of the ice was broken up where the waterbeast had plowed through, and the reek of oil was stronger than ever.

"Kallik, we have to go this way," Ujurak said.

"He's right," Toklo agreed impatiently. "It'll be dark soon, and we can't stay here all night."

"I'll find a good place to slide in," Lusa announced, scampering along the ice at the very edge of the channel.

Suddenly there was a loud crack, and the ice underneath Lusa's paws shattered, pitching her into the sea. Kallik started toward her, only to halt as Lusa's black head bobbed up again.

Lusa spat out water, her forepaws working vigorously. "Spirits, that's cold!" she exclaimed. "But I'm in now. I may as well keep swimming. It's like when we first swam out to the ice," she added over her shoulder as she struck out for the far side of the channel. "I don't know why, but it's much easier to swim in the sea than it is in rivers. You were right when you told us that, Kallik."

Facing forward again, she paddled strongly across the stretch of water, and Toklo slipped in after her.

"You next, Kallik," Ujurak prompted.

"I—well . . ." Kallik began to protest, then let her voice die away. She realized there was no point in arguing. *I helped them when we first swam in the sea. I taught them how to float when they were tired. I can't hang back and leave them alone now.*

She launched herself into the channel, and the water closed around her, cold and familiar. Behind her she heard Ujurak slide in and start swimming as well. Ahead she could see that Lusa was doing well, already halfway across the channel, with Toklo just behind her.

Suddenly Kallik spotted a flicker of movement out of the corner of her eye. Turning her head, she saw a huge black fin sliding through the water, bearing down on Lusa. The little black bear swam on, unaware of the danger.

Terror surged over Kallik like an icy wave. "Orca!" she shouted. "Swim faster!" She forced her legs to send her powering through the water, devouring the distance between herself and Lusa.

As she overtook Toklo, he turned, his teeth bared in a fierce snarl. "Help Lusa," he ordered. "I'll fight off the whale."

"No—" Kallik began to protest, unwilling to leave Toklo

to face an enemy that was far too strong, even for him. Then she saw the terror on Lusa's face as her short legs paddled furiously across the channel. Kicking out strongly, Kallik reached her and propelled her to the edge of the ice. She could hear Toklo behind her, growling and thrashing, but she had no time to turn and look.

And where's Ujurak? she wondered, fighting back panic. *Have the orca taken him already?*

Lusa was clinging to the ice with her forepaws, but she was too exhausted to haul herself to safety. Kallik tried to boost her out of the water, but the black bear was heavy, her pelt waterlogged, and she slid back again with the waves lapping around her shoulders.

Below her in the depths Kallik could see more black shapes swarming upward toward her. *So many! Is this what it was like for my mother?* Kallik asked herself as she gave Lusa another shove. *Nisa, help me!* The black shapes were perilously close; Kallik imagined she could see their gaping jaws, full of sharp teeth, and the glitter of their cold, cruel eyes.

Don't give up, a familiar voice murmured into her ear.

"Nisa!" Kallik gasped.

Strength flowed back into her body. She gave one more massive push, and Lusa slithered forward onto the ice. In the same movement Kallik turned to see Toklo surrounded by the evil black fins.

"Save yourself!" he bellowed as Kallik struck out toward him.

Kallik ignored him, forcing herself through the water. But

before she could reach Toklo, she spotted another fin, bigger than all the others, churning up the water as it charged toward her.

"Sorry, Toklo," Kallik whispered. She closed her eyes and hoped it would be over quickly.

But nothing happened. Kallik heard Lusa shriek behind her and opened her eyes to see the big fin veer to the side at the last moment, as the whale crashed into the orca that were attacking Toklo.

Spluttering and choking, Kallik was swept underwater in the wake left by the huge whale when it swept past her. As she fought to right herself, she saw the newcomer fighting with the other orca, butting them with its nose and driving them away from Toklo.

Kallik struggled back to the surface and gasped in a mouthful of air. "Swim, Toklo!" she choked out. "It's Ujurak, helping you!"

Jaws wide as he gulped for air, Toklo thrashed frantically to escape from the seething water where the orca battled. Kallik swam beside him until they reached the ice and could haul themselves out. Lusa was waiting, leaning over to grip their fur in her teeth and tug them upward.

Kallik's chest was heaving as she turned back to look across the channel. "Ujurak, get out!" she shouted. "We're all safe!"

She didn't know if the Ujurak-whale could hear her. Four more black fins were bearing down on him, cutting off his escape. They surged toward him, churning the sea to foam. Ujurak's fin was motionless as his attackers closed in.

Then, just before the four orca reached it, the black fin vanished. Lusa let out a squeal of astonishment as the four attacking whales swirled together in a chaos of bubbling water.

Baffled, the orca swam to and fro, looking for their vanished enemy. With Lusa and Toklo beside her, Kallik peered down into the sea, but she couldn't make out anything beyond the surging water and the circling shapes of the whales.

"What happened?" Lusa asked. "Where's Ujurak?"

"I don't know." Kallik glanced from Toklo to Lusa; both her friends looked as bewildered as she felt. "Did he sink?"

"I'm going to look." Toklo stepped forward, ready to leap into the water again, but Kallik blocked him and shouldered him away.

"Don't be cloud-brained!" she snapped. "What good can you do, with *four orca* swimming in there? Besides, we have to stick together."

Toklo huffed angrily, but to Kallik's relief he flopped down onto the ice and didn't try to argue.

"What are we going to do?" Lusa asked in a small voice. "We can't just go off and leave Ujurak."

"We have to wait," Kallik replied. "He's gone missing before and still come back. He'll be back this time; you'll see."

"But this isn't the same," Lusa persisted, blinking anxiously. "He was here, and suddenly he wasn't. How can a huge orca vanish like that?" She hesitated, then went on in a rush. "Suppose he's dead; then how will we know which way to go?"

"He's not dead!" Toklo growled obstinately.

Lusa's voice rose to a wail. "Then tell me where he is!

Ujurak! Ujurak!" Her voice rang out across the ice, but there was no response. "He's not coming back," she choked out at last. "What are we going to do?"

The numbness of grief crept up on Kallik as she realized that Lusa could be right, but she fought to hide it from her friends. Still, she couldn't make her paws move; continuing their journey would be to accept that Ujurak was dead. *And what will he do if he comes back and finds we've left him alone on the ice?*

She cast a glance at the channel, to see the orca finally giving up their search and beginning to glide away. At the same moment she heard a splash from the opposite direction, followed by huffing and puffing breath.

Sudden hope pierced Kallik, sharp as a shard of ice. Turning, she saw Ujurak a few bearlengths farther down the channel, pulling himself out of the water in his bear shape.

"Ujurak!" Lusa squealed, bouncing toward him. "You're okay! Where did you go?"

Ujurak plodded up to his friends, water streaming from his pelt. "When the orca attacked, I turned myself into a tiny little fish," he explained. "I swam down into the dark water and hid under the ice until the orca left."

"That's so clever!" Lusa marveled.

Ujurak let out a huff of satisfaction and flopped down on the ice beside Toklo, who pushed his snout briefly into his friend's shoulder fur. "Thanks," Toklo muttered. "Those stinking whales would have finished me off without you."

"You're welcome," Ujurak murmured.

He sounded exhausted after his battle, and Kallik realized

that he couldn't go any farther until he had rested. Besides, the short day was drawing to an end, the sun going down behind a bank of clouds in a murky red glow.

"Let's make a den for the night," she suggested. "We can go on in the morning."

None of the others argued with her. They were exhausted, cold, and hungry, and it was all they could do to scrape out a rough den in a nearby snowbank and curl up together in a mass of wet fur.

Kallik felt herself drifting in darkness, unbroken except for the shining shape of Silaluk stretched out above her, paws reaching toward her in welcome. Kallik drew in a breath of wonder, feeling that she could gaze at the vision forever.

"Don't give up," the star-bear said, speaking in the voice of Kallik's mother. "You were very brave today. Do you understand now why I would never have left you in the water? You wanted to save Toklo; I wanted to save you."

Kallik blinked, confused but feeling warm and safe. *Is she Silaluk or Nisa?* she asked herself. *And does it matter?*

"I understand," she murmured, reaching up to touch noses with the huge starry bear. "Thank you."

CHAPTER FOUR

Lusa

As soon as Lusa curled up in the den, she closed her eyes, but sleep wouldn't come. Instead the events of the day repeated themselves endlessly in her mind. She thought she would never forget the terror of swimming away from the orca, her struggles to pull herself onto the ice, and her gratitude and relief when Kallik boosted her up. She remembered her bewilderment when Ujurak vanished, and her joy when he reappeared in his familiar bear shape.

At last Lusa sank into sleep, but even then she couldn't rest. She thought she was thrashing in dark, icy water, banging her head against an endless roof of ice. Huge shapes swarmed around her; she caught the flash of cold eyes and spiny-toothed mouths gaping to tear her flesh. Her senses started to spiral away in terror.

Help me! Someone help me!

Then Lusa felt something nudging her from behind, propelling her through the water. A moment later she broke out into open air. Gasping, she plunged away from the ice and turned to see who had saved her.

"Ashia!" she exclaimed, so amazed that she almost forgot to swim.

Lusa's mother gazed at her with all the warmth and love she had given Lusa when they lived together in the Bear Bowl. But she had changed.

"Mother, there are stars in your fur!" Lusa whispered, awestruck as she gazed at the soft glimmer sifting through Ashia's black pelt.

Ashia stretched out her paws and rose from the water until she hovered over Lusa. She grew and grew, and the stars in her fur grew brighter and brighter, until she took on the form of the Great Bear, Silaluk. But when she spoke, it was still with the voice of Lusa's mother.

"You are safe now."

The starry bear alighted gently on the ice and began to amble away.

"Wait for me!" Lusa cried, scrambling out of the water and bounding in pursuit.

Silaluk glanced back over her shoulder. "You're doing fine, Lusa," she said. "I will be watching you."

She moved away once more, so swiftly that Lusa had no hope of catching her, until she dwindled to a bright star on the horizon.

Lusa let out a wail of loss and immediately felt something prodding her sharply in the side.

"Stop making all that noise," Toklo growled. "A bear can't get any sleep around here."

Blearily Lusa opened her eyes and looked around. She was curled up in the makeshift den in the snowbank, with the other bears huddled closely around her. *I'm not alone,* Lusa thought, suddenly feeling more optimistic. *I have three friends with me.*

Above Lusa's head the sky was growing pale with the approach of day, and across the ice she could see a golden flush to tell her where the sun would rise. Her belly growled, reminding her of how long it had been since they had found any food.

The sun rose as her friends clambered out of the den, and they set out again, blinking through the bright whiteness as the rays reflected off the surface of the ice. Soon they made out the shape of the land up ahead: It looked like another island, bigger than the first, rising in a dark mass from the frozen sea around it.

More willow shoots, Lusa thought hopefully, water flooding her jaws in anticipation of filling the hollow in her belly.

Toklo took the lead, breaking into a trot. Lusa and the others picked up their pace to keep up with him, and soon the island was looming above them. This time it was easier to see where the sea ended and the land began, because the land sloped more steeply upward with only a narrow strip of beach. Here and there the wind had blown the snow away, leaving patches of bare gray rock.

"I'm so hungry!" Lusa exclaimed, burrowing eagerly down through the snow.

Toklo jumped back as the white crystals splattered his fur. "Watch it!"

But disappointment flooded through Lusa as her claws scraped on stone. There were only big pebbles at the bottom of the hole she had made—no earth, no plants. "We can't eat rock!" she complained.

"We need to go farther inland," Kallik pointed out. "We'll find something to eat soon, don't worry."

"Right. What are we waiting for?" Lusa bounded a few paces away from the shoreline and glanced back to see that Kallik and Ujurak were following her.

"Stop!" Toklo exclaimed.

The big grizzly angled his ears at something in the distance, farther up the hill. Turning in that direction, Lusa saw a white bear standing on a rock. He looked young and fit, about the same size as Kallik, and his pelt had a reddish tinge. Even though he was so far away, Lusa could feel his eyes on her.

After a moment's silent scrutiny the white bear turned and galloped away, disappearing over the brow of the hill. Lusa felt a pleasant thrill of excitement as she watched him go.

It's so long since we've seen any other bears! Maybe we'll find more.

Then her excitement gave way to anxiety as she wondered whether these bears would be friendly. *What if they attack us and drive us away?* She swallowed nervousness at the thought of facing hostile bears who were so much bigger than her.

Kallik clearly didn't share her misgivings. A pang of jealousy shook Lusa as she saw the pleased expression on her friend's face. *I wonder if she'll like other white bears better than she likes us.*

But there was no time for Lusa to dwell on her feelings.

Ujurak was already heading toward the nearest rise, jerking his head to beckon the others to follow him.

"Come on!" he called. "We'll be able to check out the whole island from up here."

Lusa's short legs ached with the exertion by the time she stood on top of the ridge. Standing beside her friends, she looked out across a vast landscape of rising and falling hills. Except for the ice the bears had crossed, which now lay behind them, there was no sign of the ocean.

"Hey, this island is big!" Lusa exclaimed.

"I can't see any more white bears," Kallik added, looking around and sniffing eagerly.

At first Lusa thought that nothing at all was alive in all that rolling stretch of hills. Then she spotted movement and gasped in astonishment as a whole herd of creatures came into sight, shambling down a gully on the far side of the hill they had just climbed. They reminded Lusa of the caribou, but they were bigger and more solid, with hunched shoulders and shaggy brown fur that hung down as far as their knees. Lusa repressed a shudder at the sight of their long, curving horns.

"What are those?" she asked, hardly expecting a reply.

"Musk oxen," Kallik whispered. "I've never seen them before, but my mother told me and Taqqiq about them. She said they live near the Endless Ice, and they can feed a family of bears for a whole moon."

"Great!" Toklo bared his teeth. "Let's hunt!"

Ujurak was giving the musk oxen a doubtful look; Lusa shared his misgivings. They were bigger by far than any animals the bears had ever hunted.

"Are you sure we can catch one?" she asked Toklo.

"We can if we work together," he replied confidently.

He led the way down the hillside, and the bears hid behind a rock to watch the herd. The huge animals were ambling along placidly, pausing here and there to scrape the snow with their sharp-looking hooves and munch on the grasses they uncovered.

Lusa swallowed; up close the oxen were even more frightening, and she couldn't help wondering whether even Toklo could bring one down. *What if the whole herd turns on us?*

"Seals are much less scary to hunt," Kallik muttered into her ear.

Suddenly Lusa felt more confident. "Excuse me!" she whispered back. "You fought a whole gang of orca yesterday!"

Toklo had been watching the herd closely; now he turned back to his friends. "We've got to get one," he said. "I can taste it now. . . . This is what we'll do. . . ."

A few moments later Lusa and Kallik were creeping quietly down the hill, working their way behind the herd of musk oxen to the other side of the gully. A flap of white wings made Lusa look up to see a tern skim low over their heads and circle in the air above the herd.

"There goes Ujurak," she murmured.

"I hope he waits until we're in position," Kallik replied.

Once on the far side of the herd, Lusa and Kallik took shelter behind a huge boulder. Lusa gagged on the strong scent of the musk oxen.

"At least they'll never pick up *our* scent through all of that!" she whispered.

The tern-Ujurak swooped down toward them and let out a screech as he rose into the air again. At the signal Toklo burst out from the cover of a scrawny thornbush and launched himself down the hillside toward the herd.

The musk oxen bellowed in panic and turned to run, heading for the boulder where Lusa and Kallik crouched in hiding.

"Now!" Kallik said.

She and Lusa sprang out of their hiding place and sprinted toward the herd. The roaring and the pounding of the oxen's hooves terrified Lusa, but she swallowed her fear and ran on.

The leaders of the herd spotted Lusa and Kallik and tried to turn back, but they were pushed from behind by the other oxen fleeing from Toklo. The strung-out herd quickly became a mass of milling, panic-stricken animals.

In the confusion Lusa spotted Toklo running alongside the herd; he leaped on a smaller, young-looking ox and brought it crashing to the ground. Its hooves flailed as it rolled in the snow, trying to stand up. Kallik sprang on top of it, and Lusa avoided the thrashing hooves to get a grip on its haunches.

We're good *at this,* she thought as she struggled to hang on. *We're no longer weak, silly cubs—we know how to work as a team.*

The musk ox gave one last convulsive jerk and then went limp as Toklo dealt it a massive blow across the neck. Panting, the three friends relaxed, gazing at one another across the body of their prey, while the rest of the herd stampeded away up the gully.

"We did it!" Kallik exclaimed joyfully.

"I knew we could," Toklo growled, his eyes blazing in triumph.

Lusa said nothing, but warmth flooded through her at the closeness she felt to her friends and the way they had worked together. *That's it. . . . Together we can fight orca and musk oxen and anything!*

Ujurak came trotting down the gully, back in his bear shape, and the four friends feasted on their prey. The musk-ox meat was rich and warm, and they gulped it down eagerly. It tasted good, even to Lusa. She couldn't remember the last time they had been able to gorge until they were full.

"Thank you, spirits," Ujurak said, when none of them could manage another mouthful. He cast a hopeful glance up at the sky.

The sun was already sinking behind the hills, and twilight gathered in the gully while the last scarlet rays lingered on the ridges. There was still no sign of the fire in the sky. Lusa opened her jaws to ask Ujurak why not, then closed them again. She could tell all her friends were just as worried as she was, and none of them was prepared to talk about it.

"We'd better make a den," Toklo said, sighing with satisfaction as he swallowed one last mouthful of the prey.

Ujurak nodded. "If only the days weren't so short. We'll never get anywhere at this rate."

Lusa agreed. She missed warm sunshine more than anything. Here the sun hardly had time to come up before it went down again.

But at least we're well fed.

She felt a twinge in her belly as she padded over to the side of the gully where Toklo and Ujurak had begun to scrape out a den.

Maybe too well fed, she added to herself as she scrabbled in the snow to find some grass and gulped down the stalks to ease the pain from so much rich food.

The den grew quickly with all four bears digging their way into the snow. As Lusa paused for a brief rest, panting, she looked up and spotted the watching shapes of more white bears standing on the horizon.

Shuddering, she nudged Kallik's shoulder and pointed her muzzle at the pale figures outlined against the darkening sky. "Look up there."

"Don't worry," Kallik responded. "They won't come near us."

I hope that's true, Lusa thought. *But sooner or later we'll have to meet them.*

When Lusa scrambled out of the den at sunrise the next day, there was no sign of the other white bears. She let out a sigh of relief. *I don't care what Kallik thinks. I think they look scary.*

"Hey, Lusa!" Ujurak was crouching beside the carcass of the musk ox they had killed the night before. "Come and eat."

Lusa still wasn't hungry after their previous feast, but they couldn't carry the prey with them, so it made sense to eat as much as possible before they left. She joined Ujurak, to be followed a few moments later by Toklo and Kallik, still blinking sleep out of their eyes.

"This is cold and hard now," Toklo grumbled, giving the prey a prod.

"Hey, it's food. We'd have been glad of this when we were out on the ice," Kallik reminded him.

Lusa felt optimistic as they set out, enjoying the dazzle of sunlight on the snow. With Toklo in the lead, they crossed a valley, pausing to dip their snouts for a drink from a half-frozen stream.

"I've almost forgotten what running water sounds like," Lusa remarked, listening to the gurgle of the icy current, so different from the silent depths of the sea.

Splashing through the stream, the bears headed across an open space where snow and earth had been churned together.

"The musk oxen have been here," Ujurak said as he peered at the hoofprints.

"There are so many of them!" Kallik exclaimed.

Toklo swiped his tongue around his jaws. "Good!"

They were still too full to think of tracking down the musk oxen, so they kept going to the far side of the valley. Here the ground sloped steeply upward to a ridge, but when they tried to climb, the loose snow gave way beneath their paws, and they slid helplessly back again.

"Now who's stuck?" Lusa teased as Toklo pawed his way out of a drift, scattering snow as he shook his pelt.

Toklo just growled in annoyance.

They tried again and again, and before long Lusa was too wet and exhausted to think about teasing anymore. "There has to be an easier way than this," she muttered as she struggled to climb through thick snow.

Glancing around to make sure she hadn't lost sight of her friends, she realized that Kallik wasn't with them. Anxiety stabbed through her, until she spotted the white bear farther up the valley, nosing around at the bottom of the slope.

"Look over here!" Kallik called.

Lusa trudged over and found Kallik standing at the mouth of a gully leading upward, where broken rocks poked out of the covering of snow.

"This looks easier," Kallik went on.

The two she-bears waited while Toklo and Ujurak came plodding over. Toklo gazed up the gully, then nodded. "It seems to cut through the ridge," he said. "We might as well try it."

Kallik took the lead, bounding easily up the broken rocks. Lusa found it harder—sometimes she had to bunch her muscles for a long leap—but she kept going, her breath puffing out in clouds in the cold air.

A breeze was blowing from the top of the gully; Lusa picked up a salt tang carried along with it and realized that they were heading toward the sea.

As they reached the top of the gully, Kallik halted suddenly.

"What can you see?" Lusa asked.

She scrambled up to peer out from behind her friend; Ujurak and Toklo caught up a moment later.

In front of Kallik the ground leveled out, stretching in front of them for many bearlengths until it stopped abruptly.

The salt tang of the sea was even stronger.

"Cliffs," Ujurak murmured. "We can't go that way. They'll just lead us down to the sea again, if we don't fall off and break our necks."

"Hey, look!" Toklo pointed with his snout toward the edge of the cliffs.

Lusa spotted a white bear struggling through the snow, dragging the body of a seal behind her. The seal left a furrow in the snow, smeared with blood.

"I'm surprised there are so many white bears on this island," Kallik murmured, looking puzzled. "Mostly we live alone on the ice. We don't stay together once we're full-grown."

Lusa shrugged. "Well, these ones do."

"Let's chase her off," Toklo suggested, bouncing a little on his paws. "Then we can steal her catch."

Kallik gave him a shove. "What's the point? If there are seals around here, we can hunt them fresh."

"And not risk a fight," Lusa added.

Toklo shrugged. "Okay."

"We could go and talk to her, though," Ujurak pointed out. "She might be able to tell us something useful."

When the bears emerged from the gully, they had hardly covered a bearlength before the white she-bear turned and saw them. She stared at them for a moment, her eyes wide with alarm; then she lumbered back the way she had come, abandoning her catch in the snow.

"It's okay! We won't hurt you!" Kallik called after her, but the white bear didn't seem to hear her.

"She didn't even try to defend her catch," Toklo said, sounding faintly disappointed.

"Maybe she's not really hungry," Lusa responded. "She's pretty thin, though. She looks as if she's in need of a good meal!"

Toklo padded up to the seal and gave it a quick sniff; Kallik and Ujurak gathered around, too, while Lusa headed past them to peer over the edge of the cliff. Her claws dug through the snow to the ground beneath as she gazed over the dizzying drop to the shore below, where sharp rocks were half covered by the frozen sea. Cautiously she edged backward again.

"I wonder how that white bear got down there," she murmured to herself.

"It's prey!" Toklo was arguing when Lusa rejoined her friends. "We can't just leave it here."

"But our bellies are full now," Kallik retorted. "And I don't want to drag a seal carcass all over the island. Ujurak, what do you think?"

"It won't be too hard to carry if we all take turns," the smaller brown bear pointed out.

"Well, maybe . . ." Kallik still sounded doubtful.

Lusa bent her head to sniff at the seal, wondering if she felt hungry enough to eat some now. A strange, rank scent was rising from the carcass, like a mixture of rotten fruit and fire-beasts.

"Yuck!" she exclaimed, flinching. "I'm not eating that. It's disgusting!"

All her instincts were telling her that they shouldn't eat the seal, but the others had hardly noticed her reaction and were still continuing to discuss whether they should take it with them or not.

"Have you smelled it?" Lusa interrupted. "We really shouldn't eat it. There's something wrong with it."

Her friends broke off their discussion and stared at her.

"Lusa, it's *prey*," Toklo pointed out, as if he were trying to explain something to a very small and stupid cub.

Kallik let out a huff of laughter. "You'll be glad enough of it when your belly is empty again."

"No, I *won't*," Lusa retorted, furious that they were laughing at her; even Ujurak's eyes gleamed with amusement. "It smells wrong. No bear should eat it."

"Well, *I'm* going to eat it," Toklo announced. "So it smells a bit weird. So what?"

Lusa gazed at him in horror as he began to drag the seal toward him. "No!" she screeched, leaping across the carcass and butting Toklo in the chest.

Toklo was so astonished by her attack that he backed off, letting the seal drop. "Are you bee-brained, or what?" he demanded.

Lusa didn't bother to answer. Giving the seal a strong shove, she tipped it over the edge of the cliff and drew a breath of relief as she watched it splatter on the rocks below.

"Lusa, what are you doing?" Kallik asked, anger in her voice. "That's a waste of good food."

"It's *not* good; that's the point." Lusa knew she had to stand up for herself and what she had done. "Eating that seal would have made us ill."

"You don't know that," Toklo growled.

Lusa tried hard to think of a reason her friends would accept. *How could they smell that seal and think it was good to eat?* "I just do—okay?" she said defensively. "And we can easily catch something else later."

"Easily?" Toklo huffed scornfully. "There are lots of white bears living around here, or haven't you noticed? That means there's going to be plenty of competition for prey."

Guilt stabbed Lusa like a thorn in her heart, but she still didn't back down. *There was something wrong with that seal, and I'm not going to say I'm sorry for saving the stupid fluff-brains!*

She noticed that Ujurak's anger had faded and he was giving her a very odd look. Lusa almost asked him what the matter was. Then she realized he probably thought she had bees in her brain for throwing prey over a cliff.

I don't care, she told herself. *Somehow they'll find out that I was right.*

CHAPTER FIVE

Kallik

Kallik felt sorry for Lusa as she watched the small black bear trying to defend herself. Whether she was right about the seal or not, she was only trying to help.

"Well, the rest of us are going to look for the seal hunting ground, and when we find it, we'll catch some prey," Toklo growled, thrusting his snout aggressively at Lusa. "If you don't want to eat it, you can keep your mouth shut and stay away. I'm not going to gnaw frozen twigs, even if that's good enough for you."

He marched off, following the seal track in the snow, then halted and looked back over his shoulder. "Are you coming or not? I think that if we follow this track back, it will lead us to the place where that white bear caught the seal."

"Okay." Ujurak set off, trotting in Toklo's wake.

Kallik exchanged a sympathetic glance with Lusa before following, aware that the smaller bear was trailing unhappily behind.

She herself was feeling optimistic. Toklo thought that with

so many white bears on the island there would be competition for prey, but Kallik didn't think he was right. So far they had seen plenty of prey, enough to support a good number of bears.

She wondered whether this place was still part of the Endless Ice. It certainly felt as cold as it did on the frozen sea. She reveled in the frosty air as she followed Toklo along the track of bear pawprints and seal blood.

"Look, I can see the pawprints the white bear made when she ran away," Lusa said after a while. She was sounding more cheerful again, as if she was putting the quarrel behind her.

Kallik padded over to see. The pawprints were clearer here, undisturbed by blood or the marks of where the seal was dragged through the snow. A feeling of uneasiness crept up on Kallik as she looked at them.

"There's something wrong here," she said to Lusa. "The prints are uneven, as if she was stumbling through the snow. What was the matter with her?"

Lusa shrugged, unable to reply, though Kallik saw that her friend was looking uneasy, too. They followed the prints, heading in the same direction as the seal track a bearlength or so away. The tracks led to a jumble of boulders at the edge of the cliff. From here it looked as if the ground fell away to the shore.

"This is where the seals come from," Toklo grunted in satisfaction.

He quickened his pace and rounded the boulders, until he halted with a huff of astonishment. Kallik hurried forward to find out what he had seen. Peering around Toklo's massive shoulder, she saw the white she-bear, slumped on her side in the snow.

For a moment Kallik tensed, half expecting the strange bear to leap up and attack. Then she realized that the bear was hardly conscious; she let out a long moan, and her paws scrabbled feebly in the snow.

Brushing past Toklo, Kallik went up to her. "What's wrong?" she asked. "Is there anything we can do to help you?"

The white bear groaned again, struggling to breathe. "My belly . . . it's on fire."

Kallik leaned her head against the white bear's shoulder, trying to offer comfort, but the other bear jerked away from her, snapping her sharp teeth.

"Leave me alone," she growled. "I won't let you hurt my baby."

Kallik backed away, staring in surprise. As the white bear moved, she revealed a tiny cub trying to suckle from her belly. Its eyes were still closed, and its hair was so fine that it looked almost bald.

So tiny! Kallik marveled. *It must be newborn.*

"We won't touch your cub," Lusa said gently, padding up to stand beside Kallik.

The she-bear's only reply was a hostile snarl that turned to a groan as she clawed at her belly. The cub whimpered and tried to burrow deeper into its mother's fur.

"Do you live with those other bears?" Toklo asked. "Where are your dens?"

The sick she-bear glared at him. "Why would I tell you?"

"We're not here to do any harm," Kallik tried to reassure her. "We need to know about this island, that's all. And if you tell us where to find your friends, we'll fetch them and maybe they can help you."

"No bear can help me." The she-bear's words turned into a groan, and she closed her eyes.

"I wonder why she's ill." Ujurak pressed forward and gave the she-bear a sniff. "She's thin, but she's not starving. . . . You can see she's full of milk."

"But she smells weird," Kallik added, taking a good sniff in her turn.

"A bit like that seal," Lusa agreed.

As her friend spoke, apprehension began to gather inside Kallik, like a stone in her belly. *What if Lusa was right? Can seals make us sick?*

Ujurak approached the mother bear cautiously, sniffing at her fur as if he was trying to work out what was wrong.

Maybe he knows of an herb that will make her well, Kallik thought hopefully.

But the she-bear didn't understand. She snapped feebly at Ujurak and lashed out at him with one paw. Ujurak jumped back swiftly to avoid the blow.

"Come on," Toklo said roughly. "We can't do anything to help her. And our being here is only making her worse."

Kallik realized that Toklo was impatient to be hunting seals, but even so she had to admit that he was right. *I think this bear is dying. And what will happen to her cub then?*

Toklo led the way along the seal track, heading down toward the beach. Lusa and Ujurak followed, with Kallik bringing up the rear. She kept casting glances back toward the other white bear and her cub, even when they were out of sight. She couldn't get the tiny cub out of her mind. Its pink, hairless skin looked so vulnerable in the biting cold.

That night Kallik lay curled up in the snow-den she and her companions had dug out against the cliff face. She listened to the peaceful breathing of her friends, but she couldn't sleep.

If the mother bear dies, her cub will die, too. The words echoed through her mind, over and over again.

No! Kallik sat up, careful not to wake the others. She knew that she couldn't abandon the cub, not if there was something she could do to save it.

Nisa didn't let the orca take me. She gave up her life so that I would be safe. Now it's my turn; I have to help this cub, whatever it takes.

The first light of dawn was glimmering on the snow as Kallik carefully slid out of the den and retraced her steps along the seal track to the top of the cliff. Beside the heap of boulders the mother bear lay dead, cold as a stone. Kallik fought with sadness and regret. She had known from the first there was nothing any bear could have done to help the mother.

But what about the cub?

Kallik pawed through the dead bear's belly fur until she came upon the limp body of the cub. He lay so still that at first she thought he was dead, too. Her heart swelled with grief.

Oh, spirits, no! Please . . .

Then she saw, as if in answer to her silent pleading, that the cub's chest was rising and falling as he breathed: a slight movement that Kallik had almost missed. Thankfulness washed over her as she realized the tiny creature was still alive.

Cupping her paws around him, she breathed warm breath over his body until he gave a wriggle and started to whimper.

"There, small one," Kallik whispered, pushing him up against one of his dead mother's teats. "See if your mother has any milk to give you."

The cub latched onto the teat and began to suckle, feebly at first, then more strongly. Kallik waited for him to finish. Then she crouched down beside the cub and nudged him onto her shoulders. When she was sure that he was clinging securely, she turned and padded down the path, carrying the cub to her friends.

When she reached the beach, the other three bears were emerging from the den.

"There you are, Kallik!" Toklo called to her. "We didn't know where you'd gone off to. You shouldn't—" He broke off, staring. "*What* have you got there?"

"I went back," Kallik explained, trying to keep a defensive note out of her voice as she padded over to Toklo and the others. "The mother bear is dead. I couldn't leave the cub to die, too."

"And how will you keep him alive?" Toklo asked scathingly. "We have no milk."

Kallik faced the brown bear steadfastly. "I don't know, but I'm going to try."

"Your brain's full of cloudfluff!" Though Toklo's voice was angry, his eyes were haunted, as if he was revisiting some terrible memory. After his first horrified glance, he didn't look at the cub.

Kallik took a step forward, baring her teeth. She would fight for the cub if she had to. Toklo was her friend, but the rage of protectiveness that surged up inside her made her forget everything except the threat to the cub.

For a moment Toklo held the white bear's gaze. Then Kallik saw the haunted look in his eyes fade, replaced by respect.

"Do what you want," he muttered, turning aside to talk to Ujurak.

Lusa padded up to Kallik, her bright eyes alive with interest. "Can I see?" When Kallik nodded, she stretched out her neck and gave the cub a gentle sniff. "Oh, Kallik, he's adorable! Have you thought of a name for him yet?"

"Yes," Kallik replied. "I'm going to call him Kissimi. It means 'alone.'"

"But he's not alone anymore," Lusa pointed out. "He has you."

Yes, Kallik thought, deep satisfaction welling up inside her. *Yes, he has me.*

CHAPTER SIX

Toklo

Toklo sat in the shelter of a thornbush, watching Lusa and Kallik as they fussed over the white bear cub. Two days had passed since Kallik had rescued him. The day before, a blizzard had forced them to retreat from the coast and take shelter beyond the ridge of low hills. Ujurak had caught a white hare, and now Kallik was chewing up the softest part of the meat for the baby to swallow.

Toklo's hackles rose as he gazed at the scrawny little creature. "This is a waste of prey," he muttered to Ujurak, who was sitting beside him, finishing off his share of the catch. "And the cub doesn't even belong to us."

Ujurak said nothing, just touched his nose to Toklo's shoulder.

"This cub isn't part of our destiny, is he?" Toklo hissed.

Ujurak looked uncertain. "We can't leave him behind" was all he said.

"No, we can't," Toklo agreed reluctantly. "Kallik wouldn't let us." *But the cub is a weakness,* he added to himself. *And we can't afford weakness. It's already taking all we have to survive.*

"Hey, Toklo!" Lusa called, glancing across at him with bright eyes and beckoning with one paw. "Kissimi has opened his eyes. Come and see!"

"No, thanks," Toklo growled, rising to his paws. *So his eyes are open. Big deal.* "I'm going to look for some more food."

Without waiting for a response, he left the thorn thicket where they had spent the night and headed along the valley. His senses were alert for the scent or sight of hare. In the distance he spotted a cloud of snow thrown up into the air, and wondered for a moment what could be causing it.

Musk ox, he realized, picturing the way that the sharp hooves churned up the ground. His belly rumbled, and he was tempted to head in that direction.

But I'd never catch one on my own, he thought regretfully.

Toklo was still searching for hare without any success when he heard a growl from somewhere ahead. Looking up, he spotted a full-grown male white bear standing in his path. His stance was threatening, and Toklo didn't like the unfriendly gleam in his eyes.

"So it's true," the white bear said. "There are brown bears here."

Toklo braced himself for an attack, but for the moment the white bear didn't move.

"My brother Yakone saw you arrive," the white bear went on. "Where are the others?"

"Safe from you," Toklo retorted, his pelt bristling in defiance.

"That's what you think," the white bear sneered. "You are not welcome here. Brown bears and black bears don't belong on this island."

"There are no scent marks," Toklo responded. "Nothing to say that this is your territory and yours alone. We have every right to be here."

"You have *no* right," the white bear snarled. "To start with, your fur is the wrong color."

The white bear's eyes glittered with hostility, and he took a pace toward Toklo, baring his teeth. Toklo stood his ground, trying to hide how daunted he was by the bear's sheer size.

He's big, even for a white bear. But if I can dodge under his paws, I can get in a few blows to his belly.

Toklo rose to his hindpaws and parted his jaws to roar a challenge. But at the same moment he heard a new voice, shouting from the ridge behind his attacker.

"Unalaq!"

The white bear looked over his shoulder as an ancient white she-bear appeared on the crest of the ridge, flanked by more white bears. She looked older than any bear Toklo had ever seen before, like a leafless tree with a pelt hanging from its branches. But as she drew closer, Toklo saw that her eyes were black and bright. The other bears followed her down the slope; clearly they regarded her with the greatest respect.

The old bear padded down the hillside until she stood in front of Toklo, gesturing with one paw for the hostile white bear to join the others.

"But you—" he began to protest.

The old she-bear repeated the gesture more forcefully. "I don't feel threatened, with all of you to come to my rescue. Besides," she added gruffly, "this young bear doesn't look as if he would attack a feeble old she-bear."

There was a twinkle in her eyes that suggested she didn't regard herself as feeble at all. Toklo shook his head, unsettled by her; he had no idea what to expect.

"What is your name?" she asked him.

"Toklo," he replied.

"And they call me Aga. It means 'mother' in our speech. Star Island has been my home for many circles of the sun."

"This is Star Island?" Toklo asked.

Aga nodded. "They tell me you have companions," she went on. "May I meet them?"

Toklo wasn't sure. This old bear seemed friendly enough, but what if she was trying to trick him? "What for?" he asked, mustering all his courage.

The she-bear dipped her head slightly. "This is our place," she reminded him gently. "And you are strangers. We have a right to know who you are, and what led your pawsteps to Star Island."

Toklo could understand that, but he was still reluctant, especially after the hostile reception he had received from the young male.

"How do I know you won't hurt my friends?" he asked. "I'm supposed to be looking after them. I won't lead enemies to them."

Aga blinked, understanding in her eyes. "Your courage

does you credit," she told Toklo. "But you and your friends will come to no harm from me or these others. Unalaq there makes a lot of noise, but he isn't as dangerous as he looks."

"All right," Toklo agreed. *I don't have much choice; I have to trust her.* "But my friends are quite a long way off," he added, looking at Aga's frail figure.

"I'm stronger than I look," Aga assured him, again with that unsettling twinkle in her eyes. "Let us go."

As Toklo turned to lead the way, a young she-bear stepped out of the group and padded beside Aga. She gave Toklo a wary glance, as if she was half expecting him to attack.

"This is Illa." Aga introduced her.

Toklo gave the young white bear a curt nod, surprised at how thin she looked. All the bears seemed underfed, he realized. *But why should they? Between the musk ox and seal, this island is full of food.*

"Illa, you will come with me," Aga continued. "The rest of you, stay here." She gave Unalaq a hard stare, as he seemed about to protest again. "I will return soon."

As he headed back up the valley with Aga and Illa, Toklo was still aware of the gaze of the other white bears boring into his back. *I don't think we've seen the last of Unalaq. That bear is trouble.*

"Where do you come from?" Aga asked him, distracting him from worrying about the hostile bear. "Not from somewhere with ice and snow," she added, a humorous gleam in her eyes. "That brown pelt of yours stands out sharper than a walrus!"

"I'm from a place with forests and mountains," Toklo began.

"Forests?" Aga asked curiously.

Of course—she's never seen a forest! Toklo realized. "A forest is a place with a lot of trees. And trees are like bushes, with leaves and branches, only bigger. Where I come from, you can walk among the trees for days and days and never come to the end."

Aga blinked in wonder. "Truly the world is wide," she murmured. "And why have you come here?" she went on. "Why did you leave your . . . forests?"

Toklo wasn't sure how to reply. *If I tell her about Ujurak and his quest, she'll think my brain is full of cloudfluff!*

Before he could decide what to say, he was distracted by a flicker of movement. An Arctic hare had sprung up from a dip in the ground and was racing up the valley a few bearlengths ahead.

Without thinking, Toklo took off after it, his powerful paws scattering the snow as he ran. Beside him he was aware of Illa, running with longer strides, much more experienced in the snowy landscape.

Veering to one side, she careened into Toklo, knocking him off balance and nearly sending him rolling in the snow.

"Hey!" he protested.

"This is our prey," the young she-bear growled.

We'll see about that. Determined not to be put off, Toklo pounded after Illa, catching up with her so that the two bears were racing neck and neck for the hare. Suddenly the hare swerved toward Toklo; with a spurt of energy, he reached out for it and brought it down with a deft blow to its head.

"That's mine!" Illa said indignantly, coming to face Toklo, her eyes blazing with frustration. "I chased it into your paws. Hand it over!"

"No. It was a fair catch," Toklo argued.

"But you don't understand." Illa's voice grew quieter, filled with desperation. "We need that hare far more than you do."

Why? Toklo wondered. *What are these bears not telling me?*

"I need it, too," he told the young she-bear. "My friends rely on me to hunt for them."

Illa opened her jaws to go on arguing, but at that moment Aga padded up.

"Let Shesh have the hare," she ordered.

"Shesh? That's not my name," Toklo said, surprised.

"But it is what you are," Aga explained, dipping her head to him. "'Shesh' is the word for a brown bear."

"You're really giving this hare to him?" Illa broke in, sounding surprised.

Aga nodded. "There's no reason to make these visitors feel unwelcome."

Toklo was struck by how calm she was, and how she seemed to know all about him and his friends. *It's almost as if she was expecting us,* he thought, then pushed the thought away. *Bee-brain! You're starting to sound like Ujurak!*

Carrying the hare, Toklo led the way along the valley until they reached the thornbushes where he had left his friends. Lusa was on watch, and she let out a squeak of alarm when she spotted the white bears.

Toklo heard Aga whisper, "So you have come at last." He stared at her. *What does she mean?*

"It's all right, Tungulria, black one," Aga said aloud.

Lusa gave the white bears a panicky look, then ducked out of sight into the makeshift den among the thorns. Toklo heard some shuffling and tensely whispered conversation before she reappeared with Ujurak and Kallik. He looked for Kissimi; the cub was nowhere to be seen, and Kallik was looking particularly tense and determined.

"These are my friends," Toklo said, dropping the hare at his paws. "This is Lusa, the brown bear is Ujurak, and the white bear is Kallik."

As Toklo introduced them, Aga and Illa gave their visitors a formal nod, which Lusa and the others returned awkwardly. Ujurak seemed most comfortable with the white bears, giving them a friendly and curious stare.

"How many white bears are there here on the island?" he asked.

"Many," Aga replied.

"And have you lived here all the time?"

Aga didn't seem upset by the young brown bear's questioning. "We have lived here on Star Island for as long as my mother's mother could remember."

"Star Island!" Ujurak's eyes brightened; Toklo gave him a warning look. He didn't want his friend giving away too much about their quest.

"And where have you come from?" Aga turned her attention to Kallik, who was shifting from paw to paw and looking as if she would rather be anywhere but there.

"From . . . from the Melting Sea," Kallik stammered.

"So it really exists!" Aga sounded impressed. "I have heard rumors of it before, from bears who traveled very, very far. You have clearly come on a long journey." She paused, then added, "Do you have the Iqniq where you come from?"

"What's that?" Ujurak asked.

"Iqniq is the fire in the sky," Aga explained. "The Iqniq is our name for the spirits of our bear ancestors."

"Yes, we have the Iqniq," Ujurak told her. "We believe that the spirits of our ancestors watch over us."

Aga nodded sadly. "We believe that, too—or we did once. But now we are suffering from terrible pains in our bellies. Some bears believe that we have been cursed by the Iqniq and that they are abandoning us." The ancient bear's voice grew deeper and more rhythmic, almost like a chant. "The Iqniq do not walk among us as they did of old, and no bear knows why. Their fires are fading from the sky, and when they have gone altogether, the sacred link between the world of the living and the world of the spirit-bears will be broken. Then living bears will be cut off altogether from their ancestors. They will be alone. The time of the bears may soon be over."

Aga fell silent and gazed long and hard at the bears who were listening to her. At last she fixed her gaze compellingly on Lusa. "Or maybe not," she added softly.

Toklo couldn't think what to say. He sensed a world of pain that the old bear suffered, and he found it hard to understand. *And why is she looking at Lusa like that?*

It was Ujurak who broke the silence. "Are the white bears really dying?" he asked.

Illa nodded. "We just found the body of my sister, Sura. There was no reason for her to die! She was young and strong, and she had a cub."

Toklo's paws itched with apprehension; he forced himself not to look at Kallik.

"Did . . . did you find the cub?" Lusa stammered.

Illa shook her head sadly. "No. We assumed the poor little thing fell over the cliff. Why? Have you seen a lost cub?"

"No!" Kallik spoke far too loudly. "No cubs at all."

Oh, no . . . Toklo thought. *Now there* will *be trouble.*

Aga was still looking at them closely, and Toklo wondered whether she suspected that Kallik was lying. But all she said was "Please keep a lookout for him. Meanwhile, you are welcome on Star Island."

As Aga spoke, Illa gave her a startled glance, as if she thought the old bear was out of her mind. But she said nothing.

"Take care, Tungulria," Aga said to Lusa as she turned to go. "We will see you again."

Toklo and his friends watched the two white bears as they padded down the valley, until their pelts were lost against the background of snow.

Lusa was squirming uncomfortably, shuffling her paws. "Why did she look at me like that?" she asked. "And why did she call me by that name? It was weird. I didn't like it!"

Toklo didn't like it, either, but he was more concerned

about what Kallik had said. "Why did you lie about having the cub?" he demanded. "He belongs with his family. If they find out that you stole him, we won't stand a chance!"

Kallik faced him defensively, her lips drawn back in the beginnings of a snarl. "You saw how thin they looked. They can't take care of themselves, let alone a cub. Kissimi is mine now!"

Toklo was taken aback. "Are you so bee-brained that—"

"Stop!" Ujurak yelled. His eyes were focused on the sky. Toklo was surprised by the unusual note of authority in his friend's voice. "The Iqniq are leaving," he whispered. "Then this is our destiny: to make them return."

CHAPTER SEVEN

Lusa

Lusa squirmed uncomfortably in the snow-den beneath the thorn-bushes. Sleep had never seemed so far away. She couldn't forget the way that Aga had looked at her, with eyes as piercing black as holes in the ice.

Why did she call me Tungulria . . . "black one"? Is it just her name for me? It sounded more like . . . It sounded as though she was expecting me.

Lusa shivered at the thought that the old bear had seemed to know so much about her. There had never been black bears on Star Island before.

I'm the very first one!

Lusa gave another massive wriggle, feeling as though she were lying on the sharpest pebbles on the whole island. Toklo, curled up next to her, gave an irritable grunt, and from her other side Lusa heard Kallik's voice, raised in anxiety.

"Kissimi? Are you all right, little one?"

"Sorry to wake you," Lusa muttered.

Trying her best not to disturb her friends even more, she

pushed her way out of the den and through the thorn branches into the open. The moon was floating high above in a clear sky, washing the snow-covered hills with silver.

Lusa skirted the bushes and climbed a little way up the hill, above the den, staring up at the moon and the thick sprinkle of stars. But there was no sign of the spirit-fire.

What did Aga call them? The . . . the Iqniq. Have they left us already? Are we too late?

Below her, through the snowy roof of the den, she could hear Kallik's voice. "Now that your eyes are open, little one, you can look up at the sky and see the stars in the shape of the Great Bear, Silaluk. She runs around and around the Path-way Star, hunting seals and beluga whales. She is the greatest hunter in the world."

Lusa's belly rumbled, distracting her from the sound of Kallik's voice. Scrabbling around in the snow, she found a piece of lichen she had hidden there earlier. It was crispy from the cold as she bit into it, but still tasty.

Out in the open Lusa felt more at ease, but she still couldn't forget what the old bear had said.

She told us the white bears are dying. Could it be a curse from the lights in the sky, from the Iqniq?

Lusa wasn't sure why the bear ancestors would want to pun-ish the living bears. Maybe there was another reason why the bears were getting sick. Her mother, Ashia, had been taken out of the Bear Bowl when she was sick and taken back there once she was well again. Lusa had no idea what the flat-faces had done to help her. She didn't even know what had made her mother sick in the first place.

What makes bears get sick?

She remembered how sick she had felt when she was out on the Endless Ice, eating nothing but meat. And she remembered further back still, when Ujurak had fed her herbs to help her heal after she had been hit by the firebeast.

Maybe the bears are eating something that is making them sick. Like those horrible-smelling seals.

Lusa gasped. What if that was it? *The white bear Sura ate the seals, and then she* died. *What if it's the* seals *that are killing the bears, and not an Iqniq curse?*

Lusa sprang up and charged back into the den, spraying snow behind her as she ran. "Listen! Listen, everyone! I know why the bears are dying!"

Toklo blinked at her blearily. "Great, Lusa. Now leave us to get some sleep." He closed his eyes and wrapped a paw over his nose.

There was a faint wail from Kissimi. "Look what you've done!" Kallik exclaimed crossly. "I'd just gotten him to sleep!"

To Lusa's relief Ujurak sat up, looking alert, and gave Toklo a prod in the side. "Wake up. Lusa just said something important. Go on, Lusa."

When Toklo had heaved himself up with a drawn-out sigh, Lusa explained her theory that Sura had died after eating the disgusting seal.

"But seal is a good food for white bears," Kallik objected.

"Lusa, just because too much seal makes *you* feel sick, it doesn't mean that it's the same for every bear," Toklo pointed out. "You're just assuming that there's something wrong with the seals."

"No, I'm *not!*" Lusa insisted. "The seal smelled wrong, and Sura smelled the same when we found her before she died. Maybe every other seal in the world is safe to eat, but not the seals here."

Excitement flooded over Lusa as she imagined making the white bears better. *My mother told me to "save the wild," and here's my chance!* Saving the white bears on Star Island wouldn't save the *whole* wild, but it would be a big pawstep in the right direction.

"I'm going to tell the white bears not to eat seal anymore," she announced.

"What?" Toklo huffed in contempt. "Don't be salmon-brained! The white bears are being generous enough to let us stay here. They won't take too kindly to some upstart little black bear telling them not to hunt seals!"

Sighing, Lusa had to admit that Toklo was right. *Why would Aga and the other bears listen to me? I'm too small, and I don't belong here.* But she couldn't shake the conviction that she was right, too. *If only I could find where the white bears go to hunt seals. Then I might be able to work out why the seals are getting sick. . . .*

Tiredness overcoming her, she curled up against Kallik's back and fell asleep. In her dreams she found herself hunting seals, which vanished as she drew near, leaving behind only a stench of firebeasts and sickness.

Movement from Kallik woke Lusa; pale snow-light was filtering into the cave, and she realized that dawn was breaking. Toklo and Ujurak were stirring, too.

"I'm going out to hunt for food for Kissimi," Kallik announced.

Lusa jumped to her paws. "I'll come, too." When Toklo had brought back a hare the night before, Kallik had patiently chewed some of the meat into a pulp and coaxed Kissimi to choke it down. Maybe if both of them searched together, they would find something better for the tiny cub to eat.

Kallik gently picked up Kissimi, who let out a drowsy squeak, and set him down between Ujurak's front paws. "Look after him," she directed.

Ujurak yawned. "He'll be fine with me, Kallik."

Lusa was aware of Toklo's gaze on her as she left the den with Kallik. It was definitely a "don't do anything stupid" look.

I won't, Lusa promised silently. *Not yet, anyway.*

Kallik glanced at Lusa as they walked side by side away from the den. "I was going to look for the seals."

"I hoped you would," Lusa responded. "I want to see them." *If we can find where the seals live, we might find out what's the matter with them.* She could see that Kallik wasn't convinced by her theory that the seals were making the white bears sick.

Together Lusa and Kallik padded along the shore and around the base of a hill. They had never traveled in this direction before; Lusa's paws itched with curiosity to see what lay beyond the snow-covered slopes.

It was good to be exploring with Kallik, too, without risking an argument over Kissimi. Kallik was looking much more friendly now, more like the bear she had been before she found the cub.

As they reached the inlet beyond, Kallik, who was a few pawsteps ahead, halted, glancing back over her shoulder at Lusa. "No-claws!" she hissed.

"Here?" Lusa edged forward. "I didn't think there were any no-claws on this island."

"No-claws get everywhere," Kallik replied glumly.

Peering over a boulder, Lusa saw a small flat-face denning area on a bluff above the beach. The dens had flat roofs; they were small and square, built out of white stone. Among them stood tall sticks, made out of shiny stuff, and lots of chunky green firebeasts. Flat-faces were walking to and fro among the dens.

"Why are all the no-claws dressed the same?" Kallik wondered. "Their pelts are all green, like leaves."

"Maybe they're made of leaves?" Lusa guessed.

"Where would the leaves come from?" Kallik gestured with one paw toward the bare landscape, where nothing grew except for a few straggly thornbushes poking above the snow.

Lusa shrugged. "Flat-faces are weird."

Keeping well inland, Lusa and Kallik skirted the denning place and approached the shore again on the other side.

Lusa pointed with her chin. "Look! White bears!"

A whole group of white bears had gathered on the shore near the denning area. Some of them were venturing close to a line of the silver cans that flat-faces put their unwanted food in. It looked to Lusa as if an argument was going on, as if some of the bears wanted to stop the others from going near the cans.

Lusa recognized one of the bears who had planted himself in front of the row of cans, blocking his companions from approaching. His fur had a reddish tinge, as if the sun were rising behind him.

Kallik recognized him, too. "That's the bear who watched us arrive on the island," she murmured.

Lusa and Kallik cautiously drew closer to the white bears. "There's Illa," Lusa whispered. She looked around to see if Aga was there, too, but there was no sign of the ancient bear.

The young she-bear was talking to a couple of the males who were trying to get at the cans. "I know you're hungry, Tunerq," she said. "We're all hungry. But we're bears. We shouldn't be taking food from no-claws."

"They don't want it," the smaller of the two males replied sulkily. "And it smells really tasty."

"That's not the point! We—"

"Stop telling us what to do," the bigger male interrupted. "I want food, and I'm going to get it."

"Are you as fluff-brained as you look, Unalaq?" Illa began scathingly. "We should be hunting seals. That's what white bears do."

"I'm going to talk to them." Taking a deep breath, Lusa began marching toward the bears, unsure of what she would say when she reached them.

"Be careful!" Kallik called after her.

Lusa glanced back. "Aga said we were welcome," she reminded her friend.

"Well . . . okay." Kallik followed at a distance, looking wary.

Lusa's confident pace faltered as she drew closer to the white bears. *Am I brave enough for this? I didn't realize how much bigger than me they are!*

First one bear spotted her, then another, until the whole group was staring at her in astonishment.

"I told you so!" Illa said.

"You didn't say she was the size of a hare!" Tunerq retorted. *I'm bigger than that!*

Lusa's indignation gave her courage. At least the bears were only looking at her; none of them had tried to attack.

She marched up to the white bears and stood gazing up at them. "You mustn't eat any more seals," she told them, trying to make her voice sound bold and certain. "It's the seals that are making you sick."

Tunerq looked pleased. "You mean we should just eat what's in these no-claw cans?" he asked, obviously trying to use Lusa to bolster his own argument.

Lusa glanced at the silver cans, then back at the bears. She knew how tasty flat-face food could be; she had relied on it in the first days after she escaped from the Bear Bowl. *But it's flat-face food, not bear food. . . .*

"No," she replied. "If you do that, you might forget how to hunt and be wild. You need to find something else to eat."

"Lusa . . ." Kallik's voice, full of foreboding, came from just behind her.

The white bears huddled together, muttering to one another and casting glances now and again at Lusa. She heard one of them say, "It's Tungulria. . . ."

Lusa tensed as she heard the name Aga had called her, remembering the strange look the old she-bear had given her.

Then Unalaq, the huge male, stepped forward; his eyes glittered with hostility. Lusa swallowed her fear and made herself stare back at him, though when he loomed over her he was almost big enough to block out the whole sky.

"You're lying!" Unalaq growled. "You just want all the food for yourselves. All the seals, and what's in these silver cans!"

"Right!" Tunerq agreed, coming to stand beside Unalaq. "But you won't get it."

Most of the other bears gathered around, muttering threateningly, though Lusa noticed that Illa and the bear with the red-tinged pelt hung back, looking uncertain.

"That's not what I want at all!" Lusa protested. "I'm trying to help, if you'd only listen. The seals—"

Kallik jabbed Lusa hard with one paw. "Er . . . I think we ought to go."

As she was speaking, Unalaq stepped forward with a fierce roar. Lusa and Kallik spun around and fled. Lusa could hear the white bears pounding after them, and imagined she could feel their hot breath on her pelt.

They raced past the denning area and down to the shore, fleeing along a stony beach that ended in an outcrop of sharp rock.

"We can't climb that!" Lusa gasped.

"We've got to!" Kallik's voice was grim.

Putting on an extra burst of speed, they reached the bottom of the outcrop. Kallik gave Lusa a boost; as she scrambled over the pointed rocks, Lusa looked back to see the white bears charging after them along the beach, with Unalaq in the lead.

She pulled herself up and over the summit of the rocks and practically fell onto the snow-covered beach of a cove beyond. Kallik sprang down after her a moment later; together they crouched, panting, behind a heap of boulders and waited.

They could hear growls and snarls from the white bears on the other side of the outcrop. After a few moments Unalaq's voice rose above the others. "Stay away from our hunting ground! These are our seals. We'll be watching to make sure you don't steal any."

Lusa and Kallik remained silent, huddled in hiding behind the boulders. For a few moments they could hear pawsteps and snuffling on the other side of the outcrop; then the sounds faded to silence.

"They've gone!" Kallik gasped with relief.

Now that the danger was over, Lusa was able to look around her. The cove felt safe, small and sheltered between looming cliffs. Out on the sea-ice she spotted the dark patches of seal breathing holes, showing that there would be good hunting here for the white bears.

"Why did Unalaq say this was their hunting ground?" Kallik wondered. "White bears don't really have hunting grounds like brown bears do. And they don't live in groups together, either. These white bears are really weird."

"I suppose they come here because this is where the seals are," Lusa replied.

She noticed there was a harsh tang in the air, as if firebeasts had been breathing smoke everywhere. And beneath that stench was something sharper, like some sort of liquid; Lusa gagged as she breathed it in.

"I don't like it here," she said. "It smells terrible."

"Then let's go back," Kallik suggested, rising to her paws.

"No," Lusa said stubbornly. "We have to find out what that stink is first."

Peering around more carefully, she noticed that the ice and snow had melted from some of the rocks farthest away from the shoreline, and that steam was rising from them.

"Look at that," she said to Kallik, pointing with one paw. "That's not right. I'm going to see what's causing it."

She bounded up the beach, with Kallik following more slowly. Scrambling over the rocks, Lusa spotted a flat-face pipe, like the ones they had seen where the flat-faces were taking oil from the ground, only smaller. This pipe was cracked, and foul-smelling black stuff was oozing out of it.

"It looks a bit like oil—but it doesn't smell like it." Lusa turned away, clapping a paw over her nose as if she could block out the stench. The stuff smelled like the dead seal, and like Sura, but here the smell was so strong that it made Lusa's eyes water and her belly flip over.

"This place is *really* bad," she choked out.

Even Kallik was looking worried by now as she stared at the pipe and the oozing stuff. "You're right, Lusa," she murmured. "We have to tell Ujurak and Toklo about this."

CHAPTER EIGHT

Ujurak

"Okay, little cub," Ujurak said. He crouched down just outside the thornbushes that screened the entrance to their den, so that he was eye-to-eye with Kissimi. "I'm a seal. What are you going to do to me?"

Kissimi let out a squeak of delight and pounced on Ujurak, batting at him with small, soft paws. Ujurak rolled over, paws in the air. "Oh! Oh! A big, fierce, white bear got me!"

"Oh, please . . ." Toklo muttered from where he sat a little way up the hill from the mouth of the den. "You're getting as bad as Kallik."

Ujurak sat up, shaking his pelt, and gently brushed the snow from Kissimi's fine white fur. "We're just playing," he replied mildly. Affection washed over him as he glanced over at Toklo. He knew very well that whatever the big grizzly said, he wouldn't let the little cub die. "I told Kallik I'd look after him, and—"

He broke off as he spotted movement farther down the valley and made out Kallik and Lusa racing toward him.

"Toklo! Ujurak!" Their agitated cries rang through the air.

Toklo sprang to his paws, and Ujurak scanned the valley behind his two friends, half expecting to see some of the white bears chasing them. But nothing else moved in all the snowy landscape.

"What's the matter?" Ujurak asked as the two she-bears panted up to him and flopped down on the snow. Anxiety clawed at him as he saw the distraught expression in their eyes.

"The white bears chased us," Lusa panted. "Into a cove . . ."

"There's foul stuff leaking out," Kallik added, stumbling over her words in her eagerness to tell the story. "Sickness!"

"Sick seals! Sick bears!" Lusa wailed.

"Calm down." Toklo strode over to them, authority in his voice. He rested a paw on Lusa's shoulder. "Start at the beginning."

As the two she-bears caught their breath, Kissimi wobbled over to Kallik, letting out squeaks of joy at seeing her again. Kallik let him climb onto her back and snuggle into her fur, while Lusa began the story.

Ujurak listened with growing concern as he learned what Lusa and Kallik had discovered. He could see that Toklo, too, was finally taking Lusa's ideas more seriously.

"So we climbed out of the cove on the other side," Kallik finished, "and sneaked past the no-claw dens so that the white bears wouldn't see us."

"What are we going to do now?" Lusa asked.

"That leaking stuff sounds really terrible," Toklo said. "I feel like I can smell it now."

Ujurak raised his snout into the air and sniffed experimentally. "I *can* smell it!" he exclaimed, gagging as the rank smell drifted into his nostrils. "Lusa, do you have some on your fur?"

Lusa twisted around, trying to see all her pelt at once. "Oh, yuck, I do!" she complained, rolling in the snow in an attempt to clean off a patch of her shoulder fur. "I don't think I'll ever get rid of it."

Ujurak reeled back from the stench, his mind spinning. *That stuff is really bad.* He remembered the last time he'd been a flat-face on the ice, helping to rescue the creatures who had been poisoned by oil from the rig. *This must be a different kind of poison.*

"If the stuff smells as horrible as this," he said, "it must be poisoning the seals and the fish and everything in the sea. And then the bears that eat them." He paused, then added decisively, "We need to tell Aga."

Kallik rose to her paws. "We'll have to find out where the white bears are denning. Come on."

"Hey, Kallik." Toklo stopped the white bear before she had gone more than a couple of pawsteps. "You'll have to leave that cub behind."

Kallik spun around; Ujurak saw how she fired up as soon as Toklo mentioned separating her from Kissimi. "No. He's coming with us," she stated flatly. "He can't stay here on his own."

"But you can't let the other white bears see him," Toklo argued. "Not after you lied about him to Aga."

"Then I'll stay here with him," Kallik said, turning back.

"The rest of you can go."

Toklo blocked her as she tried to return to the den. His tone was determined, but not hostile. "Kallik, we've come this far together. You can't let the cub change that."

"He hasn't changed that!" Kallik snapped back. "I'm still loyal to my friends."

"Come with us, then," Ujurak said, becoming impatient with the delay. "We'll think what to do about Kissimi later."

Kallik flashed him an uncertain glance, as if she was still torn between their friendship and her care for Kissimi. "Okay," she agreed reluctantly.

With Kallik in the lead, Kissimi on her back, the four bears headed down the valley.

"This is the way to the place where I first met Aga and Illa," Toklo pointed out. "Maybe the bears' denning area is near there."

Kallik grunted agreement; Ujurak could tell she still wasn't feeling too friendly toward Toklo.

As they padded farther down the valley, Ujurak fell into step beside Lusa. "You've been digging into the snow for plants," he began. "Do you know where the snow is thinnest?"

Lusa considered for a moment, glancing around and sniffing the air carefully. "There might be a place over there," she replied, angling her ears toward a rough slope a few bear-lengths away.

Ujurak bounded over to the place she showed him; pushing his nose down into the snow, he sniffed deeply. He smelled the tang of moss, then shook his head. *That's not the right kind. I'll know the smell when I find it.*

Toklo and Kallik padded up, gazing curiously at Ujurak as he raised his head and shook snow off his muzzle.

"What are you doing?" Toklo asked curiously. "You won't find any prey under there."

"I know," Ujurak replied absently, still sniffing and not paying much attention to what Toklo was saying.

The big grizzly let out a grunt. "Well, don't be too long about it, whatever it is," he said. "We're going to see the white bears, or have you forgotten?"

He turned and plodded on, and after a moment's hesitation Kallik followed him.

Ujurak went on checking a few more spots, instinctively aware of which herb he was looking for, even though he couldn't remember ever having used it before. *My mother must be sending me a message.*

At last the scent he was looking for flooded over him, tangy and clean. Scraping through the snow, he unearthed some delicate silver-gray shoots of moss. With a huff of satisfaction, he dug up some of them.

"Lusa, can you carry this under your chin?" he asked. "Take as much as you can manage."

"What's it for?" Lusa asked curiously.

"You'll see."

Ujurak bounded forward to catch up with Kallik and Toklo, Lusa behind him, carrying the moss. When they reached them, Kallik was digging a hole in the snow.

"You stay there," she told Kissimi, nudging him gently

into the hollow she had made. "You'll be nice and warm. And you're not to move, whatever happens, until I come back for you. Do you understand?"

Kissimi let out a squeak; then he crouched down and wrapped his paws over his nose, looking up at Kallik with wide eyes.

"That's a good little cub," she murmured, touching her nose to his. "Okay," she added to the others. "Let's go."

"The white bears should be just over this ridge," Toklo said. "That's where they were coming from when I first met Aga."

As they crossed the ridge, Ujurak noticed that a white bear was on watch again; he had a red tinge to his pelt, and Ujurak thought he recognized the bear who had been watching when they first arrived on the island.

The reddish bear came to meet them as they padded down the slope, and he gave a nod of recognition to Kallik and Lusa. "Have you come to tell us not to eat hares as well?" he asked.

He sounds almost friendly, Ujurak thought, surprised and pleased. "We need to speak to Aga," he announced.

The bear hesitated for a moment, then gestured with one paw. "Sure. Follow me. My name's Yakone, by the way," he added, looking at Kallik as he spoke.

"I'm Kallik," the she-bear replied. "This is Lusa, and the brown bears are Toklo and Ujurak."

Yakone narrowed his eyes, looking at Kallik with interest. He led them down the slope, from the crest of the ridge to a wide, flat expanse of snow with the mounds of several dens visible just above the surface. A few white bears, looking thin and ragged, were wandering among the dens.

Ujurak spotted a couple of the bears lying stretched out on the snow. "What's the matter with them?" he asked Yakone. "Are they sick?"

"It's nothing," Yakone replied. "Just bellyache."

Sniffing the air, Ujurak could smell the sickness even at a distance, and he knew the trouble was worse than that. *Does Yakone really not know, or is he lying to us, to hide these bears' weakness?*

"We're not going to attack you, you know," he murmured.

Yakone turned his head to look at him, half surprised and half amused. "Four of you against all of us?" he responded. "No, I wouldn't think so."

Yakone led the way to a den with two bears outside; Ujurak recognized the younger of them as Illa. More of the bears gathered around as they approached, looking curiously at the newcomers.

As soon as Illa spotted Ujurak and the others, she rose and stretched out her neck to speak into the mouth of the den.

"Aga, you have visitors. Shesh and Tungulria are here."

Aga's rasping voice came from inside the den. "I'll come out."

When she emerged, Ujurak was shocked by her appearance. The ancient she-bear looked thinner and older than ever, though it was only the day before that they had seen her.

"I heard what happened beside the no-claw dens," she said, dipping her head in greeting.

Lusa stepped forward and laid down the moss she had been carrying in front of Aga; Ujurak admired her courage. She was trembling with a mixture of fear and anxiety, but her voice was steady as she spoke.

"You have to listen to us, please. We don't want your food. We want to help you."

Aga fixed her eyes on Lusa in a long, considering look. "Well, Tungulria," she said at last. "I'm listening."

Ujurak took a pace forward to stand by his friend's side. "We know why your bears have been getting sick," he explained. "There is a leak in the rocks near your seal hunting ground that is poisoning the seals. When the bears eat the seals, they get poisoned, too."

"How do you know this?" Aga asked. Her voice was guarded, as if she had not decided whether to believe the story.

"I found the poison!" Lusa told her, bouncing a little on her paws. "Kallik and I did."

She launched into the story of being chased into the cove by Unalaq and the others, and how she and Kallik had found the stinking stuff leaking out of the pipe.

She's exaggerating a bit! Ujurak thought, remembering how Lusa had first told the story. *She's making it sound as if there's a whole river of the stuff pouring into the sea!*

Finally Toklo halted Lusa with a grunt. She flashed a glance at him and stopped speaking.

Ujurak waited as the silence stretched out. *What will they decide?*

At last Aga blinked. "What can we do?" she asked.

Illa moved closer to the old bear, her face showing shock and confusion. "Are you going to believe them?" she asked.

Aga nodded gravely. "I will believe Tungulria," she said. "The Iqniq told me to. Long ago."

Ujurak heard Lusa gasp with astonishment. Aga had been *expecting* Lusa—or at least a black bear. *She must have had great faith to keep believing among all this snow!*

"They must have been told about you by the spirits of their ancestors," Ujurak whispered to Lusa. "To these bears you're special!"

Lusa looked shocked and unnerved, shaking her head as if she wanted to deny what she had just heard.

"Don't worry," Ujurak reassured her, pushing his snout briefly into her shoulder fur. "We can use this to help them. Tell them that they must eat this special moss to make themselves sick."

Lusa swallowed nervously, then reached out one paw to touch the moss she had placed in front of Aga. "My friend says that if you eat this moss it will make you sick," she explained.

To Ujurak's dismay there was a murmur of protest from the other bears who stood around listening.

Aga clearly shared their anxiety. "My bears are already sick," she said. "Why would I make them worse?"

"This sick will make you feel better in the end. The moss will clear out your insides and take all the poison away," Ujurak told the ancient bear. "But you must not eat any more seals. Not one. There may be other seals near here that aren't poisoned, but unless you learn to tell them apart from the ones in your hunting ground, you can't risk eating them."

Aga's eyes widened in anguish. "Then we will starve," she whispered.

"Why?" Toklo asked. "There's other prey on this island. Hares and musk ox, and—"

"But not enough," Aga interrupted. "Yes, we can catch hares and birds, but only the strongest of us can hunt the caribou. And no bear is strong enough to bring down a musk ox."

Ujurak exchanged a glance with Toklo. When they had first arrived on the island, they had worked together to hunt and kill a musk ox. But clearly these bears had never thought of hunting together like that.

"Without the seals we will starve," Aga repeated.

"No, you won't!" Lusa's voice was strong and excited once more. "You'll be fine, because we'll move the seals away from the hunting ground."

Every bear stared at Lusa as if she had grown another head. Ujurak heard Toklo mutter, "Oh, yeah, we'll just tell them all to grow wings and fly!"

"Don't you see how it makes sense?" Lusa went on. "If the seals are healthy, then the bears who eat them are healthy. So we need to move the seals somewhere healthy." She let her gaze travel around the group of gaping bears. "All you need to do is look after the animals that feed you. That means moving the seals away from the leaking pipe."

For a moment there was silence as Aga and the others thought that over. Then Ujurak spotted a disturbance in the crowd as a huge male barged his way to the front. "This is madness!" he growled. "And you're crazy, Aga, if you agree with it. It's just a trick! There's nothing wrong with the seals. It's been a hard season, so it's no wonder if the seals taste a bit odd. These bears are just trying to poison us with their plants so they can take the seals for themselves."

Ujurak dug his claws into the ground with frustration as he heard a murmur of agreement from the crowd. Some bear called out, "Unalaq's right! We shouldn't trust them."

So that's *Unalaq.* Ujurak remembered what Toklo had told him about how the huge bear had threatened him, and how he had chased Lusa and Kallik. *We might have known he would make trouble.*

"Well, I think we should listen to them." Yakone shouldered his way forward and stood beside Unalaq. "You're too hotheaded, brother; you should think before you open your jaws." Unalaq drew back his lips in a snarl, but Yakone ignored him and went on. "Has any bear seen these newcomers eating seals?" His gaze raked the crowd. "No? Then maybe that's not their kind of food."

Ujurak was grateful that one bear at least could see sense. He could smell the taint of sickness on Yakone and see it in his drooping head and dull eyes. He pushed a little of the moss toward him.

"Eat this," he said. "It will help."

Yakone eyed the moss uncertainly. Before he could do anything, Aga thrust herself forward to his side.

"I will eat it first," she said. "Before any of my bears."

Ujurak admired her nobility, but he stretched out a paw to stop her as she lowered her head toward the moss. He gave her a careful sniff and realized that she hadn't eaten any of the poisoned seal.

"You aren't sick," he said. "The moss will only make you ill unnecessarily."

"But—" Aga began.

"I'll eat it," Ujurak interrupted. "Then you'll see what will happen to you. It's not nice, but it will make you better, I promise you."

Ujurak bent his head, licked up some of the moss, chewed, and swallowed, feeling the gaze of every bear boring into him as he did so. Unalaq looked suspicious, and Lusa had alarm in her eyes, while Aga's gaze was full of mysterious wisdom.

The juices of the moss had a clean, astringent taste, and almost at once Ujurak could feel his belly start to revolt. Stumbling through the crowd, which parted to let him pass, he heaved and heaved up vomit into the snow until his belly was empty. Spitting out the last of the bitterness, he gulped in some fresh snow to clean his mouth and tottered back to the assembled bears.

"See?" he rasped. "That's all that will happen. The moss will get rid of the poisoned seal."

Aga looked at Lusa. "And you? You're sure about this?"

Lusa nodded vigorously. "Ujurak is never wrong about herbs," she assured the ancient bear. "And . . . and I know that it will help your bears."

Aga gave a brisk nod, suddenly looking less old and frail. "Illa, go and fetch all the sick bears," she ordered. "Bring them here to eat the moss."

"Toklo, could you go and fetch some more?" Ujurak asked. He still felt too shaken to go all the way back to the valley. "Lusa will show you where it came from."

"I'm on my way," Toklo replied, heading back the way they had come with Lusa beside him.

Kallik remained by Ujurak's side. "I'm not leaving you alone with that Unalaq around," she whispered.

One by one the sick bears came up, took a mouthful of the moss, and went away to be sick. Unalaq stood watching, and he gave the moss a contemptuous kick with one hindpaw.

"I'm not eating that!" he snarled. "You might trick all these others, but you won't trick me."

"You're not sick," Ujurak pointed out, giving the big bear's pelt a quick sniff. "So you don't need to eat it."

"I wouldn't touch it even if I *was* sick!"

Two others—young males like Unalaq—were standing close behind him, and they nodded in agreement as he spoke.

"You're right, Unalaq," one of them said. "Why would these strange bears want to help us?"

Ujurak felt a flash of frustration burning through him like a bolt of lightning. *How can they be so stupid? They just don't want to be helped.* "If you eat the poisoned seals, you will die!" he warned them.

Before Unalaq or the others could respond, Kallik nudged Ujurak away. "Come on; calm down," she murmured. "There's no helping them if they're that bee-brained."

As Ujurak turned away, he spotted Yakone, looking very

shaky as he plodded up. Ujurak caught the smell of vomit on his fur.

"You were right," Yakone said hoarsely. "I got rid of all the seal I ate yesterday. It . . . it smelled really bad."

"You'll be fine," Kallik assured him. "Lie down and rest, and I'll fetch you some fresh snow to lick."

"Thanks." Yakone flopped down into the snow, his chest heaving with deep breaths.

Leaving him to Kallik, Ujurak turned away to see Toklo and Lusa returning with more moss, weaving a path among the retching bears.

Toklo dropped the moss at Ujurak's paws. "I can't believe they did what you told them!"

Ujurak shook his head. "No, they did what Lusa told them. I think Aga has been waiting for a black bear to come and save her people."

Toklo blinked disbelievingly. "Lusa?"

Lusa butted him in the side. "Show some respect!" she exclaimed with mock indignation.

"Don't forget," Ujurak reminded her, "you still have to fulfill your promise of moving the seals away from the leak."

Lusa gulped, suddenly serious again. "Do you think we can?"

Ujurak met her gaze, suddenly feeling what a huge task lay ahead of them. "We have to," he replied.

CHAPTER NINE

Kallik

When Yakone had gotten rid of the taste of vomit from his mouth, he settled down to sleep. As Kallik headed back to where Ujurak was dosing the last of the sick bears with the healing moss, she spotted Aga padding up to her. Her belly fluttered nervously. *Does Aga know about Kissimi somehow? Can she smell him on my fur?*

But when the old bear reached Kallik's side, her look was friendly. "You have traveled far, young one," she said. "It's strange to me, to see one of my kind together with brown bears and a black bear."

"It feels strange to me, too, sometimes," Kallik confessed. "But they are my friends—and they would never dream of harming any bear here," she added.

Aga nodded. "I can believe that now." Her bright eyes seemed to pierce Kallik to the depths; Kallik felt that somehow she must be able to see the truth about what had happened to Sura's cub. She braced herself for an accusation.

"The bears here are strange to me, too," she began, desperate to distract Aga from asking questions. "Where I come from, white bears live alone, not in a group as you do."

To her relief Aga's look was still penetrating, but full of interest. "This is our way," she replied. "Perhaps it is because we live on an island. Even if we tried to live alone, we would always be tripping over one another!"

Kallik cast a glance to where Ujurak, Lusa, and Toklo were still dividing up the last of the moss. *Come on! Get me out of this!*

"Why do you have special hunting grounds?" she asked Aga. "My mother, Nisa, told me that white bears range all over the Endless Ice and take their prey where they find it."

Aga blinked sadly. "Again, our island is small, young one," she replied. "Our task is hard enough: to find food for all of us. The cove where the seals live is our best source of prey."

"I'm sorry," Kallik said. *Everything is connected,* she thought. *The sick seals, the way no-claws spoil the hunting grounds . . . Somehow we have to find out how to save the wild!*

She started at the touch of Aga's snout on her shoulder.

"Your friends are coming." The old bear pointed to where Toklo, Lusa, and Ujurak had left the other white bears and were heading toward Kallik. Giving Kallik a look of great kindness, she added, "Perhaps we will talk again soon, young one."

Once she and her friends had left the sick bears to recover, Kallik couldn't wait to get back to Kissimi. She bounded ahead, following their tracks back through the snow, straight to the snow hollow where she had left him.

When he spotted Kallik, the tiny cub bounced up, letting out happy squeaks. Kallik bent over him, nuzzling his belly and reveling in the feeling of his soft paws batting her ears.

I could stay like this forever, she thought.

Behind her Toklo's gruff voice broke into her absorption in her cub. "Come along. It's getting dark, and we need to figure out where we can put the seals to make them healthy."

Kallik could hear the frustration in his tone.

"I don't know why we're doing this," he grumbled as Lusa and Ujurak caught up. "If these bears are too dumb to see that the seals were poisoned, how will they know when they're safe to eat?" He kicked the snow irritably. "We should be concentrating on finding the end of our journey, not messing around like this for strangers."

Ujurak gave his friend a long, solemn look. "Toklo, what if this *is* the end of our journey? Helping these bears matters as much as helping any animals." He hesitated, then added, "Besides, they've been waiting for Lusa."

Toklo huffed contemptuously. "That's just a BirthDen story!"

"It feels pretty real to me!" Lusa retorted, her fur bristling with indignation.

Kallik tickled Kissimi's belly lightly with her claws. "We *should* help the white bears," she insisted, without taking her eyes off the cub.

"You're just saying that because *you're* a white bear," Toklo pointed out.

Kallik rounded on him. "That's not true! I'd help any bears

who were starving to death because their food had been poisoned."

She flashed back to Yakone. *His eyes were so tired and scared, even though he was acting brave around the other bears.*

An unfamiliar pain quickened in Kallik's belly at the thought of what Yakone had suffered.

Why do I feel like this? Why is Yakone different from all the other bears?

"Please help the bears," she begged, turning to Lusa.

Lusa nodded, and brushed her muzzle against Kallik's flank. "I'm going to try," she promised. "But I'm not doing it on my own."

"Of course not," Ujurak said instantly. "We'll help you."

Kallik glanced at Toklo, who still looked unconvinced. "I suppose I've stuck with you this far . . ." he muttered.

"That's great!" Lusa blinked with relief. "First we have to find somewhere safe for the seals to live."

"Tomorrow," Kallik said; Kissimi's head was drooping, and he parted his tiny jaws in a huge yawn. "Now let's get back to the den."

Gray dawn light gleamed on the snow as the bears set out the following morning to find a new home for the seals. A fresh breeze made Kallik's eyes water, and she checked that Kissimi was bundled deep into the fur on her shoulders.

"Did any of you notice that the sky was completely empty last night?" Ujurak asked as they left the den behind. "There were no spirits—not even the faintest trace of them. No Iqniq, as the white bears call them. Could they be right, that the spirits are abandoning us?"

Kallik felt a stab of dismay at Ujurak's words. *Could my mother really be leaving me, now that we're so close to the end of our journey?*

Desperately she tried to hear Nisa's voice on the wind, or recall the touch of her fur, but there was only an empty silence.

Mother, please don't—

Kallik's frantic thoughts broke off as she realized that Kissimi was slipping off her shoulders. Halting, she boosted him back up. "Hold tight, little one," she said gently, then hurried to catch up with her friends.

Avoiding the no-claw denning area, they headed for the edge of the cliff not far away from where they had first seen Sura dragging her seal along.

Lusa pointed with one paw. "The seal hunting ground is that way."

"Then we should go the other way," Toklo suggested. "As far away from that stinking stuff as we can get to find clean water."

He took the lead along the edge of the island. Worried that Kissimi might fall, Kallik kept well away from the precipice, while the others searched for a way down to the shore.

"We could try here," Toklo reported, peering down over a dip in the cliffs. "I'll go first, and for the spirits' sake watch where you're putting your paws."

He vanished over the cliff edge with Lusa after him and Ujurak a few moments behind. Kallik turned her head to look up at Kissimi. "Remember I told you to hold tight?" she asked. "It's going to get bumpy now, but it won't be for long."

Kissimi squeaked a reply as Kallik began edging down the broken rocks to the shore below. The others were waiting for her. She reflected that she would have climbed down quickly only a few days before, but that now she had her cub's safety to think about.

"Nice job," Ujurak murmured as she reached the safety of the beach. He touched his nose to Kissimi's tiny one. "Well done, little cub. You're brave!"

Kallik stared out across the frozen sea as she and her friends made their way along the beach. She felt they needed to get much farther away from the cove with the leaking pipe before they could be sure that the water was free of poison.

Then, rounding a spur of rock jutting out from the cliff face, they found the way blocked by a pile of boulders stretching for many bearlengths above their heads.

Toklo let out a growl of frustration. "We can't climb that!"

"Then we'll have to climb the cliff again," Ujurak said calmly. "I think I saw a place just back here."

Kallik's shoulders drooped as she retraced her steps, padding behind Ujurak. Her legs ached with weariness, and her belly was grumbling for prey. *Kissimi needs food, too.*

Ujurak led them to a place where there was a deep cleft in the cliff face, full of debris. "We should be able to claw our way up here," he suggested.

Without waiting for a response, he pushed his way into the cleft and scrambled upward, sending a shower of grit and pebbles and melting snow down on the bears behind him.

"Ugh!" Lusa exclaimed, flicking dirt off her fur.

She began to climb after Ujurak. Kallik waited for her to get well ahead before she started to follow, warning Kissimi again to hold on tight.

"I'll be right behind you," Toklo said. "If he falls, I'll catch him."

Kallik flashed the big grizzly a grateful look. *Toklo might be grumpy, but I know I can trust him.*

She scrabbled her way to the cliff top, barely squeezing between the narrow walls of the cleft. Kissimi clung to her shoulders, squeaking excitedly as if this was a big adventure.

Not long after they regained the top of the cliff, the land fell away steeply into a gorge, where bare, gray boulders poked up out of the snow. The bears half slid, half scrambled down into the bottom and hauled themselves up the other side.

"We've got to get back to the beach," Lusa panted. "We'll never find a home for the seals at this rate."

"And we need to hunt," Toklo added. "If we don't eat, we'll be too weak to help the other bears."

He headed toward the sea again. Kallik realized that the ground was sloping downward more gently here, and soon they came in sight of a huge bay, a wide half circle like an enormous bite out of the land. At each side the cliffs gradually sank to meet the shore, and between them a frozen river ran into the sea.

"This looks promising," Ujurak said.

Lusa's eyes were bright and optimistic. "It looks great!"

Their weariness vanishing, all the bears picked up speed until they were racing down the slope to the edge of the river. Kallik loved the feeling of cold air flowing through her pelt and the keen scent of the ice.

They reached the riverbank a few bearlengths away from the shore. Snow-laden plants hung over the surface, and the air was filled with a soft gurgling sound from the river water flowing underneath the ice. Kallik took a long breath and let it out again in a sigh.

It's so peaceful here. I hope we've found the right place for the seals.

Ujurak headed farther down the beach, while Kissimi crouched down at the very edge of the river and reached out with one paw to pat the frozen surface. "Ice!" he squeaked. "Ice!"

Kallik gasped with surprise. "Hey, did you hear that?" she exclaimed. "Kissimi said *ice!*"

"He's so clever!" Lusa marveled.

Toklo groaned. "I suppose now he'll never stop talking. Just like a certain annoying black bear."

Lusa turned around and kicked out with her hindpaws, showering snow over Toklo. "I'll show you how I can be *really* annoying!"

She dashed off, following Ujurak, and Toklo lumbered after her.

Meanwhile Kissimi was still crouching over the river, peering in fascination at the shapes made by the flowing water.

"Stay here and play, little one," Kallik told him. "Don't wander away. I'll come back for you very soon."

Kissimi nodded happily; Kallik made for the beach, where the others were padding up and down, exploring the bay. She stood still and sniffed; close to the sea the ice still smelled clean. There were no leaking pipes here; there was no disgusting black mud to defile the sea with its stink.

"This place looks good for seals," Toklo remarked, halting beside her.

"It does, but we can't be sure yet," Kallik replied. "Not until we've looked under the ice. That's where the seals and fish spend most of their time. We have to be certain that there's no poison in the water."

Lusa stared out at the ice, her eyes wide with dismay. "But how will we be able to do that? That ice is thick!"

"I'll look for a breathing hole," Kallik replied, beginning to head out onto the ice.

"But won't that mean there are other seals living here?" Lusa asked. "They might not let the seals from the cove come live here."

Kallik glanced back. "Maybe. But I don't have a better idea."

She ranged back and forth across the ice within the curve of the bay, but at first she found nothing. Almost ready to give up, she was on her way back to the beach when she spotted a darker patch a little farther ahead. Drawing closer, she found a ragged hole in the ice, already starting to close up.

It looks as if there was a seal here, but quite a while ago. If there were seals here now, there would be more than this one hole.

Taking a deep breath, Kallik plunged her head through the

hole, right down into the sea. The cold shock rushed through her, sending a tingle of energy through her whole body to the tips of her paws.

Opening her eyes, she saw that the sea was dark but there was no dirt in it. With a satisfied grunt she pulled back, taking a huge gulp of air. Carefully she swiped her tongue around her jaws; all she could taste was salt and the wild tang of the ocean.

"Well?" Toklo was plodding over to her across the ice, followed closely by Lusa and Ujurak. "What did you find?"

"It's clean," Kallik reported. "This really could be what we're looking for."

"Then we should go and tell—" Lusa began.

She was interrupted by a loud squeaking from farther inshore. "K'lik! K'lik!" Kallik turned her head to see that Kissimi was scampering across the ice toward them.

Warm happiness spread through Kallik. *He knows my name!*

As Kissimi hurtled toward her, his paws skidded on the ice. He let out a shrill cry of exhilaration as he slid forward with the wind flattening his soft fur to his sides.

Kallik's happiness turned to horror. "Kissimi, watch out!" she shouted, hurling herself toward him.

But she was too late. Before any bear could reach out to stop him, Kissimi fell with a splash into the breathing hole. His excited squeal became a startled wail; then his head went underwater.

"No!" Kallik exclaimed.

For a moment of heart-stopping panic she thought that the

young cub had vanished completely. Then she spotted him underneath the ice, scratching feebly at the underside with his paws. His eyes were wide and terrified.

Kallik crouched beside the hole and plunged a paw into the water, but Kissimi was just too far away for her to grab him; all she managed to do was push the cub farther away still.

Beside her Toklo reared up on his hindpaws. "I'll break the ice," he grunted, his forepaws poised to crash through it.

"No!" Kallik thrust herself in front of him. "You'll hurt him!"

"I'll save him." Ujurak spoke behind them, tense but calm. "Wait here."

He bounded over to the hole. Kallik watched in breathless hope as his body shrank and his brown fur vanished, to be replaced by a gleaming gray-brown pelt. In the shape of a sleek seal he dove into the hole, his slim form just brushing the sides.

Gazing down, Kallik saw Ujurak's dark shape curl around Kissimi. The cub thrashed with his paws as if he was afraid and trying to escape. But Ujurak nudged him safely back to the hole, where Kallik bent down and sank her teeth into the cub's scruff, hauling him out onto the ice.

"What did I tell you?" she growled as Kissimi lay with his paws splayed out, coughing up water. "I said stay by the river! You might have died!"

"Hey, take it easy." Lusa pressed comfortingly against Kallik's side. "He's only little. He doesn't understand about danger."

"Then it's time he learned!" Kallik snapped. She thought that her heart would never stop thumping. "Oh, little one, what if I'd lost you?" She bent her head and started to lick the seawater out of Kissimi's fur.

"He got a bad scare," Lusa went on. "And on top of being stuck under the ice, the way he was fighting looked like he thought Ujurak-seal was going to eat him! I'm sure he's learned his lesson."

"I hope so," Kallik muttered between licks.

Ujurak pulled himself out of the hole, changing back from a seal to a brown bear and shaking the water from his pelt. Kallik looked up to see a huge fish flapping helplessly in his jaws.

"Great catch!" Toklo said, his eyes gleaming hungrily.

Ujurak dropped the fish on the ice and killed it with a bite to the back of its head. "There," he said. "It smells fine. Proof that the water here is clean."

All the bears gathered around. Kallik felt herself growing calmer as she took her first bite, relishing the delicious taste. "Here, Kissimi," she said, tearing off a small shred of the fish and chewing it up before dropping the pulp in front of her cub. "You can try your first taste of food from the ocean."

She watched the tiny cub as he nibbled the fish cautiously at first, then gulped it down with gleaming eyes and looked around for more. Kallik's heart pounded painfully in her chest; she had never imagined that loving someone could hurt as much as this.

"Ujurak, thank you," she said. "I'll never forget how you saved Kissimi."

Ujurak dipped his head. "Anytime."

Kallik blinked at him, wanting to say more, then was distracted as Kissimi nudged her paw impatiently with his nose.

"Okay, okay, more fish coming up," Kallik said. "Soon you'll be catching these yourself," she promised, preparing another mouthful for him.

Kissimi glanced back at the breathing hole, shuddered, and let out a squeak.

Lusa huffed with amusement. "He says not if he has to go near the water again!"

When the last scraps of the fish were eaten, the bears headed back toward their den. While they were still climbing up the slope from the bay, the first flakes of snow began to fall, rapidly growing thicker and thicker until the way ahead was almost hidden behind a whirling white screen.

"This is all we need," Toklo grunted.

The wind picked up, blowing into their faces, until they were forcing their way into the teeth of a blizzard. Kallik could hear Kissimi whimpering unhappily and realized how cold and tired he must be. She felt his tiny paws clinging to a tuft of her fur.

"Don't let go, little one," she warned him. "I'd never find you in all this snow."

Lusa had taken the lead, with Toklo just behind her, nose to tail so as not to lose her, then Kallik, and last of all Ujurak. They plodded through the thickening snow; Kallik wasn't sure if they were heading in the right direction any longer.

Up ahead a startled yelp came from Lusa, and her black shape, scarcely visible through the driving snow, suddenly vanished. Toklo stopped so abruptly that Kallik almost blundered into him.

"What happened?" she asked.

"This is the gorge," Toklo replied, glancing over his shoulder at Kallik. Snow was thick on his muzzle and around his eyes, and he sounded as if he was struggling to repress panic. "Lusa stepped over the edge."

Kallik's belly lurched with anxiety. "Is she okay? Lusa!"

"The snow's thick enough," Ujurak pointed out as he joined them. "It would be soft to fall on." Kallik suspected he was trying to sound more confident than he felt.

"I'll probably have to drag her out of another drift," Toklo muttered under his breath as he began heading down the steep slope, stepping sideways through the deep, soft snow so that he wouldn't slip.

Kallik and Ujurak tried to walk in his steps, but the shifting snow made it almost impossible.

"Lusa! Lusa!" Kallik called as she floundered around in the sea of white, and she thought she heard an answering cry beneath the whining of the wind.

Peering through the snow, she spotted a black boulder just ahead; as she drew closer it turned into Lusa.

"Thank the spirits!" Kallik exclaimed. "Are you all right?"

"I'm fine," Lusa replied, though she sounded shaken. "Do you think we should shelter down here until the wind drops?"

Through the whirling snow Kallik could see that they had reached the bottom of the gorge. "We could make a temporary den," she began, "Kissimi could do with—"

She broke off. A rumble of thunder sounded through the gorge.

"Thunder?" Ujurak sounded puzzled. "In a blizzard?"

For a moment Kallik froze. She knew something was wrong. The sound was growing louder and louder with every breath she took. The snow beneath her paws was trembling, and a thin layer started to shift around them.

"Something's coming down the gorge!" she exclaimed.

"Run!" Toklo barked.

Side by side the bears struggled to scramble up the far side of the gorge. But the newly fallen snow was soft and powdery, and it shifted under their paws. Kallik found that she was sinking into it as far as her belly fur, and there was nothing solid for her paws to grip. She floundered a few steps upward and slid down again in a flurry of snow.

The thundering sound grew louder still, and suddenly a herd of caribou lurched out of the blizzard. Something had spooked them, and their hooves pounded through the snow as they galloped down the gorge in terror, a moving wall of hooves and antlers, bearing down on Kallik.

The white bear froze, staring in horror. *Kissimi! What can I do?*

"Kallik!" Toklo's voice sounded urgently from just above her. "Kallik, up here!"

Kallik looked up to see the brown bear perched on a rock

a couple of bearlengths above her head. He was peering down at her, gesturing urgently with one paw.

"Up here!" he repeated.

Desperately Kallik launched herself upward, thrusting Kissimi in front of her. Toklo leaned down from the rock and grabbed the cub in his jaws. Kallik tried to follow, but as she scrambled toward the rock, she felt her paws slipping under her. Snow cascaded around her as she fell back to the bottom of the gorge, under the hooves of the caribou.

One pointed hoof struck her on her shoulder as she struggled to regain her paws. She fell back again, scrabbling sideways toward the foot of the slope, but another set of flying hooves caught her on her back. The terrified caribou trampled her as she fought frantically to climb back up. In the chaos of thundering hooves she thought she could hear the bears calling her name. Then blinding pain shot through her head; the gorge wheeled around her, a sickening whirl of white. She gave up her struggles, lying limp and helpless. The white gradually darkened to gray as her senses faded, then to a black sky filled with stars, and the tumult of the fleeing caribou faded to silence.

Kallik opened her eyes on a world of unbroken white. There was no wind, no falling snow, no sound of thundering hooves.

Am I dead? she wondered. *Nisa, where are you?*

A face loomed over her, but it was black, not white; blinking, Kallik recognized Lusa. Toklo and Ujurak were just behind her; Kissimi was clinging to Ujurak's fur.

"Thank Arcturus you're all right!" Lusa gasped.

Kissimi let out a loud squeal. Wriggling out of Toklo's grasp, he hurled himself at Kallik's chest, bouncing up and down.

"Gently, little one," she muttered, encircling him with a paw.

Kallik's heart thumped harder as she realized that she had thrust Kissimi to safety just as her mother, Nisa, had thrust her away from the orca. She would have died for Kissimi, just as Nisa had died for her. New strength and determination gathered inside her as she felt herself treading in her mother's pawsteps.

Slowly the white bear rose to her paws, testing each leg to make sure she could stand on it. Her body ached all over from the caribou's hooves, but nothing seemed to be seriously damaged. "I'm okay," she said.

All along the gorge the caribou had churned up the snow, a trail that broke up the untouched whiteness as far as Kallik could see in both directions.

"What on earth spooked them?" she asked, not expecting a reply.

Toklo shrugged and shook his head.

"They went past too quickly," Ujurak said. "I couldn't sense anything from them except fear. But I think we should get out of here, in case they come back."

"Good idea," Toklo agreed.

He led the way a little farther up the gorge until they came to a place where the sides were lower and it was easier to climb.

Twilight was falling by the time they reached the top.

As they trudged on, the lights of the no-claw denning area came into sight; Kallik could hear noise coming from there, and the sound of seals barking.

"We did it!" she said, satisfaction flooding through her. "We found clean water, and we got back safely."

"We did." Lusa's voice was confident. "And tomorrow we move the seals."

CHAPTER TEN

Ujurak

Black waves lapped at the pebbles as Ujurak padded down the beach and waded out into the ocean. As the water's icy claws sank deep into his fur, he scanned the surface for the bobbing heads of seals, but he couldn't see a single one.

Strange. This is the bears' hunting ground, so where are the seals?

The black water rose rapidly around Ujurak as he waded farther, and he plunged downward as it closed over his head. Swimming underwater, he kept his bear shape, resisting the urge to take the sleek form of a seal.

He felt a stab of panic as the water grew darker and darker and he still couldn't find any seals.

Have they all left? Will I ever find them?

Then suddenly the seals were all around him, shadowy, supple shapes swarming everywhere, gliding around him but never touching him. Their eyes glinted at him, shining brighter and brighter in the dark depths of the ocean, until Ujurak suddenly realized that they weren't eyes—they were stars.

The water had vanished. Now Ujurak was swimming through the night sky, surrounded by stars that blazed so brightly he had to blink against them. When he looked down, he could see the icy island far, far below him, and on the seashore three tiny dots that he knew were Toklo, Lusa, and Kallik.

No! Ujurak's panic returned, flooding over him in vast waves. His paws thrashed helplessly at the air. *I'm going to fall!*

Then a quiet voice sounded alongside him. "Don't be afraid. You're quite safe with me."

With a rush of relief and love, Ujurak recognized the voice of his mother, Ursa. She was all around him, her starry body enfolding him with the softest brush of fur. Ujurak reveled in her touch, realizing that he had never felt more at home.

Looking down at himself, Ujurak saw that his fur was full of stars, too, blending into his mother's fur so that he couldn't be sure where he ended and she began. He gazed up into her shining eyes, content not to question.

"Do not fear," Ursa whispered. "I am waiting for you."

The cold touch of snowmelt trickling through his fur woke Ujurak. He was curled up in the snow-den under the thorns, tucked in among the sleeping bodies of his friends. Pale dawn light was seeping through the entrance.

For a moment Ujurak blinked in disappointment, yearning for the stars and the soft touch of his mother's fur again. Then he remembered that this was the day they had to move the seals to the bay they had discovered, and his memory of the dream was swallowed up in apprehension.

The other bears began stirring around him; Toklo parted his jaws in an enormous yawn. Ujurak wriggled between him and Kallik and scrambled out into the crisp dawn air, waiting for the others to join him.

They were all quiet, exchanging quick glances with one another. Their confidence of the previous day had ebbed like the tide. Ujurak could tell that they were all sharing the same thought: *This is a huge task! Can we really do what we promised?*

Lusa was the first to break the silence. "Come on! We have to do this."

Pride in her courage warmed Ujurak like a ray of sunlight. He remembered how Aga had called Lusa "Tungulria."

"Hurry up, Kissimi." Kallik nuzzled her cub and crouched down so that he could scramble up onto her shoulders. "We're going to visit some seals."

The little cub let out a plaintive wail as he settled himself in Kallik's fur. Ujurak guessed that he was hungry; it had been a long time since they'd shared the fish he had caught.

"I don't blame you, little one," Ujurak muttered; he could feel the hollowness in his own belly. "I'm hungry, too!"

"Are you sure you should take Kissimi with you?" Toklo asked. His voice was concerned; he seemed to have lost a lot of his hostility toward the cub. "Remember what happened with the caribou."

"I'm not leaving him behind!" Kallik's head whipped around, and she gave Toklo a searing glare. "You never know what might be lurking, just waiting to take a cub who can't defend himself."

Toklo shrugged. "Okay, calm down. It was just a suggestion."

Kallik hesitated, then nodded, her anger fading as if she realized that Toklo was concerned for Kissimi, too. She set off in the direction of the old seal hunting ground, with a glance back to see if the others were following.

Is she really afraid that something will harm Kissimi? Ujurak wondered as he padded after her. *Or is she worried that one of Aga's bears will find the cub?*

With Kallik in the lead, they skirted the flat-face denning area, where a few lights were showing among the dens. The only sound was a flat-face voice, then another answering it, but they were faint with distance, and Ujurak realized they were no threat.

Several firebeasts were crouching here and there among the dens. Toklo glared at them as they padded past, and a low growl came from his throat.

A shiver went through Ujurak as he waited for the firebeasts to open their glaring eyes and break into a menacing roar. But they stayed dark and silent.

"It's okay. They're asleep," he whispered.

"They'd better stay that way!" Toklo muttered back.

Keeping their distance, the bears headed down to the shore and scrambled over the boulders into the cove.

"Thank Arcturus there aren't any of the white bears here!" Lusa exclaimed as she leaped down onto the pebbly beach. "They listened!"

Toklo gave a huff of agreement. "We have enough to worry

about without them coming around."

Gazing out to sea, Ujurak spotted several seal breathing holes, and even some seals basking on the ice, well away from the shoreline. He took a pace toward them, then stopped, realizing that he had no idea what to do next.

"How are we going to get them to move?" Lusa asked, echoing his doubts. "I thought we could show them the poison trickling out, but how would we get them close enough to see it? Or we could get the stuff on our paws and then—"

"You can forget that right now," Toklo interrupted. "I'm not getting that stink on my paws, not for all the bears on the ice!"

Lusa sighed. "You're right; it is horrible. And we would still have to show them where it came from. Kallik, you know more about seals than the rest of us," she went on. "How can we make them understand?"

"We can't," Kallik replied. "Bears don't talk to seals."

"Then maybe we can chase them into the other bay," Toklo suggested, hunching his shoulders as he gazed out at the distant seals.

"We can try," Kallik agreed dubiously. "But what if they dive back into the water? We can't chase them there."

Toklo hesitated, then shrugged. "We'll have to stop them from going back through their breathing holes."

Kallik gave Toklo a look that told Ujurak she didn't think that would work, but she said nothing.

"We can't just stand here," Lusa said. "Let's give it a try."

Toklo lumbered out onto the ice, picking up the pace as

he drew closer to the seals. Lusa dashed after him. Ujurak exchanged a doubtful glance with Kallik, then followed.

But well before the bears reached the first breathing holes, the seals were aware of them. They started hauling themselves across the ice, slipping down through the holes into the safety of the ocean. There were too many holes for the bears to intercept the seals. Ujurak could sense their panic.

"Cloud-brains!" Toklo halted and let out a roar of frustration. "We want to help you!"

"They don't understand," Lusa panted.

Kissimi squealed with excitement as Kallik hurled herself across the ice, trying to intercept a seal as it dove down through a hole. It slid past her, barely a muzzlelength ahead of her claws, and vanished with a farewell flick of its tail.

Lusa charged into a group of seals, biting and snapping in her efforts to herd them toward the new bay, but the seals just scattered in terror. Lusa lost her footing on the ice and thumped down hard on her haunches.

"Why won't they do as they're told?" she gasped.

Ujurak heard a panic-stricken screech behind him and spun around to see that Toklo had flung himself on top of one of the seals, which lay limp under his claws, its eyes glazed with fear. Toklo was poised to sink his teeth into its throat.

"No, Toklo!" Ujurak yelled. "We're not hunting! The seals are poisonous!"

Toklo let out a snarl of rage and scrambled off the seal. The terrified creature lay frozen for a moment, then dug the claws on its front flippers into the ice and flung itself down a breathing hole.

"This feels all wrong," Toklo grumbled. "Seals are *prey*."

"Not these seals," Lusa reminded him.

Glancing around, Ujurak saw that almost all the seals had vanished, and those that were left were moving rapidly toward the nearest holes. Chasing them hadn't worked.

"Now what do we do?" Kallik panted.

Lusa shook her head helplessly. "I have no idea."

"It was a dumb idea anyway." Toklo glared at the breathing hole where the seal had vanished. "We couldn't have chased them all the way to the new bay."

"We could have if they'd stayed on the ice," Kallik argued.

Ujurak listened to his friends bickering and realized that there was only one answer. He let out a long sigh. "I know what to do," he said reluctantly.

He concentrated as he headed toward one of the breathing holes, feeling his fur shrink back until a smooth gray pelt covered all his body. His legs changed into flippers. By the time he reached the hole, he had taken on the complete shape of a seal.

As Ujurak slid easily through the conical tunnel into the dark water beneath, a nearby seal swerved away from him in alarm, with a soft grunting noise. Ignoring it for the moment, Ujurak drew a little of the water into his mouth, aware right away of its sickening taste, and he saw how cloudy it was because of the poison leaking from the pipe.

This is disgusting, he thought. *I wonder why the seals haven't moved already. They must know about that beautiful clean bay; it's not so far away.* Hope surged through him. *It's so clear they must move. Maybe this task will be easy, after all.*

Ujurak swam among the seals, who were hovering in the water, reminding him of the shapes that had swirled around him in his dream. They were all staring at him with solemn eyes in whiskered faces.

I'm surprised they know I'm a stranger, he commented to himself, finding it hard to tell one seal from another.

Then as his gaze traveled around the group and he looked more closely with his seal eyes, he realized that he was wrong to think they looked alike. One seal had more of the silver-gray dappling on its back than any of the others. Another had especially long whiskers. Yet another was very fat. Ujurak realized that each of them was subtly different.

As different as one bear is from another.

Ujurak swam on, looking for a breathing hole so he could take in air, but also wondering which of the seals was their leader. Spotting a circle of light above his head, he headed for it, only to find a big, whiskered seal floating just beneath the hole.

His senses spinning from lack of air, Ujurak wondered if the big seal would try to block his way. He braced himself for a fight, but at the last moment the big seal swam aside.

Ujurak popped out through the hole, gulping in huge mouthfuls of air. He hauled himself out onto the ice and dragged himself awkwardly a bearlength forward.

Cautiously Ujurak scanned his surroundings. To his relief

none of the white bears were waiting for their prey to appear. Toklo, Lusa, and Kallik had disappeared, too; Ujurak guessed they were hiding so as not to spook the seals.

Hearing a grunt behind him, and the sound of a large body flopping onto the ice, Ujurak turned to see that the big seal had followed him out of the hole.

"Who are you?" the seal asked. "Where have you come from?"

"I come from far away," Ujurak replied, hope surging up inside him at the chance of explaining. "I have something important to tell you."

The big seal blew out a noisy breath, riffling his whiskers. "What?"

Ujurak glanced around. More of the seals were appearing through the breathing hole, staring curiously at Ujurak as they formed a ragged circle around him and the big seal. This time Ujurak had no difficulty reminding himself that he wasn't one of them. The urgency of his mission kept his mind focused.

Taking a deep breath, Ujurak raised his voice to carry to all of them. "This place is making you sick!"

The big seal narrowed his eyes, giving Ujurak a suspicious look. Ujurak expected him to deny that there was anything wrong, but he said nothing, as if he was taking his time to weigh what Ujurak told him.

The other seals, Ujurak could tell, were more shocked by his announcement. One or two of them shot him hostile glares. Others bent their heads close to one another and muttered anxiously.

One young male with silver markings clustered thickly on his back leaned forward and slapped one flipper threateningly on the ice. "Go away and mind your own business!" he barked.

"Leave him alone, Silver!" an older female snapped, shouldering the young male back. "Maybe he's got a point."

"But how does he know?" another seal asked warily.

"I have found the place where the poison leaks into the water," Ujurak explained.

"Poison?" The word was echoed by more than one seal in the crowd.

"What is he talking about—poison?"

"I'll show you," Ujurak answered. "Follow me."

Sliding down through the breathing hole, he swam farther inshore, until he spotted another hole near the rocks. When he hauled himself out, still clumsy in this new shape, he found himself close to the place where Kallik and Lusa had found the leaking pipe.

"Look," he said to the big seal as his whiskery face popped up out of the hole. Ujurak pointed with one flipper toward the place where the brown stinking liquid was oozing out onto the rocks.

The big seal pulled himself out onto the ice, followed by his companions. Shocked exclamations came from some of them; Ujurak realized how strong the stench was to his sensitive nose—stronger even than when he was a bear—and he could understand how the seals must be revolted by it. One or two of them even plunged straight back into the hole.

Anger jolted through Ujurak at the thought that the seals

had stayed in the cove when something was so obviously wrong. "You must have known this was here," he accused the big seal. "Why haven't you moved away? I know it's been making you sick. The water is poisoned. The fish you eat have been poisoned."

Ujurak's heated tones didn't seem to affect the big seal. "This is our home," he growled. "And the no-swims helped us make our home here. So why would they do something that would drive us away?"

No-swims? Ujurak wondered. *Does he mean flat-faces? And what does he mean by saying that they helped the seals?*

The big seal loomed over him. "I don't trust you," he went on. "You don't live here, you're not one of us, and yet you're so anxious for us to leave? This feels like a trap. Did the bears send you?"

CHAPTER ELEVEN

Ujurak

Fear surged through Ujurak, and he had to force himself not to recoil in front of the big seal. He didn't know how the seal could have come so close to the truth.

"Of course the bears didn't send me!" he snapped. "I'm a seal!"

The big seal still loomed over him, stretching out his whiskery snout to sniff at Ujurak's skin. Frantically Ujurak wondered if some of his bear scent was still clinging to him. *No other creature has mentioned it before, but then, this is the first time I've drawn attention to myself like this.*

"There's something strange about you," the big seal growled, still sniffing.

"Yes." Ujurak forced himself to speak steadily, not showing his fear. "I'm the only seal here who seems to realize that this water is making you sick."

Before the big seal could reply, a smaller female edged forward timidly. "I thought the water was bad, too," she said. "But no one listened to me."

Instantly Silver, the aggressive male with the silver back, rounded on her. "Splash, how dare you say that about our home? Remember how hard we fought to win this place!"

Ujurak glanced up at the big seal. "What does he mean?"

"Tell him, Dark," Silver said, with another hostile glare at Ujurak. "Then we'll drive him off."

Dark, the big seal, gazed out across the frozen sea for a moment; Ujurak could see memory flickering through him like shoals of fish.

"Our mothers and our mothers' mothers have calved in this place for longer than any seal can remember," he began. "Yet there came a time when we were almost driven out. Orca came—"

"I know that story!" a young seal calf interrupted, slapping his flippers against the ice. "You told it to me in our snow-den," he added, nudging up against a female with a dappled pelt.

"That's quite enough from you." His mother cuffed him lightly over the head. "We don't interrupt when Dark is speaking."

"Thank you, Dapple." Dark gave her a brief nod. "Orca came to the cove, many sunrises ago, and attacked us," he went on. "A lot of seals died. We tried to fight, but there were too many orca. And they came back, time after time, until few of us were left."

"I remember that," an older male said, his head bowed in sadness. "My mate was one of those who tried to drive the orca away, and she never came back."

"My father was another," Silver added, the aggression in his voice giving way to pain.

Murmurs of agreement came from the other seals, as they remembered their own losses. Ujurak could sense the horror that enveloped all of them like a cloud.

How could they have lived through that, day after day? They must really love this place.

"In the end," Dark continued, "we decided that we couldn't fight them. We would have to leave. We—"

"I wish I'd been there! I wouldn't have been scared," blurted the young seal calf. In the midst of his tension Ujurak had to stifle a huff of amusement at the youngster. "*I'd* have killed all the orca!"

"No, you wouldn't have! I would have!" Another calf butted his friend from behind. "You be an orca, and I'll show you!"

Dapple let out a growl as the two calves started to shove each other. "Stop showing off, both of you!"

"What happened then?" Ujurak asked.

"Swift, who was the head seal, was ready to lead us in search of a new home," Dark replied. "But at the last moment the no-swims came." He nodded in the direction of the flat-face denning area.

"And you'd never guess what happened." Splash, the small female who had backed up Ujurak about the poison, broke in, her timidity forgotten as her eyes glowed with the memory. "The no-swims started killing the orca!"

Ujurak was astonished. "They what?"

"They killed the orca," Silver repeated. "Open your ears, mud-brain!"

"Finally the last of the orca fled." Dark took up the story again. "And so we stayed here. And ever since then we have looked on the no-swims as our saviors."

Dapple nodded. "We like living close to them. The no-swims don't hunt us, so we must be special to them."

"And that's why we have to stay," Dark finished.

Ujurak's head was spinning. He couldn't understand why the flat-faces would have hunted the orca to save the seals. Then he remembered Sally and the other flat-faces who had helped the animals and birds trapped in the oil.

Sally and her friends really cared. Maybe these flat-faces are like them? But that still doesn't mean the seals can stay here. . . .

Ujurak let his gaze travel over the listening seals. "How many of you have been sick?" he asked.

Dark let out a growl of annoyance and glared at the other seals as if he was daring them to answer. But to Ujurak's relief he didn't manage to silence them all.

"I have," Dapple said.

Splash gave a vigorous nod. "I have, too. I *told* them it was the water!"

A voice spoke from farther back. "My calf died."

"Can't you see that Splash is right?" Ujurak asked. Once again he pointed with his flipper to the stinking liquid oozing out of the pipe. "It's the water that's making you sick—the water and the fish that swim in it. You can smell that the stuff coming out of there is all wrong. It's bad no-swim stuff."

The words were hardly out before Ujurak realized he had made a mistake. Dark loomed threateningly over him again. "The no-swims aren't bad!" he insisted.

Ujurak saw that the head seal was ready to fight, and that there were others, like Silver, who would back him up. *Arcturus, tell me what to say!*

"No, the no-swims aren't bad," he agreed, realizing he would have to handle this carefully. "They haven't poisoned the water deliberately. It's an accident."

"What? How?" Silver demanded, while Dark still glared at Ujurak and the rest of the seals muttered urgently among themselves.

"I don't know," Ujurak replied. "But I know it isn't the no-swims' fault. If they want you to be safe, they'd be happy for you to move."

To his relief Dark backed off slightly. He seemed to be thinking about what Ujurak had said. The other seals looked at one another anxiously.

At last Dapple spoke up. "I'd be willing to move. I don't want my calf getting sick."

"I'd go, too." A younger male pressed forward, his whiskers twitching eagerly. "I'm sick of living near that stench."

"But what about the orca?" The older male, the one who had lost his mate, looked Dark in the eye. "They'll attack us again if we don't have the no-swims to protect us."

"You're right, Shade," Silver said. "Besides, why should we move away just because this mud-brain tells us to? Maybe he planned this with the orca!"

There was a chorus of agreement. Ujurak could feel the mood of the gathering swinging against him, as if the seals were prepared to admit that the leaking pipe might be causing their sickness, but they were too terrified to move away from it.

Give me the right words now, Arcturus! he begged.

"Where is your pride?" he asked challengingly. "Can't you fight for yourselves? There are many, many seals in the ocean—as many as there are stars in the sky. They don't all have no-swims looking after them."

Dark struck the ice with a flipper. "Are you saying we're scared? I'm not, and I'll prove it to you! Maybe we should move after all. . . ."

"Then I know where you can go," Ujurak said eagerly. "There's a bay farther around the island—" He gestured with a flipper. "A river runs down into it. The water is clean, and there are plenty of fish."

"Yes! Let's go there now!" Dapple's calf bounced up again. "I'm hungry!"

A loud discussion broke out. As he listened, Ujurak spotted Toklo, Kallik, and Lusa looking down at him from the top of the cliffs.

They're probably wondering what's taking so long, he thought.

As he watched his friends, Ujurak saw some of the white bears coming up behind them. Even at that distance he picked out the huge shape of Unalaq. Toklo, Lusa, and Kallik rounded on them.

"Stay away from the seals!" Toklo's roar reached Ujurak down on the ice.

Gesturing vigorously down into the cove, Lusa added something Ujurak couldn't hear; he guessed she was telling the white bears yet again about the poison in the water.

But the white bears clearly didn't want to listen. Unalaq and Toklo were facing off against each other; Ujurak realized that a fight could break out at any moment.

A pang of alarm shot through him. *I have to get a move on! I wouldn't put it past Unalaq to eat Lusa!*

Down on the ice the seals were still trying to decide what to do.

"We *have* to go," Splash urged them eagerly. "If we don't, the poison will kill us all."

"And if we do go, the orca will get us," Shade replied somberly.

"Well, I'd rather take my chance with the orca than live near that stink anymore," a young male declared.

Ujurak tried to think of what more he could do to stop the seals from hesitating. *I could turn into a flat-face and attack them. . . . No, too complicated.* He thought of drinking the poisoned liquid himself, to prove that that was what was making them sick, but he knew that he might never recover. *And it would take too long. . . .*

Somehow he had to prove to the seals that they weren't dependent on the flat-faces. Then they would have the courage to move to a new home.

Turning back to the seals, he felt his heart sink as he saw Shade and some of the older seals clustered around Dark.

"I know of seals who used to live in that bay he told us

about," Shade was saying. "They were driven out by walruses!"

"There are no walruses there now," Ujurak assured him, hurriedly hauling himself across the ice to join the group. "It's perfect!"

"So *you* say," an older female retorted. "I don't want to risk it."

"I think you're wrong." Ujurak tried to force down his desperation and speak calmly. "Plus you could learn to defend yourselves against an orca attack. Or a walrus attack, if they ever came back."

Silver let out a scornful grunt. "And how do you suggest we do that?"

"You could . . ." Ujurak thought rapidly. "You could swim into shallower water, where the orca couldn't reach you. You could hide under rocks. Or—" A picture suddenly flashed into his head. "You could make a wall of seals, all thrashing and impossible to catch. Fight back against the orca, together!"

He was encouraged to see that Dark was looking interested, his hostility gone. But Shade and the others were still shaking their heads doubtfully.

"Why should we do that?" Shade asked. "We're safe here because of the no-swims. The orca don't come near us."

Then an idea came to Ujurak.

"I think you ought to consider moving," he told the seals. "I think you should have faith in your own strength. But I don't want to argue with you anymore. It's time for me to move on."

He could see that Dapple and Splash looked disappointed, but most of the seals seemed relieved, and he heard

Silver mutter, "Good riddance!"

Dark gave Ujurak a dismissive nod and waved one flipper. "Thank you for coming. We will think about your words." But the tone he used convinced Ujurak that once he was gone, most of the seals would do their best to forget about him.

Ujurak slid back into the breathing hole. He could feel his friends' stares of disappointment from the cliff top when they saw that none of the seals followed him.

With a flick of his powerful body, Ujurak headed for the mouth of the cove. He reflected how strong and graceful his seal shape was in the water, when he had felt so awkward on land. He was aware of other seals looking at him suspiciously as he swam past.

Ignoring them, Ujurak swam out of the cove, diving deeper and deeper until the water was black around him and there were no more seals. He listened for any other signs of life, but there was nothing. Pushing away a sudden pang of desolation, he pictured an orca in his mind, making it as clear as he could: the powerful black-and-white body, the sleek shape, the jaws with their rows of spiny teeth.

Pain rippled through him. Ujurak had only once before transformed from one creature to another without becoming a bear again in between. That was when he had changed from an orca to a tiny fish, to save himself from the vicious creatures who were attacking him.

With danger so close, he had changed almost without thinking. Now he had time to think about how hard it was to tear his mind away from everything that made him a seal and plunge into the thoughts and being of an orca.

Not a small hunter of fish anymore . . . a huge hunter of seals. No more fear . . . I'll be stronger than anything in the sea!

Ujurak gasped as the pain of his transformation suddenly intensified. His body stretched and expanded, and water churned around him as he took on the shape of the orca. Sensations rushed over him; the water was full of the smell of prey. He visualized warm, fat seals, tempting mouthfuls of fur and flesh. His jaws gaped in anticipation.

No!

Ujurak dragged his mind back, clinging to his knowledge of who he really was, and focused on what he had to do. As he powered through the water, back toward the seals, his senses told him that the water was tainted. He knew it was a bad place for hunting, but the instincts of the killer whale were so strong that they were overriding that knowledge. His mind drifted, his awareness slipping away and sinking into the orca's overwhelming urge to kill and eat.

Suddenly grunts and squeals of panic surrounded him. Bodies thrashed past him, and he realized that the seals had spotted him. Ujurak darted toward the nearest of them, all his senses screaming for food.

No . . . I'm a bear . . . a bear. . . .

With a massive effort Ujurak swerved away. He knew that he wasn't there to hunt. Instead he had to scare the seals into defending themselves. But his belly was hollow with hunger, and the seals smelled so good. . . .

Thud!

Ujurak's body rocked as a seal slammed into him. Then another. Then a whole line of them. His whale mind shrieked in fury, braced to fight back, wanting to teach these miserable bits of food a lesson. But his bear mind rejoiced.

Yes! The seals are defending themselves!

Through the blurry, stinking water Ujurak made out Dark, directing his community of seals. Sharp satisfaction shot through him as he realized the head seal was using the suggestions he had made. Splash chivvied the calves and the smaller seals into shallow water or the cover of rocks, while Dark, Silver, Dapple, and the others formed a line and hurtled toward the whale's flank.

They were too fast for Ujurak to turn and face them. The line of seals crashed into him with their blunt noses, and the shock of their heavy bodies made him roll in the water.

Surrendering to his whale instincts, Ujurak recoiled and snapped at them, but the sleek seal bodies evaded his jaws and re-formed the line to attack him again. Driven back, Ujurak's fear of the shallow water stopped him from following them.

Water thrashed around him as the seals darted in again and again to strike his body. At last Ujurak turned, swimming away into deeper water. As the blackness closed around him, the scent of prey cleared from his nose, and he became fully aware of himself as a bear.

Let's hope I've done enough. I can't do any more.

Ujurak swam around the entrance to the cove and headed for some rocks. Relief flooded through him as he returned to his familiar bear shape and clambered out of the sea. Every muscle in his body was aching as he padded up the beach and found a spot where he could scramble up the cliff.

Lusa, Toklo, and Kallik were still peering over the edge, looking down at the seals. The other white bears had disappeared. His friends must have convinced them to go. As Ujurak trudged up from behind, Lusa spun around, her eyes stretching wide with surprise as she spotted him.

"What are you doing here?" she asked. "Are you giving up? Did you get attacked by that orca?"

"No, that was me." Ujurak flopped down beside her, unable for the moment to answer her urgent questions.

Kallik swung around to stare at him, almost dislodging Kissimi from her shoulder fur. "Are you crazy? Now they'll never leave if they think there's an orca waiting for them out at sea!"

"Wait," Toklo said, before Ujurak could respond. The big grizzly was still staring down into the cove. "Something's happening."

Together all the bears gazed down. Ujurak saw that the seals had bunched into a tight group and were gathering at the mouth of the cove, their dark bodies circling below the ice. The seals still on the surface slipped one by one into breathing holes to join their companions. Every so often Ujurak spotted Dark popping his head up, barking at them to hurry.

"They're leaving!" Kallik whispered in relief.

Ujurak could hardly believe what he was seeing. Though he was battered and exhausted from his fight, he felt that every ache was worth it. "They know now that they are brave and strong," he murmured. "They know that they can make their own safety without relying on the no-swims."

Toklo let out a grunt of astonishment and gazed at Ujurak as if he thought his friend was crazy. Ujurak was too tired to explain.

Together he and his friends stood on the cliff and watched the last seals vanish; Ujurak pictured them swimming beneath the ice until they reached their new home in the bay.

"It will be a while before the seals are free of the poison inside their bodies," he said, "but it will happen in time."

"Then the white bears will be able to hunt without getting sick." Lusa's voice was full of satisfaction.

A pang of conscience shook Ujurak like a gust of icy wind. When he'd been in seal shape, and even more as an orca, he had begun to respect the seals. *Was I right to send them to a place where the white bears will be able to hunt them more easily?*

But Ujurak realized that the bears would hunt the seals no matter what he did, wherever they lived; that was the way the world worked, just as the seals ate fish and the orca ate seals and bears.

At least we've given them the chance to lead healthy lives.

Ujurak gazed up at the gray sky, wondering if his mother, Ursa, was watching. *It has begun,* he told her silently. *We are fighting back.*

CHAPTER TWELVE

Kallik

"*So from now on the seals* will be living in the bay beyond the steep gorge," Lusa explained. "You'll be able to hunt them safely there."

Aga and the other white bears were pale shapes in the twilight. Kallik watched them anxiously as Lusa finished her account of how she and her friends had managed to move the seals.

Will they believe what Lusa is telling them?

Aga nodded slowly as Lusa finished speaking, but Kallik saw that her eyes were wary. "This tale is strange to me," she said at last. "But I am willing to hear the words of Tungulria."

"Well, I'm not!" Unalaq pushed forward to stand at the front of the crowd of bears, next to Aga. "I can't believe they just walked in here and interfered with our hunting! We should drive them out now!"

Kallik's belly lurched to see the threatening look that Unalaq gave the small black bear. But Lusa faced him bravely.

"Fine!" she snapped. "Don't bother to thank us for saving your lives!"

Unalaq opened his jaws for an angry retort, but Aga silenced him by raising a paw. "No bears will be driven from this island," she announced. "Especially not when we have waited so long for Tungulria to come."

"But what do we need to do now?" Illa asked. Kallik could tell that the young she-bear was puzzled rather than hostile. "If we move over to the other bay, how will that help? The seals are still poisoned."

"That's right," another bear muttered in the background. "I like my den here. I don't want to leave."

Kallik listened anxiously as the white bears clustered together, casting doubtful glances at Lusa. What would happen if they agreed with Unalaq and decided not to believe Lusa?

"Yeah, but if the water's poisoned here . . ." another of them began.

"We *know* it's poisoned. Haven't you smelled that stuff? Yuck!"

"I was really sick until I ate that moss, but I feel fine now." That was Yakone. "I say we should trust them."

Kallik focused her attention on Aga. Her decision was the one that would count. Toklo and Ujurak were watching Aga closely, too, while Lusa held the ancient she-bear's gaze without flinching.

She knows Aga will listen to her because of the prophecy about Tungulria, thought Kallik.

Pride in her friend's courage coursed through Kallik, but all the while it was battling with her longing to return to Kissimi. She had hidden the cub in the shallow hole in the valley where she had placed him the first time she and her friends had gone to talk to the white bears. She knew he would be safe there, but her need to be with him was like a constant tug on her fur.

Did my mother feel like this? Kallik asked herself. *How terrible that she had to die and be separated from her cubs forever!*

"It's not far to the new hunting ground," Toklo began, stepping up to stand beside Lusa. "Just follow the cliffs until you get to the gorge. The bay is on the other side. Then—"

"We know our own island, cloud-brain!" Unalaq interrupted.

"Then you'll need to wait a while until the seals are free of the poison," Toklo went on. He glared at the big white bear but otherwise ignored him. "Meanwhile you should be careful to just eat seals that smell of clear water and nothing else."

Aga shook her head uncertainly. "How long will that take? And what are we going to eat in the meantime?"

"You'll have to hunt other prey," Lusa replied. "If you like, we'll teach you how to catch a musk ox."

"What?" Unalaq let out a snort of contempt. "A puny scrap of fur like you, killing a musk ox? I'd like to see that!"

"You can see it." Toklo took a pace forward and confronted the big white bear, showing his teeth. "I'll lead a group of you and show you." Dipping his head respectfully to the old she-bear, he added, "With your permission, Aga."

A touch on her shoulder made Kallik jump. She had been so busy thinking about Kissimi that she hadn't noticed Yakone padding quietly up to her. Even though she was glad to see the bear with the reddish pelt, she found it hard to drag her thoughts away from her cub.

Kallik turned to Yakone and dipped her head politely. "Hi. I'm glad you're feeling better now that—"

She was interrupted by a huffed complaint from Unalaq, and Aga's sharp voice reprimanding him.

Yakone's eyes glimmered with amusement. "Sometimes Unalaq doesn't know when to keep quiet!"

"At least he listens to Aga," Kallik responded.

The amusement faded from Yakone's eyes, and he shook his head uncertainly. "I'm not sure how much longer Aga will be in charge," he said. "She's growing old and frail—frailer than any other bear on the island. Besides, she might not want to go on being leader now that the prophecy about Tungulria has been fulfilled."

"I don't understand all that," Kallik told him, a powerful sense of strangeness sweeping over her. "Has Aga really been waiting for Lusa to come?"

Instead of answering right away, Yakone gestured with one paw, drawing Kallik away from the group of bears gathered around Aga. He led her to the crest of the hill, from where they could look down over one side of the island. The snow-covered hillside fell away in front of them as far as the cliff edge and the frozen surface of the poisoned cove. By now night had fallen; lights glimmered in the no-claw denning place, and stars glittered in the sky, though there was still no sign of the dancing spirits.

"It's weird," Yakone murmured. "White bears have always eaten seals. It's hard to accept that they were making us sick." He fell silent with a sigh.

Kallik nodded sympathetically. She remembered how her mother had taught her and Taqqiq how to crouch beside a breathing hole and wait for the seal to appear. None of them had ever dreamed that seal might not be good to eat.

"We white bears have been getting sick for a long time now," Yakone began again. "Ever since the pale no-claws came to the island. At first we thought the sickness was a curse from the Iqniq because we hadn't chased the no-claws away."

"But chasing them away would be too hard." Kallik touched the young male's shoulder sympathetically with her snout. "No-claws go where they want."

Yakone nodded. "But then Aga had a dream," he went on. "The Iqniq came down to the ground and told her that we had to wait for a black bear, Tungulria, who would save us." He sighed and glanced away from Kallik, staring at his paws. "Not many of us believed her," he confessed.

"I can understand that. I don't suppose any of you had ever *seen* a black bear before!"

"None of us had," Yakone agreed. "I couldn't believe it when I saw the four of you coming across the ice." He hesitated, then added, "Has Tungulria done other special things before now?"

Kallik stared at him, not sure how to reply. In one way

their whole journey had been special. *I'm traveling with black and brown bears, for a start!* But she didn't think that was the kind of answer Yakone wanted.

"I think we've all come here for a reason," she responded thoughtfully. "Moving the seals was part of it. Maybe we each have our own role to play."

Could my role be to become Kissimi's mother? she wondered. A shiver of mingled fear and delight ran through her as she realized that she wasn't a young cub anymore. *Could I really care for Kissimi as Nisa cared for me? Oh, spirits, I do hope so!*

"How did you four meet?" Yakone asked.

Kallik looked into his eyes and saw nothing there except honest curiosity. Surprising herself, she realized how much she liked the young white bear. *He's friendly, and I can talk to him.*

But as she became aware of her feelings, she realized that she didn't want to tell Yakone everything. She was afraid that he would think she was strange for coming all this way in search of her mother's spirit, or for leaving the white bears behind at Great Bear Lake.

And now Nisa's spirit seems to have faded away, Kallik thought sadly. *Was the whole journey about Lusa all along?*

"I was born on the Frozen Sea," she told Yakone. "And when my mother died, I set out in search of the Endless Ice. I was so lucky to find Toklo and Lusa and Ujurak to travel with."

Yakone bent his head closer to Kallik's. "And now that you've found the Ice, will you stay?" he asked.

Kallik's belly lurched in surprise. *Is Yakone asking me to stay with him?* Then she told herself not to be so cloud-brained. He was just being friendly.

"I don't know," she admitted hesitantly.

She couldn't make that decision without thinking of Kissimi. Part of her wanted to blurt out to Yakone that she had found the dead Sura's cub. She had to bite the words back like a hard mouthful of prey. If Yakone knew, he might force her to stay or take Kissimi away from her.

Kissimi must have family here. Sura is dead, but she must have had brothers and sisters. Didn't Illa say she was her sister?

"Hey, Kallik!" Toklo's voice interrupted her thoughts. "We're leaving!"

Glancing back the way she and Yakone had come, Kallik saw Toklo waiting at the bottom of the slope with Lusa and Ujurak. Illa and Tunerq were with them. Trailing a few paw-steps behind them, clearly reluctant, was Unalaq.

"Sorry, I have to go," she said to Yakone, running down toward her friends.

She could feel Yakone staring after her. Suddenly there was a flurry of pawsteps, and the young male caught up with her in a shower of snow. Kallik stopped and turned to him.

"Kallik, will you come hunting with me?" Yakone asked. "You can show me around the new place."

"Yes!" Kallik replied without thinking. "I'll meet you at the new bay at first light."

Yakone blinked happily, and Kallik gazed into his eyes, not sure whether she needed to say any more.

"Kallik, come *on*!" Lusa barked impatiently behind her.

With a swift nod to Yakone, Kallik headed down the slope again.

"See you tomorrow!" Yakone called after her.

CHAPTER THIRTEEN

Toklo

As Toklo led the way along the top of the cliffs from the white bears' denning place, he realized that Kallik had caught up and was pacing alongside him.

"How long is this going to take?" she asked in a low voice, with a glance behind to make sure none of the other white bears could hear. "I need to get back to Kissimi."

Toklo shook his head in exasperation. "How do I know? We've got to find the musk oxen first. And then we have to show these other bears how to hunt them."

"And I'd bet a whole seal Unalaq will make it hard for you," Kallik said, glaring over her shoulder at the big white bear. "Toklo, do I *have* to come with you? Kissimi will be scared if I leave him alone for much longer."

Or one of Aga's bears might find him. Toklo had more sense than to speak his thought aloud. He didn't want his ears clawed off. "Okay, Kallik," he replied. "Just slip away quietly. Take Kissimi back to our den—I'll make sure we don't hunt anywhere near there."

Kallik's eyes were warm with gratitude. "Thanks, Toklo."

She dropped to the back of the group, next to Ujurak. A few moments later, when Toklo had to leave the edge of the cliff to skirt a large clump of thornbushes half buried in snow, he noticed that she was no longer there. He just hoped that none of the white bears would start asking awkward questions.

Not long after, Toklo left the cliff edge and struck across open ground to the head of the gully he and his friends had followed when they had first arrived on the island. Tunerq picked up his pace until he reached Toklo's side. Toklo tensed, expecting a question about Kallik, but all the young bear said was "Where are you taking us?"

"To the place where we found the musk oxen," Toklo replied. "Unless you know anywhere closer where they might be."

Tunerq shook his head. "We never bother much with the musk oxen," he told Toklo. "We always thought they were too big to hunt."

"Too big and too tough," Unalaq growled, pressing up to join Toklo at the head of the group. "Who'd want to eat musk ox when they can get seal?"

Toklo swiveled his head to glare at the big white bear. "But you *can't* get seal, cloud-brain," he snapped. "Not until they're clear of the poison. We already told you that. Are your ears stuffed with snow, or what?"

Unalaq glared back. "I think you're lying about the seals. And the musk oxen. No bear can catch one of those."

Toklo shrugged. "Watch and learn, fish-breath."

Ignoring Unalaq, Toklo led the way down the gully and toward the stretch of ground where the musk oxen had been feeding. There was no sign of them now, but the snow was churned up by the marks of their hooves. Toklo sniffed, picking up fresh scent.

"This way," he said, flicking his ears in the direction of the scent.

Instead of following the trail immediately, Toklo beckoned to the three white bears. "The only way to do this is to work together," he instructed. "When we catch up with the musk oxen, wait for me to put you in position. Understand?"

"Yes, Toklo," Illa said. Her eyes were gleaming eagerly.

Tunerq nodded, and Unalaq let out a grunt that could have meant anything. Toklo exchanged a glance with Lusa, who just rolled her eyes. Ujurak was pawing at the snow, impatient to be on their way.

"Let's go," Toklo said.

Following the musk oxen's trail, Toklo spotted fresh droppings and places where the snow had been pushed aside to reveal the plants the oxen fed on. Then, as they reached the top of a shallow slope, they spotted the musk oxen in the valley ahead. They had stopped again to graze, their hunched shoulders and shaggy pelts standing out dark against the snow.

Toklo paused. He had forgotten how big these animals were. But he knew that this was no time to lose confidence. He knew that Unalaq would love it if he made a mess of this. *We've got to catch something.*

"Right," he began. "Lusa, you take Tunerq and work your

way around to the other side of the herd. Ujurak, take Illa and get into position on that side." He pointed with a paw. "Unalaq, you come with me. We'll scare them and get them confused like last time, and then I'll pick one of them out. We all get together to bring it down."

"Will that work?" Tunerq asked doubtfully.

"Wait and see." Lusa gave an excited little bounce. "Toklo's really good at hunting!"

She led the white bear down the slope toward the herd. Toklo watched them for a moment, giving the herd a wide berth and using rocks and bushes for cover. Once they were well on their way, Ujurak set off with Illa for the opposite side of the herd.

Toklo waited until he could see them in position, aware of Unalaq fidgeting and huffing impatiently beside him.

"Okay," he said at last. "We're going to charge down there and roar at the oxen to scare them. Don't try to grab one until I tell you."

Without waiting for a response, he headed down the hill, picking up speed as he went and stretching his jaws wide to let out a roar. Unalaq paced him, roaring even louder. The musk oxen raised their heads, then began to move farther down the valley, slowly at first and then picking up speed as the bears drew nearer, until they were running.

Above the pounding of their hooves Toklo could hear answering roars from the other bears. The musk oxen checked; the ones in the lead tried to turn back, but those in the rear were still trying to flee from Toklo and Unalaq. Soon the middle of the valley was full of a panic-stricken crowd of oxen, milling around and trampling to and fro as they let out deep-throated bellows of terror.

Exhilaration flooded through Toklo as he realized that the plan was working. At the edge of the crowd he spotted one ox that was limping. "Over here!" he yelled, hurtling toward it.

Unalaq was pounding alongside him; just ahead Illa and Ujurak appeared, veering toward the limping ox to cut it out of the herd. Illa reached it first and heaved herself onto her hindpaws to score her claws down the ox's shoulder.

The ox half reared, then turned, trying to flee, only to meet Unalaq head-on. The big white bear sprang at it, with Toklo a pace behind; together they knocked the ox off balance. It fell to the ground, legs thrashing, while Ujurak and Illa seized its haunches to hold it down. Lusa and Tunerq came up, panting, in time to grip its forelegs, while Toklo made the kill by slashing his claws across the ox's throat. The creature jerked once and lay still.

"That was great!" Illa exclaimed. "There's enough prey here to feed every bear."

Unalaq was already sinking his teeth into the ox's shoulder, tearing off a huge mouthful of meat. Toklo bit back a growl. Just for a few moments he had hunted side by side with Unalaq, feeling a brief companionship with the big white bear. Unalaq was a good hunter.

But he's still a pain in the fur, Toklo thought, watching him tucking greedily into the ox.

"Eat," Ujurak encouraged Illa and Tunerq. "Then you can

take some back for Aga and the others."

"And now that you know how, you can catch more," Lusa added enthusiastically. "You'll have prey to eat until the seals are ready."

Tunerq dipped his head, gratitude in his eyes. "Thank you, all of you. We won't forget this."

Together Toklo and his friends waited until the white bears had taken what they wanted from the ox carcass.

"Is that what we were meant to do?" Lusa asked as she watched them go, dragging part of the meat with them. "To move the seals *and* teach the white bears to hunt new prey?"

Ujurak blinked, watching as Unalaq and the others disappeared over the brow of the hill. "I don't think so," he replied. "It's important, what we've done, but none of that is going to bring back the spirits."

CHAPTER FOURTEEN

Kallik

It was still dark when Kallik crept out of the den, leaving her friends asleep. Pale dawn light reflected off the frozen surface of the river by the time she reached the meeting place near the bay where the seals had made their new home. There was no sign of Yakone; no pawprints disturbed the fresh covering of snow. Kallik guessed that the white bears were waiting for the seals to recover from the poison before they moved their dens to this part of the island.

"Stay here, little one," Kallik murmured to Kissimi as she scraped a hollow for the cub to hide in. "You must keep very still."

Kissimi nodded as he clambered down from Kallik's shoulders and curled up in the hole with his paws over his nose. He was quieter than usual, Kallik realized; his head drooped, and he looked thinner.

Eating seal fat and chewed-up fish isn't agreeing with him, Kallik admitted to herself reluctantly. *He needs milk.* The realization welled up from deep inside her, but she did her best to push it down again. *I love him so much; I have to be able to take care of him. He'll be fine when he's older and doesn't need milk; I just have to hang on until then.*

"Kallik! Hi!"

Kallik jumped at the sound of Yakone's voice. Looking up, she spotted the young bear's reddish pelt standing out against the snow as he looked for a way down the cliff. Quickly she kicked snow over Kissimi, hiding him from Yakone's gaze.

"Hey! *Cold!*" Kissimi protested.

"Keep very still and quiet," Kallik reminded him. "I'll come back for you soon."

Satisfied that the cub was well hidden, she bounded away and met Yakone at the edge of the beach. The young male was staring out over the frozen bay, his jaws parted in astonishment and his eyes gleaming.

Following his gaze, Kallik spotted several dark patches on the ice; more breathing holes had appeared since she and the others had first discovered the bay. She could even see one or two seals a long way out from the shore. Triumph surged up inside her.

Ujurak, you did it!

"The seals really have moved!" Yakone echoed her thought. "And the air smells different. . . . There's none of that awful sickly scent."

The excitement in his tone thrilled Kallik, and she felt answering high spirits bubble up inside her. Playfully she butted her head into Yakone's flank. The young male swung around with a huff of laughter and swiped her with one paw. A moment later they were tumbling together in the snow, wrestling in a mock fight.

Kallik wriggled to one side as Yakone tried to pin her down. She realized he was bigger, but her long, hard journey had given her muscles strength. When he leaped on her again, she brought her hind legs up against his belly and sent him toppling into the snow. Before he could get up again, she hurled herself on top of him and clamped a paw down on his neck.

"Wow! You're strong!" Yakone gasped.

Pleased that she'd impressed him, Kallik stepped back and let the male bear scramble to his paws.

"Where did you learn to fight so well?" he asked as he shook clumps of snow off his reddish pelt.

Kallik didn't want to talk about her journey. "Hey, let's hunt!" she suggested.

Together the two white bears headed out across the ice. The seals on the surface slid down into the water long before Kallik and Yakone could reach them, but it didn't take long to find a breathing hole.

"Smell that?" Kallik asked as they stood side by side gazing down into the hole. "That's what healthy seawater smells like."

Yakone took a long sniff. "It's good. Much tangier than the water around our old hunting ground."

"Now we have to wait for a seal," Kallik said, settling down beside the hole and making herself comfortable. "But it has to smell of clear water and nothing else."

Yakone nodded and crouched down beside her. Kallik

couldn't help noticing how soft his reddish fur looked. Dar-
ingly she reached out and brushed her paw gently along his leg.

It is so soft!

Embarrassment flooded over her as she realized Yakone
was giving her a surprised look. "Uh . . . there was a bug crawling over you," she muttered.

Amusement sparkled in Yakone's eyes. He reached out and
gave Kallik a playful pat. She responded by prodding one paw
into his side.

I haven't had so much fun since Taqqiq and I were cubs together! Kallik
thought. *I don't want to sit here and be patient.*

"We're never going to catch a seal if we play around like
this," Yakone said, nudging her with his head. "We have to
concentrate."

Kallik realized he was right. Forcing down her surging
high spirits, she stared into the hole, resisting the temptation
to give Yakone a sidelong glance.

The moments seemed to drag by. Kallik listened to the
whisper of the wind blowing across the surface of the ice, and
she wondered how Kissimi was doing in his snowy den. She
had enjoyed playing with Yakone so much that for a short
time she had almost forgotten her cub. Now her paws began
to itch with impatience to head back to him.

Maybe with some good, healthy seal for him to eat.

The thought had scarcely crossed Kallik's mind when
she spotted a swirl in the water and a dark shape rising
up through the breathing hole. Quicker than Yakone, she
flashed out a paw and grabbed the seal as it surfaced. At the

same time she gave it a good sniff.

"This one is fine," she told Yakone, dragging the struggling seal out onto the ice and dealing it a sharp killing blow to the neck.

"That's great!" Yakone's eyes were wide with admiration. "You hunt as well as Unalaq, and he's the best."

Warm pride flooded through Kallik. "It's not hard," she murmured. "You just have to keep very still and be ready to move as soon as you see the seal coming up to breathe. Let's try again, and you can catch the next one."

This time it didn't seem so long until a seal poked its whiskery head out of the water. Yakone was ready, but as he reached for it, Kallik knocked his paws aside. The seal took a swift gulp of air and vanished.

"Hey!" Yakone exclaimed indignantly. "I could have caught that."

"I know," Kallik said. "But it was poisoned. Just smell the water that it left behind."

Yakone lowered his snout and sniffed at the seawater that had spilled out of the hole when the seal surfaced. "You're right," he said with a sigh. "I can see we'll have to be careful when we hunt here. It's a tough lesson for us."

"I know," Kallik replied, brushing her pelt against his. "But it will get easier with time."

Together she and Yakone dragged the first seal across the ice and up to the beach so that Yakone could carry it home later. Kallik was pleased; she knew the other white bears were more likely to come to the new bay if they realized there was good hunting in its waters.

"How about a swim?" Yakone suggested when they had deposited the seal in the shelter of a pile of rocks. He jerked his head back toward the sea. "I noticed a channel of open water out there."

"I don't know. . . ." A thrill of fear rushed through Kallik at the thought of the last time she and her friends had swum from one stretch of ice to another, and of the circling orca that had almost killed them. "What if there are orca?"

"We'll keep a lookout," Yakone replied. "Come on. It'll be fun."

Kallik was tempted; it *would* be fun to swim with Yakone. Murmuring agreement, she followed the male bear back onto the ice. The sun had risen while they'd been crouching beside the breathing hole, and the ice gleamed dazzling white, stretching out in front of Kallik as far as she could see. The channel was a long, thin crack, reflecting the blue of the sky.

Yakone plunged into the sea with a huge splash, sending water washing over the ice around Kallik's paws. Kallik slid in after him, diving deep beneath him and surfacing on his other side to splash water in his face.

"Hey, I'll get you for that!" Yakone huffed, paddling toward her.

Kallik swam away, glancing back over her shoulder at the male bear chasing her. She felt strong and confident, her fear of the orca thrust to the back of her mind. *This is where I belong. This is what it really means to be a white bear.*

Yakone caught up to her, and they wrestled in the water,

their heads dipping under the surface and bobbing up again.

"I used to swim like this with Sura," Yakone said, shaking water out of his ears. "She loved swimming, before she got sick."

Kallik felt a stab of jealousy that Yakone had been friends with Sura before she came to the island, mixed with guilt at the reminder that she had stolen Sura's cub.

Not wanting to talk about the dead she-bear, she slid behind a chunk of floating ice when Yakone was looking the other way. When he turned back, he glanced around in bewilderment.

"Kallik? Where'd you go?" Anxiety sharpened his voice. "Kallik?"

"Here!" Kallik plunged out of hiding and threw herself on Yakone, wrestling him under the surface.

"You scared me!" he exclaimed when they popped up again. "I thought an orca had gotten you."

"I feel as if I could fight every orca in the sea," Kallik responded. "I—"

She broke off as she spotted movement on the distant shore. A white bear was prowling down the hillside toward the bank of the frozen river. Even from so far away, Kallik couldn't mistake the huge, menacing shape of Unalaq.

He's heading straight for the place where I left Kissimi!

Terror slammed into Kallik's throat. Scrambling out of the water, she raced across the ice, water droplets streaming from her fur as she ran.

"Kallik, what's the matter?" Yakone's confused voice came

from behind her; Kallik could hear his paws slapping against the ice as he followed her.

Panting, Kallik reached the shore and confronted the huge bear.

"What are you doing here?" Unalaq snarled. "Have you come to steal our seals, now that you've hidden them here?"

"We haven't hidden them!" Kallik flashed back at him, desperate to distract him from Kissimi's hiding place. "They're right here." She pointed with one paw at the dead seal lying beside the heap of rocks. "Look, Yakone and I just caught that one."

To her dismay Unalaq narrowed his eyes suspiciously. "There's something wrong," he declared. "I can tell. What have you been up to?"

"She helped me hunt," Yakone puffed, coming to stand beside Kallik. "And then we went for a swim." He raised his head defiantly and glared at the bigger bear. "What's wrong with that?"

Unalaq ignored him. Swinging his head around, he gave the air several deep sniffs. "I smell a cub," he growled.

CHAPTER FIFTEEN

Toklo

"There's no sign of them. They could be anywhere by now."

Lusa's fretful voice woke Toklo in the snow-den under the thornbushes. The little black bear was peering into the den, anxiously talking to Ujurak, who was just rousing from sleep.

"What?" Toklo stretched his jaws in a yawn. "What's the matter?"

"Kallik and Kissimi are gone," Lusa told him. In her agitation she scraped the snow at the mouth of the den with her front claws.

Blinking, Toklo woke up enough to realize that the white bear and her cub were nowhere to be seen. "Keep your fur on." He spoke around another yawn. "Kallik will be fine."

"She's probably gone hunting, if Kissimi was hungry," Ujurak suggested.

Reluctantly Toklo heaved himself to his paws and pushed past Lusa into the open. "We'd better go and check that the white bears aren't chasing her off," he rumbled. "They might not want to share their new hunting ground."

With Lusa and Ujurak beside him, Toklo headed along the top of the cliffs toward the new bay. The wind had risen, and snow flicked into Toklo's eyes as he stomped along with his head down.

I wish we were back in the forest. A pang of longing shook him. *It would be calm and peaceful, with a breeze rustling the treetops, and the sun shining down. . . .*

But what he was faced with was this snow-covered island and a blustering wind nearly strong enough to blow Lusa off her paws. Toklo gave her a helpful nudge, placing himself to shelter her from the worst of the blast, and the black bear shot him a grateful look as she struggled on.

Toklo was the first to reach the top of the hill that led down into the bay, with Lusa and Ujurak huddling together in his wake. Down below he spotted a big white bear swinging his head around, sniffing the air.

Unalaq! Oh, spirits, no. . . . This means trouble!

Kallik was pacing anxiously toward the big white bear; her voice floated up to Toklo, just clear enough for him to make out the words.

"There's no cub here. What are you talking about?"

The reddish-pelted bear—Toklo remembered he was called Yakone—was trotting anxiously behind Kallik. "We weren't doing anything wrong," he told Unalaq. "Just hunting and swimming."

Before Toklo could decide what to do, Lusa let out a squeal. "Unalaq is looking for Kissimi!" She gave Toklo a sharp prod in the shoulder with her snout. "We have to do something!"

"Lonely Star, help us all now!" Toklo muttered as he launched himself down the slope toward the white bears.

Pesky cub, he added to himself. *We might have known this would happen.*

A mixture of rage and protectiveness swelled up inside Toklo. He reached the bottom of the slope in a flurry of flying snow, with Ujurak and Lusa just behind him. "You heard them!" he roared at Unalaq. "They were just hunting!"

Unalaq spun around, staring at Toklo in astonishment. Then gradually his surprised look faded, and a pleased expression crept over his face.

Is he looking forward to a fight? Toklo braced himself.

"This isn't your hunting ground," Unalaq snarled. "Anything you eat from here is theft."

"That's bee-brained!" Toklo retorted. "Kallik says white bears don't even have hunting grounds."

Unalaq thrust his snout aggressively into Toklo's face. "Well, *we* do!"

Over Unalaq's shoulder Toklo spotted Kallik staring at him frantically. She gave a tiny jerk of her head toward a spot on the bank of the frozen river, and Toklo realized that that was where she had left Kissimi.

So that's where he is. I've got to make Unalaq move away.

"You don't own all the seals in the sea," he growled, padding a few pawsteps toward the beach. "And you couldn't even figure out that the seals were making you sick. I hardly think you have the right to drive us away from this hunting ground."

"Yes, you should be grateful to us!" Lusa put in.

"Grateful?" Unalaq pulled his lips back into a snarl, swinging his head around to glare at Lusa. "Aga was fluff-brained to think that a black bear like you could save us, you pitiful scrap of fur!"

Indignation flashed in Lusa's eyes, and Toklo was suddenly afraid that she might hurl herself at the big white bear.

"We *have* saved you, cloud-brain!" he snapped. "We taught you to hunt musk oxen. And we've moved the seals to a place where the sea is clean."

Unalaq let out a huff of contempt. "The seals were fine where they were," he retorted, lumbering toward Toklo and thrusting his snout into the brown bear's face. "*I've* eaten them, and I haven't got sick. If weak bears die, that's their fault."

Toklo backed up a few more pawsteps in front of Unalaq, and Unalaq padded toward him. *That's right,* Toklo thought. *Just follow me a bit farther over here—well away from Kallik and her cub.*

"Wow, I can see you really care about your friends," Toklo taunted the huge white bear. "You must have been so sorry when Sura died."

"Sura was always whining," Unalaq retorted. "Bellyache. Not enough snow. Too much snow. That wretched cub of hers. They deserved to die if they couldn't hunt for themselves."

Retreating still farther, Toklo felt rock at his back. *Uh-oh! I didn't mean to get myself trapped!* He was conscious that he was much smaller than the full-grown, hefty Unalaq, and thinner from his long trek across the ice. Bunching his muscles, he prepared to dodge aside and make a run for it. He knew that fighting Unalaq would just make more trouble. *Besides, if he chases me, Kallik can escape with Kissimi.*

But before Toklo could move, Unalaq gave the air another suspicious sniff. "I know I can scent a cub," he insisted. His eyes narrowed as he raked his gaze over the newcomers. "Maybe Sura's cub didn't die? Maybe you know something about it?"

Toklo saw Kallik's eyes stretch wide with horror, and he knew that at any moment Unalaq would track down the cub by his scent. He couldn't let that happen.

With a full-throated roar Toklo hurled himself on Unalaq, raking both sets of foreclaws down the white bear's shoulders. Unalaq let out a howl of mingled pain and fury. He slammed Toklo back against the rocks and dealt him a blow to the side of the head with one massive paw.

"I'll teach you to come here and interfere," he growled.

Pain pierced Toklo's head, and for a moment all he could see was glittering darkness. Blinking, he made out Unalaq's gaping jaws, poised to bite down on his neck.

Toklo hunched his shoulders and lowered his head, driving it hard into Unalaq's chest. He heard the huff of the white bear's breath and splayed his forelegs, slashing at his enemy's fur.

"Get lost, fish-breath!" he hissed through gritted teeth.

As Unalaq drew back, Toklo spotted Ujurak and Lusa circling around, ready to dart in and join the fight. "No, keep back!" he growled, knowing that Unalaq was far too strong for either of them. "I can deal with this lump of white fur."

With a snarl Unalaq flipped Toklo's paws out from under him and flung him back against the rock, driving the breath out of his body. Looking up, dazed, Toklo spotted Kallik digging in the snow on the bank of the river. She unearthed Kissimi and fled, the cub dangling limply from her jaws.

Unalaq reared up and lashed out with both forepaws, digging deep into Toklo's shoulder fur. Toklo smelled the hot reek of his own blood and felt his strength beginning to ebb, but he forced himself back onto his paws. He lunged at Unalaq and sank his teeth into the white bear's leg, hanging on with teeth and claws as Unalaq tried to shake him off.

Behind Unalaq, Kallik was dragging Kissimi up the slope toward the crest of the hill, while Yakone looked on, his eyes wide with disbelief.

I forgot about Yakone, Toklo thought, his heart sinking. *We're in trouble now! The white bears know we stole their cub.*

But Unalaq still hadn't looked around. Shaking off Toklo, he trampled over his body, pummeling him with all four paws. Toklo struggled to escape, but he was pinned against the rock.

Through blurred vision he spotted Ujurak flinging himself at Unalaq and starting to bite his fur, but the huge white bear shook him off and swatted him to the ground as if he were a fly. Ujurak scrambled up and darted in to give Unalaq a nip on his hind leg.

"Make them stop!" Lusa shrieked, bounding up to Yakone. "Help them, please!"

Yakone was still gazing after Kallik, who had reached the top of the slope and vanished down the other side with

Kissimi dangling from her jaws. At Lusa's plea he turned slowly to look at her.

He won't help, Toklo thought despairingly, as Unalaq gouged out another pawful of Toklo's fur. *He's one of them.*

Then to Toklo's astonishment Yakone strode across to the rock where he was trapped. "Unalaq, that's enough!" Yakone roared. "Stop this now!"

Unalaq ignored him. Toklo could see the rage for blood in the big bear's eyes and wondered if he had even heard Yakone.

"Unalaq, stop!" Yakone repeated.

He thrust his shoulder into Unalaq's side, sending the white bear staggering back from the rock. Unalaq turned on him, rearing up and raising his forepaws threateningly.

"You're my brother," he growled. "You should back me up, not fight on *their* side. And if you can't, you should stay out of it. Brown bears don't belong here."

Yakone hurled himself forward, forcing the bigger bear backward until he was backed up against the cliff face at the side of the beach. "You've taught them a lesson," he said. "Now leave it."

Struggling to his paws, shaking his head to clear it, Toklo could see that Unalaq was already tired and hurt from the fight. He wasn't going to make things worse by attacking Yakone.

"Who told you to interfere?" he muttered, pushing Yakone to one side and padding forward a pace to glare at Toklo. "If you know what's good for you," he snarled, "you'll stay away from this hunting ground."

Turning away, he lumbered off up the hill.

Toklo turned to Yakone, ready to thank him, but the red-pelted bear backed away from him, fury and disbelief in his eyes.

"I trusted you!" he hissed. "Unalaq is right. Stay away from here."

Watching him as he followed Unalaq, Toklo was vaguely conscious of his own blood dripping onto the snow, spattering the white surface with scarlet blotches. His legs were shaking from the effort of fighting Unalaq, and pain was surging through his whole body.

"Are you badly hurt?" Lusa asked anxiously, padding up to him.

"I'll be fine," Toklo said, though he didn't know if that was true.

"Here, this should help." Lusa scooped up a pawful of snow and pressed it against one of Toklo's bleeding gashes.

The icy touch was soothing; Toklo stumbled across the beach to an untouched snowbank and settled down in it, bathing his wounds with snow.

Ujurak came to join him. He was bleeding, too, though he wasn't as badly hurt as Toklo. Lusa fussed around them, piling snow onto the wounds they couldn't reach.

"We have to find Kallik," Ujurak said after a moment.

Anger flared up inside Toklo at the mention of the white bear. "If she hadn't insisted on taking Kissimi, none of this would have happened," he growled. "She doesn't belong here any more than we do!"

"We still have to find her," Ujurak insisted.

"We should go now." Lusa gave a quick, uneasy glance around. "What if Unalaq comes back with more white bears to chase us away?"

Toklo let out a grunt, reluctantly agreeing. Hauling himself to his paws, he limped away from the shoreline. His belly rumbled as he passed the dead seal that Kallik and Yakone had caught, but he didn't dare stop to eat. Lusa was right to be afraid that more white bears might come looking for them.

We're the hunted now, he thought. *We'll have to leave this place and find somewhere else with food and shelter.* He let out a weary sigh. *Has our journey really ended like this, chased off because of a stolen cub?*

Ujurak and Lusa had plodded on ahead and were casting back and forth at the foot of the hill. "Over here!" Ujurak called.

Trudging up to join them, Toklo spotted Kallik's pawprints in the snow, and a scuff mark left by Kissimi's dangling rump. "This way," he said.

Ujurak bounded off, following the trail, with Lusa scrambling hard on his paws. Toklo stayed where he was for a moment, staring after them.

Is this really what I want? he asked himself.

Right from the beginning, when he'd first met Ujurak running away from the flat-faces, he had been the strong one, the one who had to protect the others. He had grumbled, he had felt resentful, and once he had even left them, to live alone in the forest as a brown bear should. But in the end he had never let them down.

A hollow space opened up inside him as he watched the small figures of Ujurak and Lusa dwindling into the distance.

I don't have to follow them. I could make my own way back to the forest. I don't even know if they'd want me around if I wasn't strong. They expect me to get them out of trouble, and that's all. The bitter thought, sharp as his wounds, was followed by another. *I could leave right now.*

Toklo let his mind wander back to the forest. For a moment he could almost hear the rustle of the trees, smell the prey lurking in the bushes, and feel the warmth of the sun on his back.

When did they ever ask me what I want?

Then he let out a long sigh. Whatever he might feel, he knew that his pathway led alongside Ujurak's. Until he had fulfilled his quest, it was Toklo's destiny to journey with him.

"I'd better get going," he muttered, and he lumbered after his companions, following their pawprints in the snow.

CHAPTER SIXTEEN

Lusa

Lusa stumbled along beside Toklo and Ujurak. Fear shook her like wind in the trees; she thought she could hear the thudding pawsteps of white bears in pursuit and feel their hot breath on her fur.

Risking a glance over her shoulder, she saw that the long valley behind them was empty, but they still had to keep going, struggling up a hill whose crest never seemed to draw any nearer. Lusa's legs hurt with the continual pumping up and down; she was gasping for breath, and her belly felt sore and empty.

What's going to happen now? she asked herself. *Did Aga's ancestors warn her that* this *would happen—that the black bear who came to save them would bring with her a white bear who would steal a cub?*

Her mind whirling, Lusa slogged on up the slope. At last Toklo and Ujurak reached the top, and they stood there waiting for her to catch up. But Lusa had scarcely set paw on the crest of the hill when the snow gave way beneath her. Legs flailing, she let out a frightened squeal as she slipped and fell.

"Lusa!" She heard Ujurak's startled cry, then nothing but the rushing of wind.

The slope beyond the crest was much steeper. Lusa tumbled head over tail, cushioned by snow as she bounced, grabbing with her claws at the soft stuff, which gave way as she clutched at it. Finally she landed with a massive *floof*, and snow closed over her head.

Gasping and scrabbling, Lusa broke out into the open air. A furry white face hovered over her; she let out a squeak, thinking that Aga's white bears had caught her.

Then she made out the concern in the bear's eyes and recognized Kallik gazing down at her. Kissimi was clinging to the white bear's shoulders.

"Lusa, are you okay?" she asked anxiously.

Lusa scrambled to her paws and shook clotted snow from her pelt. "I'm fine," she gasped, warmed by her friend's concern. "Just a bit shaken."

Toklo and Ujurak hurried down, panting, in time to hear what she said.

"It's a wonder you didn't break your neck!" Toklo growled, butting his head against Lusa's shoulder with rough affection. "When will you start watching where you put your paws?"

Lusa leaned into him for a moment, comforted by his strength. "I just came down the quick way," she murmured.

Kallik's gaze was fixed on Toklo, and Lusa realized that she was staring at the wounds Unalaq had given him in their fight. "You didn't kill Unalaq, did you?" she asked nervously.

"No." Toklo's voice was scornful. "If I had, every white bear on this island would hunt us down. As it is, we just have to hope that that red bear doesn't tell the others about the cub."

At the mention of Kissimi, Kallik's expression changed from concern to defiance. "I have to take care of him. Kissimi is mine now!" she asserted.

Irritation swept over Lusa. "No, he's not, Kallik!" she exclaimed. "Don't you think this has gone on long enough? You know that Kissimi belongs to Aga's bears."

Lusa couldn't believe how stubborn Kallik was being about the cub. Kissimi was looking more feeble than ever, his head lolling and his eyes barely open. Pity churned in Lusa's belly, along with her conviction that the tiny bear didn't belong with them.

"You should give him back," she said.

Kallik drew her lips back in a snarl, looming threateningly over Lusa, and Lusa gasped with shock and recoiled a pace.

Would she really fight with me over Kissimi? Doesn't it matter that we've been friends for so long?

To Lusa's relief Ujurak thrust himself between her and Kallik, and Kallik stepped back with a frustrated growl.

"It's too late to give him back," Ujurak said. "We have to keep going before the white bears find us. Our journey isn't over."

Lusa stared at him. "It's not?" she challenged him. "But we moved the seals! Aga's prophecy came true!"

Ujurak faced her, determination in his eyes. "Yes, that was something we had to do. But it's not the only thing. There's something more waiting for us; I can feel it."

"Yeah, and I know what," Toklo grumbled. "A load of white bears ready to shred our fur off."

Ujurak dismissed his friend's comment with a flick of his ears. "We must walk until it's too dark to see," he told them. "Then we'll look for shelter."

"That doesn't make sense," Lusa muttered rebelliously.

If Ujurak heard her, he didn't reply. He set off, away from the hill and farther inland, into a part of the island where they had never been before. Toklo and Kallik followed, and Lusa, with an exasperated snort, brought up the rear.

The land was flatter here, with little shelter from the tooth-sharp wind that blew snow into their faces. As the short day drew to an end, they began to look for somewhere to shelter, but there was nothing, not even a thornbush or an outcrop of rock to break up the snowy waste.

"We'll have to dig out a den," Toklo said as he began scooping away the snow with powerful claws. "If we sleep in the open, we'll be ice bears by morning."

Lusa and the others helped, scraping at the snow until they had made a hollow big enough for them all to curl up together. By the time they had finished, Kissimi had started to whimper with hunger.

"I'll find you something soon," Kallik promised, staring helplessly around at the empty landscape. "Try to sleep for now."

But the little cub only went on whimpering.

Lusa dug down where she thought the snow was thinnest, until she came to a patch of tough, springy stems and leaves.

Taking a mouthful, she chewed it into a pulp and set it down on the snow in front of Kissimi.

"Try that, little one," she said.

Kissimi sniffed the pulp suspiciously, then licked it up and looked around for more.

"Thank you," Kallik said as Lusa prepared another mouthful.

Lusa spat out the pulp. "Well, I'm not going to watch him starve, am I?" she asked crisply.

Pity for the little cub filled her and overflowed like rain in a curled leaf, but she couldn't show it. She didn't want Kallik to think that she approved of the way she was keeping Kissimi away from his kin.

When Kissimi had finished eating and huddled against Kallik's side to sleep, Lusa dug out some more of the plants for herself.

"Well, I can't eat leaves and stalks," Toklo growled. "I'm off to find a hare."

Lusa felt too cold and tired to go with him. She watched him lumber away until his shape melted into the shadows. Kallik had settled to sleep in the den, curving her body protectively around Kissimi, while Ujurak sat on the edge of the hollow, the wind buffeting his fur as he stared up at the sky.

Lusa followed his gaze; the dark expanse was dotted with faint stars, but there was no sign of the dancing spirits.

Where has the fire gone? she asked herself, feeling a tightness in her belly.

"Is that where we're going now?" she asked Ujurak. "To find the sky spirits?"

"I don't know." Ujurak didn't move his gaze from the star-studded darkness above his head. "I can still feel something tugging me, deep inside my fur, so I know that our journey isn't over yet. Moving the seals wasn't enough."

He let out a sigh and was quiet for several moments. Then he turned to Lusa, his gaze deep and serious.

"Thank you for coming this far with me, Lusa," he said. "I know you're a long way from home."

Lusa was startled. "Well, so are you," she replied.

Ujurak raised his head to gaze once more at the stars. "Somehow I don't think I am," he said softly.

Before Lusa could respond, a bulky shape loomed up out of the darkness, and Toklo dropped a skinny hare at her paws. "That was all I could find," he announced with a huff of disgust.

"It's great, Toklo." Ujurak was obviously trying to sound enthusiastic.

"Better than nothing, I suppose," Toklo grumbled.

When they had pulled all the meat they could off the meager carcass, the bears huddled together in the den. Lusa wrapped her paws over her nose, breathing deeply, surrendering herself to sleep. But she felt as though she had hardly closed her eyes when she was roused by a thin wailing.

Lusa raised her head, blinking, to see that it was still night. Across the den Kissimi was writhing around; his tiny jaws parted as he let out a pain-filled mewling.

"Belly hurts," he whimpered.

Kallik bent her head and gently nuzzled the little cub. "I should never have let him eat those plants," she fretted.

A pang of guilt clawed at Lusa. Giving Kissimi the plants had been her idea. "I was only trying to help," she murmured.

"It's too late to worry about that," Toklo muttered blearily. "Keep him quiet, can't you? The noise will bring the white bears right to us."

"Maybe it's a sign that we shouldn't have him," Lusa suggested, desperate to convince Kallik that she should give back the cub. "You can't look after him properly."

Immediately Kallik rounded on her; the gentleness she showed to Kissimi had vanished, replaced by a savage glare. "I *can* look after him!"

The tension between the two she-bears reached Kissimi, who began wailing even louder. With a huff of annoyance Kallik picked him up by the scruff and heaved herself out of the den, shuffling off into the darkness. The sound of Kissimi's cries gradually faded.

At first Lusa had been afraid that Kallik was leaving, but she could scent that her friend was still close by. *She must believe that we don't want her,* she thought sadly. *Or maybe she doesn't want us anymore. Only Kissimi.*

Toklo and Ujurak settled down to sleep again, but Lusa stayed awake under the dark sky, feeling miserable and lonely. She wasn't comfortable in this desolate place, and fear of the white bears made her uneasy, her senses alert for any sign that they were sneaking up on their den.

Aga was grateful to me for moving the seals, she thought, *but the other bears didn't seem all that pleased with me. What will happen if they catch up with us?*

Exhaustion plunged her into sleep at last; in her dreams she was walking through sunlit woods, with a stream splashing along beside her and the chattering of birds sounding in the trees. Lusa reveled in the warmth and the sensation of a full belly.

Happy and curious, she wandered among the trees until she heard the squeaking of bear cubs from just ahead, along with the deeper rumble of their mother's voice.

Lusa quickened her pace, still following the stream, until she reached the edge of a clearing and peered out from the shelter of a clump of ferns. In front of her she saw a family of black bears, a mother and two cubs who were tumbling and chasing after beetles. It looked as if the mother was having just as much fun as the two half-grown cubs, growling and pretending to attack them, then rolling over with them on the grass in a tangle of limbs.

It would be so much fun to go play with them, Lusa thought longingly, but caution kept her in hiding.

Then she found her gaze drawn to the bigger of the two cubs. She felt as if she knew him very well, and yet she was sure she had never seen him before. Puzzled, she gazed at him, watching him pouncing and play-fighting with his sister, until a voice seemed to speak deep inside her.

"Lusa, that is your father."

Lusa stiffened. Her thoughts flew back to King in the Bear Bowl, the big black bear whose temper was so uncertain, who had harshly forbidden her to talk about the wild. Was it possible, she wondered, staring out into the clearing, that this carefree cub had grown up into King?

"Watch me!" he boasted, bounding over to a tree on the other side of the clearing. "I can climb faster than any bear!"

He raced up the tree, and as she watched him, Lusa remembered how her father had taught her to climb, back in the Bear Bowl. Balancing on a branch, the cub clawed up a pawful of fruit, and he scrambled back down to drop it in front of his mother and sister.

"There!" he said, swelling with pride as he watched them eat. "One day I'll be the strongest bear in the whole forest!"

"Maybe you will," his mother said, gently touching his head with her muzzle. "But there's more than strength to being a good bear. Never forget that the spirits of your ancestors are watching you all the time from inside the trees."

"I know." King shot across the clearing and skidded to a halt in front of a tall birch tree. "Hey there, spirit!" he called out. "Can you see me? Watch me jump!"

His sister scampered after him and stood in front of a graceful willow tree that leaned over the stream, its twigs brushing the surface of the water.

"Look at me, spirit!" she called. "I can jump higher!"

"Can not!" King danced up to a fir tree, giving his sister a quick shove as he bounced past. "Come out, spirit!" he called. "Come play with us."

"He can't, silly." The small she-cub ran past her brother and reared up, setting her paws on the tree trunk. "He's stuck in there forever and ever!"

The mother bear strode across the clearing and gave each of the cubs a swift cuff over the ears. "Don't be so disrespectful!" she scolded. "How will you feel when you have a tree of your own, if little cubs come up and tease you?"

"I'd like a pretty willow tree just like this one," the she-cub said. "And I'd swish my branches to say hello to any bears who came by."

"*I* want to be the tallest tree in the forest, an oak or a pine, overlooking all the other trees. When the wind blows, my branches will *roar!*" King said.

He reared up and waved his forepaws in the air and nearly lost his balance, staggering around to stop himself from toppling over.

"Watch out!" his mother exclaimed, with a huff of amusement. "There's a big, big tree falling down!"

Lusa wondered whether her father's spirit had made it into a tall tree. She hated the thought of him being stuck forever in the Bear Bowl. *He needs more trees to look at, not just walls and flat-faces.*

The two cubs were chasing each other around the clearing, while their mother looked on. Lusa bunched her muscles, ready to spring out and join in the fun, but before she could move, a warm shoulder brushed against her.

"Wait, little one," a voice murmured. "One day you will go home, but not yet."

Lusa turned her head and saw Arcturus, the giant starry bear who had visited her in her dreams before. Stars sifted through his pelt, and his eyes burned with soft fire.

Gently Arcturus nudged Lusa away from the edge of the clearing and back into the woods. The sunlight vanished, and shadows gathered thickly under the trees, while a cold breeze sprang up, sending icy claws deep into Lusa's fur.

"Where are we going?" she wailed.

"You will find out," Arcturus promised.

His voice faded, and Lusa woke to find herself in the dark scoop in the snow, pressed up against Ujurak and Toklo. Arcturus's wild, starry scent clung to her fur, and the happy voices of King and his sister still rang in her ears.

Lusa let out a sigh. She was sad to be wrenched away from the dream forest, but she felt better knowing that Arcturus was always watching over her.

I'll live in a forest again one day, she comforted herself. *Arcturus said so.*

CHAPTER SEVENTEEN

Kallik

Kallik woke with her body curled around Kissimi; the little cub had snuggled deep into her fur, his snuffly breath warming her belly. Stars still shone above her head, though on the horizon she could just make out the first faint glimmer that heralded the dawn.

Is one of those stars my mother, watching me? she wondered, gazing at the glittering points of light. *If you're there, why can't I see your spirit dancing?*

But Kallik soon dismissed thoughts of her mother, looking down instead at the cub pressed so closely against her. The spirit lights weren't as important to her now that she had Kissimi. Nothing mattered more than keeping him safe and alive.

"Those white bears mustn't find you," she murmured, burrowing into his fur with her snout. "I saved you. You belong to me now."

Even while she was speaking, Kallik realized how thin and weak the cub was. *I'll hunt for him later,* she thought. *He needs meat, not plants. That's the right food for white bears.*

A few bearlengths away she could hear sounds from the hollow den where the other bears were waking up. Nudging Kissimi onto her shoulders, she rose to her paws and headed in that direction. Her cub barely roused, just letting out a whimper and lapsing into sleep again.

Her three friends raised their heads to gaze at her as she padded up; the air was heavy with tension, as if a storm were about to break. *I don't care,* Kallik told herself firmly, bracing herself for their hostility. *It doesn't matter if they're not my friends anymore. I have Kissimi.*

"I'm going to hunt," she announced.

"And I'll check that we haven't been followed," Toklo added. "The wind has covered our pawprints, but our scent is still in the air," he finished, wriggling out of the den and heading back in the direction they had come the night before, his snout raised to sniff the air.

Kallik thought that he looked more anxious than usual, however much he tried to hide it. *He feels responsible for us,* she realized. *And I can smell fear-scent on him.* A pang of guilt shook her, that she had put Toklo in the position of having to protect her from the other white bears.

But I had no choice, she protested inwardly. *I won't* let them have *Kissimi!*

Lusa and Ujurak scrambled out after Toklo and stood on the edge of the hollow, casting uneasy glances at Kallik.

A heavy weight settled in Kallik's belly, and she faced Ujurak. "I had to run away with Kissimi!" she defended herself. "Unalaq might have eaten him! That's what happens with male bears, sometimes."

Ujurak just gazed at her with limpid eyes, waiting for her to finish. Kallik's hot defiance faltered, and she had to look away.

"You think I'm wrong, don't you?" she asked shakily. "You think I should have given Kissimi back."

"You have made him part of your destiny," Ujurak said, still with the same serious gaze. "You cannot change that now."

Kallik felt a stab of alarm. "But what about our destiny? Have I reached the end of my journey?"

Ujurak didn't reply to her directly, swinging his head around to include Lusa as he spoke. "The end is close. I feel it like a storm building inside me. Something is going to happen."

"What?" Kallik took a couple of pawsteps forward, bringing her within a muzzlelength of Ujurak. "What will happen? Is it about the spirits in the sky? Will they come back?"

Ujurak was silent for a long time. "I'll hunt with you," he said at last. "We'll find some food for Kissimi and ourselves."

"And I'm going to look for plants. You can leave Kissimi in the den," Lusa added, with a return to something of her old friendliness. "I'll keep an eye on him."

Kallik blinked at her gratefully, feeling guilty for the way that her love for Kissimi was straining her friendship with the others. "Thanks, Lusa."

Relief that her friends were still supporting her filled Kallik as she and Ujurak set out across the bleak landscape. A few tufty bushes appeared, stretching their twigs above the snow, and they sniffed around them for traces of hare.

"Musk oxen have been here," Ujurak murmured, and pointed with his snout at the faint traces of hoofprints still visible in the snow.

"Yes. But we'd never bring one down when it's just us," Kallik said regretfully. She prodded hopefully at the snow, but there was no sign of prey. "Why don't you turn into a hare?" she suggested. "Then you'll be able to track down their burrows under the snow."

Ujurak shook his head. "Today I want to hunt as a bear," he told her, with no explanation.

Kallik was opening her jaws to complain when a flicker of movement caught her attention. "A hare!" she exclaimed, making out the shape of its white body and the black tips of its ears, which bobbed up and down as it ran.

Ujurak launched himself after it, and Kallik followed, veering away in a wide circle to come at the hare from a different direction. The chase led them into a valley with low ridges on either side, the ground uneven with snow-covered rocks and clumps of thorns growing among them.

The hare was fleeing from Ujurak, but it hadn't noticed Kallik, who began to home in on it. Ujurak let out a roar, panicking the hare still further. It dodged around a thornbush and raced straight for Kallik.

But just as Kallik was bracing herself to spring on it, something zipped past her head. The hare let out a squeal and fell, jerking, to the ground. A moment later it went limp; Kallik saw a stick poking out of its body, sending a trickle of blood into its white pelt.

"What happened?" she asked, bewildered.

As Ujurak skidded to a halt nearby, Kallik raised her snout to sniff the air, and froze at the scent she picked up. "No-claws!" she exclaimed. "We should get out of here."

Both bears backed off from the hare lying still in the snow. Something moved in the corner of Kallik's eye, and she spotted a no-claw in white pelts emerge from behind a snowy rock. He let out a shout and waved his forelegs as if he was trying to chase the bears away.

At the same moment a harsh caw sounded behind Kallik. She turned her head to see a raven fly up from a bush and circle over their heads; she guessed the noisy no-claw had startled it.

And he's wearing the pelt of a white bear, she thought, drawing her lips back in a snarl of outrage.

"Kallik, come on," Ujurak called to her. "Let the flat-face have his prey."

"That was *our* prey," Kallik retorted. "Are you starting to favor no-claws since you became one?"

Ujurak shook his head. "Don't be cloud-brained," he said mildly. "We can find another hare just as easily."

Still grumbling under her breath, Kallik headed farther along the valley, only to halt as Ujurak called to her again.

"Wait a moment. I want to see where that white-pelted flat-face came from."

Kallik turned to see Ujurak climbing the ridge at the side of the valley where the no-claw had appeared. With an annoyed shrug she headed toward him and caught up at the top of the ridge.

"Look at that!" he exclaimed.

Peering down, Kallik spotted a collection of small snowy humps with tunnels leading into the side. Some of the humps were linked by more tunnels. The smell of no-claws and burning meat drifted up to her. "What are those?" she asked, baffled. "Hills?"

Ujurak didn't reply; his gaze was rapt, fixed on the scene below as if he was completely fascinated by it.

Then Kallik saw a no-claw emerging from one of the tunnels. *Those humps must be no-claw dens,* she realized, *but I've never seen anything like them before.* "I guess they build their dens out of snow here," she muttered. "Just like us."

Ujurak still didn't respond. Above their heads the raven let out another harsh caw, then swooped down to the cluster of snow-dens. Ujurak's gaze followed its flight.

"We should go." Kallik shifted her paws restlessly. "What if the no-claws see us? They obviously hunt bears as well as hares. I don't want to end up as a no-claw's pelt!"

Ujurak didn't move; it was as if Kallik hadn't spoken.

"We haven't finished hunting, remember?" she said impatiently, giving the brown bear a prod in the side.

Huffing in annoyance, she realized that she wasn't getting through to Ujurak. *Fine! If he wants to stand there staring at birds and little snowy hills, he can do it by himself!*

She stomped off down the hillside into the valley and began casting about for the scent of hare. Soon she spotted tiny pawprints in the snow and started to follow them, her snout close to the snowy surface of the ground.

Then a little way ahead Kallik saw a tiny dark blob. *A hare's nose! Yes!* As she hurtled forward, the hare sprang up and fled, but frustration gave Kallik extra speed. The hare swerved around an outcrop of rock; Kallik caught up with it and killed it quickly with a paw slamming into the back of its head.

The scent of fresh prey made her belly growl, but Kallik knew that she had to save the hare for Kissimi. She glanced around, thinking that she knew the right direction, and headed back to the den.

But the valley didn't open up into the flatter area where they had dug the den, as she had expected. Instead Kallik found herself trekking deeper into the gently undulating terrain, with no landmarks or trails to follow. Turning, she began to retrace her pawsteps, still carrying the hare. Its scent and taste flooded her jaws with water; all her instincts were telling her to stop and eat, but she forced herself to go on, keeping the prey for her cub.

There was still no sign of the makeshift den, or any familiar shapes in the snow-covered ground. Kallik tried a different direction, feeling foolish and angry and tired all at once.

If I just gave up and lay down, would I turn into a tiny hill of snow like those no-claw dens? But then, what would happen to Kissimi? she wondered.

Suddenly panic stabbed through Kallik, tearing at her like huge claws. *Maybe I can't find the den because the white bears found them and killed them all!*

She began to run, faster and faster, even though she had no idea where she was going. Her panting breath billowed out in clouds, which thickened around her until she was running through mist. Soon she couldn't see a single pawstep in front of her, and she felt the presence of another bear, keeping pace beside her through the fog.

"Ujurak?" she asked nervously. "Yakone?"

"Don't be afraid, little one," a voice whispered. "You are not lost. I am here."

Kallik halted, taking a huge shuddering breath as she recognized the voice of her mother. Turning to face Nisa, she could just make out a white shape, barely visible through the mist.

The one question Kallik wanted to ask tumbled from her mouth. "Did I make a terrible mistake, taking Kissimi?"

Nisa's voice was gentle as she replied in the words Ujurak had used. "You have made him part of your destiny. Every step you take is one you have chosen; remember that."

"But I couldn't leave him!" Kallik wailed. "Not without his mother!"

Nisa's warm eyes gleamed in the mist. "Ah, you were thinking of me, weren't you? But you and Taqqiq had no one to take care of you. Kissimi has other bears."

"But I don't," Kallik whispered, feeling a terrible loneliness opening up inside her. "Not white bears, not you, and not my brother." Longing to be with others of her kind washed over Kallik and mingled with guilt as she remembered how she had left Taqqiq behind.

"Taqqiq chose his own path," Nisa told her; her warm breath drifted over Kallik, bringing her comfort. "Just as you chose yours. And you still have a choice about Kissimi. . . ."

Nisa's voice began to fade on the last words. Kallik realized she could no longer see the white shape through the mist. Then a wind rose, swirling the mist away, revealing a bare hillside, where Kallik stood with the hare in her jaws. Above her the sky was white and empty, with no sign of the spirits.

Was my mother really with me just now? Kallik wondered. *Or did I dream her?*

As she stood still in confusion, she felt a tug on her fur and recognized her bond with Kissimi, calling her back. A swell in the land in front of her looked familiar. Lowering her head against the wind, Kallik began trudging back to the den.

CHAPTER EIGHTEEN

Ujurak

Standing on the hilltop, Ujurak was hardly aware of when Kallik left him. Instead he was lost in the memory of what he had dreamed the night before.

Starlight sparkled on the snow. Ujurak gazed into the black depths of the sky, tracing out the shape of his mother, Ursa. She looked so close that he felt he could almost reach up a paw to touch her.

Then, as Ujurak gazed upward, the stars began to spin. Ursa's shape was lost as they swirled into a glittering whirl-pool, then spun outward again and began to take on a new shape.

Ujurak held his breath in astonishment as he saw the wide-spread wings, the wedge-shaped tail, and the strong beak, and heard the harsh cry that came from it.

A raven!

The star-bird swooped down, circling Ujurak's head, and landed on the snow by his side. As soon as its claws touched the ground, it began to grow, its feathers billowing outward.

Its beak shrank away, and the feathers vanished from its face and wings. A tall, imposing flat-face stood by Ujurak's side, clad in a cloak of black feathers. Snow swirled up and glittered around him, forming an icy mist.

As Ujurak watched, stunned to silence, the flat-face turned to him and beckoned. Then his form faded into the mist. Before he finally disappeared, he opened his mouth, but all that came out was the harsh caw of a raven.

Ujurak blinked, shivering, and realized that he was still standing on the ridge, looking down at the snow-dens below. He remembered the call of the star-bird and the flat-face; it was exactly the same as the cry of the raven that had swooped over his head and then flown down to the flat-face denning area.

This flat-face has something to tell me, Ujurak thought.

Glancing over his shoulder, he saw no sign of any other bears. He hesitated for a moment, then began to plod downhill toward the snow-dens. As he walked, he reluctantly let his bear shape slip away, relinquishing his fur for the almost hairless skin of a flat-face. He rose to his hindpaws, staggering a little before he found the balance of this unfamiliar shape.

By the time he reached the snow-dens, he was naked and shivering, hugging himself in a vain attempt to keep warm. His bear senses had not entirely left him; he crept up to the nearest of the dens and made sure by sniffing and listening that there was no one inside.

Ducking into the entrance tunnel, Ujurak found himself in a circular den. Pale daylight filtered in through a square of

ice set in the roof. At the opposite side from the tunnel was a
raised section of packed snow, spread with twigs and caribou
hides.

Investigating, Ujurak found some flat-face pelts there, too:
He slipped on a coat made of caribou and some pelt-wraps for
his legs. Glancing around, alert in case the flat-face who lived
there came back, he spotted a pair of pelts the same shape as
his awkward flat-face hindpaws. Ujurak slipped his feet into
them and headed out of the tunnel again.

Just as he emerged into the open, he heard a shout behind
him. Startled, he spun around to see a female flat-face—*no, a
woman*, he reminded himself, trying to gather his memories of
the language of the flat-faces. She was tall, with a tanned, lined
face and gray hair wisping from underneath her head covering.

"What were you doing in Akaka's igloo?" she demanded.

Ujurak ducked his head respectfully. "I . . . I was looking
for someone," he stammered. "I've come a long way to speak to
the man who wears a black cloak of feathers."

The woman frowned. "You mean Tulugaq?"

Hoping he was right, Ujurak nodded.

To his relief the woman's face softened. "Not many people
visit Tulugaq in the deep snow," she said. "He is an old man
now. He will be glad of someone to talk to, but you mustn't
tire him out."

"I won't," Ujurak promised.

The woman beckoned. "Come with me. My name is
Anouk," she went on as she led the way among the igloos.
"What's yours?"

"I'm Ujurak."

"Well, Ujurak, I don't know how you managed to travel in the depths of winter like this. Where did you come from?"

Even though Anouk's tone was friendly, Ujurak wanted to evade her questions. *There's no way I can tell her the truth!*

"Er . . . I'm from a tribe on a different island," he replied. "I had a dream that told me to come and find Tulugaq."

Anouk smiled. "Ah. A lot of his visitors say that."

Before she could ask any more questions, a black-haired young man appeared from behind the nearest igloo. He wore white bear pelts like the hunter Ujurak and Kallik had seen, and he carried fish fastened together with a hook through their jaws.

"Hey, Mother, who have you got there?" he called out as he approached.

"This is Ujurak," Anouk replied. "Ujurak, this is Akaka, my firstborn son. He—"

"Just a minute," Akaka interrupted. He strode up to Ujurak and stood looking down at him with a thunderous frown on his face. "You're wearing my clothes! Thief!"

"I'm sorry." Ujurak took a step backward, intimidated by the man's rough voice. "I—I lost my clothes in a storm, and I was so cold! I'll put them back before I go, I promise."

Akaka narrowed his eyes suspiciously. "Lost your clothes in a storm? What sort of a tale is that? Who are you, anyway? Did you come from the military base?" He let out an exasperated sigh. "Don't tell me you want us to move our igloos *again*?"

Ujurak was bewildered by the flurry of questions. He

didn't know what Akaka was talking about, let alone how to answer him.

"Akaka!" A clear voice rang out, and Ujurak spotted a young woman hurrying to stand at Akaka's side. Her dark hair was in a long braid down her back, and her eyes were a piercing green. "Akaka, you're scaring the boy. I'm sure he didn't mean any harm."

Akaka just snorted, but Ujurak was pleased to see that the man's frown faded as he looked at the young woman.

"This is Eva, Akaka's wife," Anouk told him. "Ujurak has come a long way to see Tulugaq," she added.

"There! You see?" Eva said to her husband, as if that were a good excuse for stealing clothes. "But you'd better come with me first," she went on to Ujurak. "Anyone can see that you need a good meal and a rest."

She pointed to a bigger igloo near the center of the denning place. The tempting smell of burned meat drifted from it, but Ujurak hesitated, hunger warring with his need to speak to Tulugaq and find the answers to the questions that were tormenting him.

"Better do as Eva says," Anouk advised, laughing. "My son's wife can be very bossy, but she has a good heart."

"And take care of my clothes!" Akaka still looked stern, but he clapped Ujurak on the shoulder before striding off with his catch.

Ujurak followed Eva into the big igloo, intrigued to meet more of her people. *They seem so different from Sally and her friends. They don't have all those firebeasts and the other machines I saw there.*

They reminded Ujurak more of the Caribou People he had
met in Arctic Village, when he had almost died from swallowing a fishhook, and the village healer, Tiinchuu, had saved
his life.

As soon as he emerged from the entrance tunnel, smoke
caught him in the throat, and he coughed. His eyes stinging,
he peered through the haze, trying to make out his surroundings.

The igloo was similar to the first one he had entered,
though much bigger: a single round space with a raised area
spread with pelts, which Ujurak guessed was where the people
slept. A second tunnel led away at the far side, probably to
another of the snow-dens. Ujurak stared in astonishment to
see that the smoke was coming from a fire in the middle of
the area. There was a hole in the roof above the fire to let the
smoke out, though it wasn't working very well.

Fire? But this igloo is made of snow! Why doesn't it melt?

A metal pot was balanced on top of the fire, with the entic-
ing scent of seal meat coming out of it. Around the fire several
people were crouching, holding out more pieces of meat and
fish, speared on sticks, to burn in the flames. They were all
dressed in the pelts of caribou or bears. They looked up as
Ujurak and Eva entered the igloo, and murmured greetings.

"Hi, everyone, this is Ujurak," Eva announced cheerfully.
She thrust Ujurak forward, and two younger men moved
aside to make a space for him near the fire.

"Hi, Nauja," Eva continued, bustling up to the pot and
stirring it with a spoon. "How's your cough?" Hardly waiting

for a reply, she went on, "Irniq, Akaka has the fishhooks you wanted. You need to go and get them."

While she was speaking, she ladled out some of the meat from the pot onto a flat metal plate, which she gave to Ujurak. "There, eat," she invited with a broad smile. "You look half starved."

Ujurak sniffed suspiciously at the meat; his bear instincts made him uncertain about eating anything that had been burned. But his flat-face belly rumbled with hunger. Ignoring the spoon Eva gave him, he picked up a lump of meat in his fingers and swallowed it in one gulp. He closed his eyes with pleasure at the delicious taste and the warmth spreading inside his belly.

This is the right sort of food for bears, he thought.

Kind laughter broke out all around him. "You certainly were hungry," someone commented.

Ujurak stared at his plate, embarrassed. "Sorry." *I've got to remember how flat-faces eat!*

Eva ruffled his hair. "Don't worry, Ujurak. I like to see people enjoying their food."

While Ujurak picked up the spoon and ate more slowly, he listened to the quiet voices of the people around him.

"I feel a storm coming," one of the older men said. "My bones ache."

"Your bones are always aching, Amaruq," the man beside him said, giving him a friendly nudge.

"And there are always storms," Amaruq responded calmly. "I hope we're sheltered enough, here below the ridge."

As soon as Ujurak had finished eating, Eva beckoned him out of the igloo again. "Now I'll take you to see my grandfather Tulugaq," she said.

She led the way to an igloo on the far side of the group. Ujurak's skin began to tingle as he drew closer, and he shivered inwardly with anticipation. A loud caw overhead made him jump, and he looked up to see a raven flying above the igloo.

"Don't be afraid," Eva laughed. "My grandfather loves to feed the birds. It's a waste of good bread," she added, but she was smiling as she said it, and Ujurak realized that she was only teasing.

Eva stooped to enter the igloo, and Ujurak followed her, all his senses alive with curiosity. Inside, the only light came from a lamp set on a snow-ledge at the far side; the air was still with the musty smell of birds and unwashed pelts. Ujurak brushed past something on the ground and realized it was the cloak of feathers, lying there folded and empty, like a fallen bird.

At first he thought that the igloo was unoccupied, until something stirred among the furs on the raised sleeping area.

"Grandfather, you have a visitor," Eva said.

A very old man peered out from the midst of the furs. His hair was white and wispy, and his face seamed with lines of wisdom and experience. His dark eyes shone brightly in the dim light.

"Can I get you some food, Grandfather?" Eva asked, bending over the old man and helping him sit up. "Or water? Are you warm enough? I could fetch you some more furs."

A thin, bony hand appeared from the coverings, motioning her away. "I'm fine, Eva. Leave me in peace."

Eva gripped his hand for a moment before turning to leave. Before she entered the tunnel again, she glanced back at Ujurak. "Remember not to stay too long and tire Grandfather," she told him.

When Eva had gone, Ujurak stood silent in front of Tulugaq. The old man fixed a piercing stare on him, for so long that Ujurak started to feel uncomfortable.

"So you came," Tulugaq said at last. "I wondered if you would figure it out."

"You . . . you looked different in my dream," Ujurak stammered.

Tulugaq let out a hoarse laugh. "In my dreams I am still a young man."

"And a raven!" Ujurak blurted; excitement surged up inside him, warring with his nervousness.

"Yes." Tulugaq bowed his head. "I am always a raven."

"Are you like me?" Now words were tumbling out of Ujurak. "Can you change into anything?"

Tulugaq raised his brows in surprise. "No, just a raven. Or perhaps I am a raven that changes into a man," he added with a sly smile.

"How do you know?" Ujurak asked.

The old man's gaze grew fixed, as if he were looking far beyond the walls of the igloo. "When I was younger," he began, "I lived for the air, the silent sea above the ground where my wings could carry me anywhere. I learned so much on those journeys; I could find answers for anyone who came to see me." He paused, sighing. "But now I am old, and I want my family around me as I prepare to join my ancestors in the sky."

Ujurak stared at him. "You mean the lights? Those are your ancestors, too?"

"Oh, yes," Tulugaq replied. "They are the Selamiut, all the people who have lived on the ice before us."

Ujurak's heart pounded, and he felt he could scarcely breathe. *So they aren't just bears,* he thought. "Do you know where the lights have gone?" he asked out loud.

Tulugaq closed his eyes. "The lights have departed before this, but they have never stayed away so long." He gave a long sigh. "Yes, I am troubled. In my dreams I have tried to look for them, but I am old and tired. It is time for someone else to look."

"I'm trying!" Ujurak assured him. "But I don't know what to do next."

The old man gazed at him for a moment from his bird-bright eyes. "Would you like to travel with me?" he asked.

"Yes!" Ujurak's excitement welled up again, and he turned toward the entrance tunnel.

"No, not like that. Lie down here."

As Tulugaq motioned to the space beside him on the sleeping area, he was shaken by a fit of coughing, scarcely able to get his breath. Ujurak wasn't sure what to do. Fighting back panic, he looked around and spotted a container made of skins. The scent of water came from it; Ujurak picked it up and held it for Tulugaq to sip.

"Shall I fetch Eva?" he asked as the old man's coughing died away.

"No." Tulugaq's voice was rough and breathy. "She'll only worry. And I shall be joining the Selamiut soon, wherever they are. . . ." He motioned to Ujurak to lie down beside him, then fumbled out a small bunch of herbs from somewhere among his furs and reached up to sprinkle them on the lamp. Finally he settled himself back, closed his eyes, and began to chant in a thin, reedy voice.

Ujurak lay down and pulled the furs around himself. The warmth and the scent of burning herbs lulled him into a half sleep. Tulugaq's chanting seemed to become more resonant, wreathing around Ujurak like smoke.

Spirits, we're coming to find you, Ujurak thought muzzily. *Show us what you want us to do.*

CHAPTER NINETEEN

Ujurak

Ujurak jerked awake to see the tall, imposing man from his earlier dream standing by the entrance to the igloo. He was enveloped in the cloak of feathers.

"Tulugaq?" Ujurak asked uncertainly.

The man nodded, beckoning. "Come."

Ujurak followed him outside into the dim light of early dawn. Tulugaq walked away from the igloos, quickening his pace as he went, until the cloak was billowing out around him like a pair of vast wings. Suddenly his shape flickered; his feet left the ground, and a raven soared into the air, wheeling over Ujurak's head.

Quickly Ujurak willed himself to change, letting black feathers grow from his flat-face arms while he felt his legs shrink into the sticklike limbs and claws of a bird. Spreading his wings, he felt a beak sprout from his face, and he let out an answering caw as he mounted into the air: younger and smaller than Tulugaq, but a raven just like him.

Tulugaq rose higher and higher into the air, until the igloos vanished into the snowy ground around them. Gazing around him, Ujurak could see the whole island, and other islands dotted in the frozen sea around it. The flat-face denning area near the poisoned cove stood out stark against the snow on the far side.

Swooping lower again, Tulugaq and Ujurak flew over the new bay, where Ujurak spotted several white bears crouched beside breathing holes, waiting for seals. *Good,* he thought. *They've moved to their new hunting ground.* He recognized Yakone from his reddish pelt, and wondered what the white bear would think if he knew who was flying overhead.

A little farther on, the snow was churned up by a caribou trail, heading inland. Tulugaq swerved to follow it, past the flat-face denning area and toward the inner part of the island, where steep mountains reared up into the sky. At last they passed the caribou herd; the powerful bodies of the creatures looked tiny as Ujurak flew above them.

Then Tulugaq led him into a deep fold in the ground, flanked by jagged hills all covered in snow. He swooped down into the valley and perched on a wind-carved point of snow halfway up the slope. "Down there," he cawed as Ujurak alighted beside him, "is a cave where our ancestors met."

My ancestors? Or yours? Ujurak wondered.

"It is known as the Place of the Selamiut," Tulugaq told him.

"Are we going inside?" Ujurak asked eagerly.

The raven shook his head. "There is something else I want you to see," he cawed.

Tulugaq flew on, and Ujurak sprang into the sky and followed him. At the end of the valley a flat-face structure came into view: It was made of dark poles tapering into the sky and flanked by brown machinery.

Tulugaq flew down and perched on top of the tall structure. As Ujurak joined him, he picked up a stench that reminded him of the creatures soaked in oil that he had helped Sally rescue, and of the oilfield he had visited at the edge of the Last Great Wilderness.

Oil! The flat-faces have even come here to find it!

He looked down at the flat-faces moving around the area, dressed in bright yellow pelts. Some of them were driving past in firebeasts; others were on foot, carrying long rods or chunky bits of machinery that Ujurak didn't recognize.

As he gazed down, his vision seemed to blur, and when it cleared again, he saw more structures sprouting from the ground, more flat-faces and firebeasts, appearing like the eruptions of some horrible disease, until the whole island was covered, as far as Ujurak could see.

The sounds of dying animals huddled below him invaded his head: cubs whimpering with hunger, birds cawing feebly, white bears roaring in anger that there were no seals left. The suffering of starving creatures filled the whole world, shaking Ujurak on his perch.

Dark, sticky oil started to well up from the ground, a black tide spreading across the snow, swallowing the whiteness and the dying creatures. Wave after wave of it flowed out around him, covering the frozen sea and encroaching on the other islands until there was nothing but stinking oil from horizon to horizon. Ujurak gagged on the stench as he breathed in the tainted air.

"Tulugaq, what—?" he began. Ujurak broke off as he turned to look at the raven and saw the gloss on his feathers covered with thick black oil. The bird was choking, his beak opening and closing silently.

Tulugaq is dying!

Ujurak couldn't think where the oil had come from, but he knew there was no way of banishing it, nothing that he could do here. They had to get back to the igloos.

"Tulugaq, you must fly with me!" he urged.

The older raven turned his head and fixed Ujurak with a despairing gaze, but he spread his wings and lurched into the sky. Ujurak flew close beside him as they struggled over the hills, beginning to panic again as he realized that he didn't know which way to head.

Tulugaq was losing height, his oil-soaked wings laboring. Ujurak swooped to follow him. Suddenly he felt a jolt as if he had slammed into the ground, and for a moment everything went dark. Then he opened his eyes and found himself in flat-face form, wrapped in furs and lying in Tulugaq's igloo.

The reek of oil still filled the air, and Ujurak gasped for breath as he thrust away the furs and scrambled to Tulugaq's side. The old man was clean, the smothering oil vanished, but he lay on his back, his chest heaving as he drew in each rasping breath. His eyes were closed, and he didn't rouse when Ujurak spoke his name.

His hands shaking, Ujurak grabbed the water bottle and raised the old man's head so that he could take a sip.

Tulugaq's eyes flickered open, and he fixed them on Ujurak as he pushed the water bottle away. "The wild is dying, and I am dying with it," he whispered. "The time has come."

"No!" Ujurak exclaimed.

The old man ignored his protest, feebly trying to raise himself among the enveloping furs. "Turn back the tide to save the island," he gasped, "and perhaps the wild will survive."

Ujurak nodded. "I will, I promise." *Anything, if it will keep Tulugaq alive!* "I'll fetch Eva," he added.

The old man's hand, thin and bony like the talon of a bird, reached out and gripped Ujurak's wrist with surprising strength. Ujurak looked down to see that his eyes were brimming with tears.

"It's all right," he murmured to the old man, compassion making his voice quiver. "I will do what I can."

Tulugaq shook his head. "It is your time, too," he whispered. "I wish it were not so." Gathering his strength, he added, "Look for me where the Selamiut are, and I will find you among the stars."

His grip tightened on Ujurak's wrist, then went limp. He let out his breath in a long sigh. His eyes were still fixed on Ujurak's face, but the light within them was gone. Shock froze Ujurak for a moment before he managed to control himself.

"Good-bye, Tulugaq." Ujurak reached out and gently closed the old man's eyes. Then he bowed his head over the body and gave himself up to grief.

Movement inside the igloo roused him some unknown time later; he looked up and saw Eva. She stood behind him, her eyes full of sorrow as she gazed down at the body of her grandfather. "I knew he was dying," she whispered. "But I thought he would stay with us a little longer."

"I'm so sorry!" Ujurak blurted out. "I tried to help him."

Eva nodded, resting a hand on his shoulder. "I know. He was an old, old man. I'm glad he went peacefully."

But he didn't, Ujurak thought. *He knew that something terrible is happening on the island, and he wanted me to stop it. But how? I had so many more questions to ask!*

As Eva bent over her grandfather's body, covering his face and beginning to arrange herbs around him from a pouch beside the bed, Ujurak slipped out of the igloo. He retraced his steps to Akaka's igloo, relieved to find that it was still empty. He stripped off the borrowed clothes and ventured out into the open again, shivering in the icy wind.

As he began to run, he transformed back into a brown bear, but for once there was no comfort in the familiar shape. Every nerve and muscle in his body felt the sickness of the raven, the anguish of the Inuit boy, the hunger of the white bears, and the confusion of the caribou as their feeding grounds were drowned under the stinking black tide of oil.

This is the place where the wild is dying faster than anywhere else!

CHAPTER TWENTY

Toklo

Toklo plodded back to the makeshift den with a ptarmigan, the chunky body with its ruffled white feathers hanging limply from his jaws. His scouting hadn't found any trace of pursuing white bears, and on his way back he had practically tripped over the bird. He felt satisfied that he'd managed to achieve something.

The wretched creature is very small, he thought, *but it's better than nothing. Certainly better than those plants Lusa is always looking for!*

When Toklo reached the edge of the den, he saw only Lusa, lying on her back and playing with Kissimi, who was dabbing at her paws. She scrambled up, gently pushing the cub to one side, when she spotted Toklo.

"Have you seen Ujurak and Kallik?" she asked anxiously.

Shaking his head, Toklo dropped the ptarmigan into the den. "Aren't they here? I thought they'd be back by now."

"No. I'm getting really worried." Lusa stroked Kissimi with one soft black paw, as if she was trying to reassure him.

Toklo lowered himself into the den, pushing his prey toward Lusa so that they could share it. Tearing off a scrap, he set it down in front of Kissimi.

"Don't stare at me!" he said gruffly, feeling Lusa's gaze on him. "We're running for our lives because of him. There's no point if he dies."

He glared at Kissimi as the little cub nosed at the meat, then set his teeth in one end of it and began chewing inexpertly. Suddenly Toklo blinked. Kissimi's fine white fur faded in front of his eyes, to be replaced by the scrawny brown flanks of his brother, Tobi.

"Yuck!" he complained.

"But you've got to eat." Toklo tried to persuade the cub, panic welling up inside him. "If you don't, you'll die."

Still the cub only spat out the morsel of meat and turned his head away, letting out a weak, mewling cry.

Toklo's fear was driven out by surging anger. "Eat!" he growled. "We're risking our lives for you! Can't you see that?" He loomed over the cub, who cringed away from him with a whimper of terror, and raised one paw ready to strike.

Before he could bring down his massive paw onto the cowering cub, a shower of snow descended from the edge of the den. Kallik hurled herself at Toklo, throwing aside an Arctic hare that she held clamped in her jaws. She looked wild-eyed and exhausted.

"What are you doing?" she snarled, rounding on Toklo and baring her teeth, ready for a fight. "Leave Kissimi alone!"

Overwhelmed by rage and frustration, Toklo advanced on

her, but before he could come within striking distance, Lusa hurled herself between them.

"Stop this at once!" she snapped. "Toklo, get out. You're scaring Kissimi."

She thrust at Toklo with her shoulder, urging him to the edge of the den. Clumsily he stumbled out. His fury ebbed, and he shuddered as he came back to himself. *It wasn't Tobi; it was Kissimi all along.* His belly churned with horror as he realized that he might have to watch another cub die.

Behind him he could hear Kallik as she fussed over her cub. "Kissimi! Are you all right? Don't be afraid, dear one; the scary brown bear has gone." She gave the cub's fur a deep sniff. "Oh, you've eaten something! Thank you for sharing," she added to Lusa.

"Well, of course we fed him!" Lusa responded indignantly. "It's not his fault!"

Kallik muttered something inaudible; Toklo hoped she felt embarrassed about the danger she had brought down on them all, and the way she seemed to think they wanted her cub to die.

"Kallik, Kissimi is s lever." Lusa was obviously trying to distract her friend and calm the tension between them all. "He knows all our names now. And he was pretending to crouch beside a seal hole. He kept so still!"

While Kallik nuzzled her cub, Toklo grumpily tried to block his ears from the she-bears' chatter. *I know I was wrong to get angry with the cub. But for a moment there he looked just like Tobi . . . and I can't stop thinking about him. Cubs die too easily!*

Staring out across the snow, he wondered what had happened to Ujurak.

If he doesn't come back soon, I'll have to go and look for him. It would be just like that cloud-brained bear to get into trouble!

Then Toklo spotted movement, dark against the snowy landscape: Something was moving fast toward him. He tensed his muscles, only to relax as the creature drew closer and he recognized Ujurak, racing up with his ears pinned back.

Toklo sprang up and ran to meet him. "What happened?" he demanded, anxiety rushing through him at the smaller bear's distraught look.

Ujurak skidded to a halt, spraying snow from his paws. "I'm fine," he panted. "But I went traveling with a flat-face—he was a raven, too—and I saw more oil! It's drowning the island, and everything wild!"

"Steady, steady." Toklo rested a paw on his friend's shoulder. "I don't know what you're babbling about. Calm down and tell me."

Ujurak took in several great gulps of air; to Toklo's relief the wild look in his eyes began to fade. "I met Tulugaq, a flat-face who could turn into a raven," he began. "He showed me a place where oil is being dug up from the ground. It's going to destroy the whole island unless we do something about it."

"Do what?" Toklo asked, beginning to be irritated because he didn't understand. "We need more direction than that."

Ujurak's eyes were suddenly flooded with grief. "Tulugaq died," he whimpered. "I can't ask him anything more."

Gazing at him, Toklo was suddenly reminded of the young

cub he had protected when they'd first begun to journey through the wild. He pushed his snout briefly into Ujurak's fur. "Tulugaq must have given you some idea," he said.

Ujurak just looked blank, shaking his head in bewilderment.

Before Toklo could say any more, he heard Lusa's high-pitched squeal behind him. "Ujurak! You're back!"

She burst out of the den and dashed up to Ujurak, pressing herself affectionately against his side. "What's wrong?" she asked. "You look so sad!"

"Let's go back to the den," Toklo suggested, hunching his shoulders against the wind. "Then Ujurak can tell us everything from the beginning."

The bears huddled together when they were all inside the den. Toklo noticed that Kissimi shrank behind Kallik when he entered, and he felt another stab of irritation with the feeble cub.

He'd be afraid of his own shadow!

Then he admitted to himself that Kissimi hadn't really deserved to be scared like that, and he squeezed himself to the opposite side of the den, as far away from the cub as he could get. Kallik hesitated, then gave him a nod of thanks as she drew Kissimi close to her with one paw curled around him. She seemed to realize that Toklo hadn't meant to frighten her cub.

Toklo made a conscious effort to relax in the warmth, listening to the sound of the wind whistling by overhead. "Okay," he said to Ujurak. "Tell us everything."

He listened in astonishment as Ujurak related how he had changed into a flat-face and then into a raven, flying with the old man Tulugaq. His eyes widened as he heard about the cave where the Selamiut, the spirits, gathered. And his heart sank as Ujurak described the spreading tide of oil, the whole island drowning in it as Tulugaq the raven had drowned.

"What about the white bears?" Kallik asked, her voice shaking with horror as she curled her paw even more protectively around Kissimi.

"Well, unless they can swim in oil, they'll die!" Ujurak snapped. His voice was unusually sharp; Toklo guessed that he was feeling helpless and frustrated.

"From what Tulugaq told you, it sounds as if the spirits can give us the answer." Lusa was frowning thoughtfully. "The flat-faces call the lights in the sky the Selamiut," she went on, half to herself. "And the white bears here call them the Iqniq. Are all the ancestors in the world up there?"

Ujurak shook his head. "I don't know. But the sky is very big," he pointed out.

Since Kallik's question about the white bears she had been silent, sunk deep in thought with her eyes narrowed. "So what should we do next?" she asked. "If the answers are in the stars, does that mean Ujurak has to go to the place where the Selamiut are?" Even as the words were coming out of her mouth, she realized, *But that's impossible!*

"In the stars?" Toklo scoffed, putting words to her thought. Even Ujurak couldn't fly so high. "Good luck with that!"

"Wait," Lusa said, stretching out a paw to silence Toklo.

"Ujurak, didn't you say that the cave is called the Place of the Selamiut? What if the cave is the place where we're meant to go?"

Ujurak gave her a doubtful look. "It's a long way."

"I think Lusa's right." Toklo hated to admit it, but what the little black bear said made sense. "Tulugaq mentioned the home of the Selamiut *and* looking for you in the stars, didn't he? Which sounds like two different places. So one *must* be the cave! Besides, the flat-face couldn't possibly have meant that Ujurak had to meet him in the *real* stars." As he spoke, a chill sank deep into Toklo's fur. *The only way a bear can get to the stars is by dying.* "He *didn't* mean that," he repeated aggressively. "So where else is there, except the cave?"

As his friends looked at one another, struck by his suggestion, Toklo's paws tingled with longing to set off, to get back to the purpose of their journey.

I've had enough of white bears and sick seals and stolen cubs. They're just distracting us from what's really important.

He started as Kissimi scrambled up his shoulder, butting his tiny head into the hollow of his neck. A tiny spark of warmth woke inside him as he realized that the cub had forgiven him.

"Hey, get off," he grunted, but he kept his paw gentle as he thrust the cub back toward Kallik. *I don't want to scare him again.*

"We can't set out now," Kallik said, nudging Kissimi into her fur. "It's getting dark. We'll start tomorrow at first light."

Toklo wondered why she sounded so eager. Then he realized why. If the cave was a long way off, it was even farther away from the white bears. They would never get Kissimi back if Kallik journeyed to the cave with him.

"And now we'd better sleep," Toklo said. "We'll travel faster if we've had a good rest."

Toklo woke in darkness, but when he raised his head above the level of the den, he managed to make out a faint milky line on the horizon. It was still too early to leave, so he watched the others as they slept, half ashamed of the affection he felt for them. He knew brown bears were supposed to live alone, but he found it hard to imagine being without his friends.

We've come so far together. Are we really near our destination at last? And what will happen then? His sense of responsibility weighed on him as heavily as if the roof of the den had fallen in on him. *Who will keep them safe when I'm not around?*

A dull pain settled in his belly at the thought of separating from his companions, but he pushed it away. Once they got moving, there would be no time to think of that, he decided, prodding Ujurak in the side to wake him.

Ujurak's jaws gaped wide in a yawn as he heaved himself up, disturbing Lusa, who was curled up by his side. The little black bear wrapped her paws over her nose and muttered, "Go away. I was just eating some really tasty blueberries. . . ."

Kallik jerked awake, flexing her shoulders sleepily as she looked around for Kissimi. The tiny cub was still deeply asleep, curled into a ball. He roused briefly as Kallik rose to her paws; then he scrambled onto her back, snuggled into her neck fur, and closed his eyes again.

As Toklo followed Kallik out of the den, he wondered whether the Iqniq had intended that the cub would come with them on the last part of their journey.

He was born here on the island, so maybe he belongs here more than the rest of us. Toklo stifled a huff of laughter at the thought. *I'm starting to sound like Ujurak,* he scolded himself. *I'll be imagining oily ravens next!*

"Let's get moving," he said aloud. "Ujurak, you know the way, so you take the lead. I'll follow behind and keep a lookout for the white bears."

The bears set off in the half-light of dawn, trudging over the snow into the unknown interior of the island. They kept on as the daylight strengthened around them; Toklo's legs began to ache, and he noticed that Lusa was starting to stumble with tiredness.

"Let's take a break," he suggested as they toiled past a clump of thornbushes that gave some shelter from the wind. "I'll see if I can find some prey."

"You need to rest as well," Lusa objected, though she had flopped down thankfully in the lee of the bushes.

"And we all need to eat," Toklo responded, swinging around and trekking off into the snow-covered landscape.

He was barely out of sight of the bushes when he spotted an Arctic hare hopping across the landscape. It was moving away upwind of him; Toklo managed to sneak up to within a bearlength of it before it realized he was there, and he pinned it down and killed it as it tried to spring away.

On his way back with his catch he spotted two more

ptarmigans huddled together in the snow. Dropping the hare, he launched himself toward them; one fluttered up out of reach, but he snagged a claw in the wing of the second and brought it down.

We'll eat well for once, Toklo thought with satisfaction as he headed back to his friends, his jaws full of warm prey. *Maybe it's a sign that the spirits want us to go this way.*

This time, as they shared the prey, Toklo chewed some of the meat into a pulp and set it down in front of Kissimi. "Try that," he suggested, trying to make his voice gentle. Maybe the cub would like ptarmigan better when it was thoroughly chewed up. "It's easy to eat."

The cub sniffed the pulp doubtfully, then managed to eat a few mouthfuls. Toklo noticed that Kallik was looking at him with warmth in her eyes. "Thanks, Toklo," she said.

When they were all crouched in the shelter of the bushes, their bellies comfortably full, Toklo rose to his paws again. "Time to be on our way."

"I'm worried that we might get lost," Kallik said, gazing uneasily at the land in front of them. "Ujurak, why don't you turn into a bird and fly up to see where we have to go."

"No." Toklo was surprised at the determination in Ujurak's voice; he could tell there would be no point trying to persuade him. "The end of our journey is very close now. I know that I have to be a bear when we reach it."

As they set off again, Toklo wondered whether there was something Ujurak wasn't telling them. *He's not usually this quiet. And there's a look in his eyes . . . as if he sees something the rest of us can't.*

Now the land began to rise ahead of them into a ridge of low mountains: jagged, snow-covered peaks standing out against a sky that was growing dark and thunderous. A few flakes of snow began to drift down, rapidly thickening, and soon the snow whirled on the wind so that the bears had to battle on with their heads lowered into the storm. Ice crystals formed around Toklo's eyes and lodged between his claws; every step was an effort.

We'll all be ice bears if this goes on, he grumbled silently.

Kallik slipped on a frozen patch of ground, jostling Toklo and dislodging Kissimi from her shoulders. The cub let out a wail, though the snow was too soft for the fall to have hurt him.

"Shall I take him for a bit?" Toklo offered, as Kallik nudged the little cub to his paws and gave him a comforting lick on the snout.

Kallik turned to him, her eyes surprised and grateful. "Thanks, Toklo."

"Come on, then, small one." Toklo crouched down to let the cub scramble into his fur, finding that he liked the warm weight lodged on his shoulders. "Make sure you hang on tight." *I'll look after you, little one,* he promised silently.

As they continued, the ground began to slope more steeply up to the ridge.

"Maybe we should stop for the night," Lusa suggested, weariness in her voice. "The storm might be over by tomorrow."

"No." Again that strange tone from Ujurak. "It's not much farther."

There's something driving him, Toklo thought, trying to crush down his anxiety for his friend. *Something more pressing than usual. I wish I knew what.*

At last the bears reached the crest of the ridge and stood there, frozen and exhausted, looking down into the valley beyond. Toklo could see nothing but snow and broken rock, but Ujurak plunged unhesitatingly downward.

"Come on! We're almost there!"

Once they were a few bearlengths down from the summit, the wind dropped, and the falling snow dwindled to almost nothing. But the going wasn't much easier. Sliding in the soft, fresh snow, Toklo felt that scrambling down was even harder than climbing up. He kept an eye on his companions, giving them a nudge when they needed help. Lusa's short legs kept sinking into the snow, leaving her trying to wade through it.

"Thanks!" she gasped as Toklo grabbed her scruff and hauled her out for the third time. "Even you can't blame me for falling into snowdrifts here!"

Toklo had hardly set off again when the snow shifted unexpectedly under his paws, and he found himself sliding down the mountain on his rump. He let out a roar of surprise, which was joined by a squeal from Kissimi as the cub lost his grip and was flung off his shoulders into a snowbank.

"Kissimi!" Kallik exclaimed, scrambling over to the spot where he had disappeared and digging frantically with her forepaws. "Kissimi, I'm coming!"

She hauled the cub out, wet and wailing but otherwise unhurt, and nudged him back into her own fur. "I'll take over for a while, Toklo," she said with a nod of gratitude. "You've been a big help."

Trudging on again, Toklo began to wonder if they were right to go on. He was exhausted from keeping watch over everyone and leaping to their rescue every time they fell into the snow. *If the spirits wanted us to find this cave, wouldn't they make it a bit easier?*

Then he realized that Ujurak had halted and was staring ahead at an overhanging ledge on the side of the valley a little lower down. "This is the place!" he exclaimed.

Toklo let his gaze travel down the valley and then up the opposite slope. At the very top he could just make out a strange flat-face structure that looked as if it were made of sticks. It was wide at the bottom, but higher up it grew narrower, until it tapered to a point, outlined against the sky. There was something sinister about the way it seemed to be peering over the shoulder of the hill.

"What's that?" he asked, jerking his head toward it.

"The oil rig," Ujurak replied tersely.

"It looks so small," Lusa said.

Toklo grunted agreement. Ujurak had worried so much about destroying it, but it looked as if he could reach out and smash it with one paw.

"There's a lot more to it than that," Ujurak told them. "You'll see, but for now we have to go down here."

He led the way slowly forward; Toklo and the others followed. A sense of awe crept over Toklo at the silence and the glimmering whiteness of the snow; he guessed that the others

felt the same, for they all padded on without a sound. Even
Kissimi's whimpering died away.

As they drew closer to the ledge, Toklo heard more pawsteps nearby; he whirled around, expecting to see the white
bears tracking them down the slope, but the slope was empty,
the snow undisturbed except for their own tracks.

Now I'm imagining things!

But as he trudged on, he heard the pawsteps again, and this
time shapes brushed past him: the huge furred bodies of white
bears; caribou and musk oxen; even the scrawny bodies of flat-
faces. Toklo screwed his eyes tight shut, then opened them
again: The shapes were still there, but shadowy, as if something blurred his vision so he couldn't see them clearly

An Arctic hare hopped by at his paws; Toklo reached out
to swipe it and found with a thrill of fear that his claws went
right through it, and he could see the snowy ground through
its white pelt. He blinked, wondering if he was going crazy or
just dreaming.

Then he heard Kallik's whisper. "Do you see them, too?"

Lusa nodded, her eyes wide with awe. "There are so many
of them!"

Ujurak glanced over his shoulder. His voice was strong and
certain, and very calm. "These are our ancestors, the ancestors
of the wild, and this is their place."

Still feeling as if he were in a dream, Toklo walked with the
others among the spirits of all the birds and creatures of the
Endless Ice, hunter and prey together, joined in one company
and purpose.

Climbing the slope beneath the overhang, Ujurak led the way to the mouth of a cave. Peering over the smaller bear's shoulder, Toklo saw a wide tunnel leading back into thick darkness. Every hair on his pelt stood on end; curiosity was driving him on, and yet he wanted to get away from this strange place that belonged to so many different creatures.

How can this place be safe if flat-faces come here?

And yet the only scents he could smell were warm and comforting, seeming to beckon him inside.

While he was still hesitating, Lusa padded up to the cave entrance and peered inside. "Hello?" she called. "Anyone there?"

Her voice echoed on and on, reverberating in the darkness.

"Wow, this is a big cave!" Kallik exclaimed.

"Come on," said Ujurak. Striding forward, he led the way inside.

The half-seen creatures halted at the edge of the cave and watched as Ujurak and the others headed deeper in. Toklo felt safe with them standing there, as if they were guarding the entrance from enemies.

Nothing can harm us here, he realized.

Darkness gathered around them as they left the entrance behind. Toklo wondered what would happen when it became too dark to see anything. Then a faint white glow woke in the depths of the darkness ahead. Toklo and the others hurried forward and halted in amazement as the stone tunnel led into a vast cavern with a roof far above their heads.

Gazing upward, Toklo saw white light filtering down

through snow that covered a hole in the cavern roof. In the middle of the floor was a pile of snow that had fallen in through the hole, but the edges of the cave were dry stone.

Toklo drew in a breath of wonder as he looked down at pawprints on the ground—as many pawprints as there were stars in the sky. All the creatures who had been in the cave had left their marks; Toklo even spotted the weird pawprints of flat-faces.

And how they manage to balance on those two skinny paws, I'll never know!

He started at a shout from Kallik. "Look over here!"

Bounding over to her side, Toklo saw that she was staring at markings on the walls: lines and blotches drawn in different colors.

"What in the world are those?" he asked, not expecting an answer.

Ujurak and Lusa came to join them, staring at the marks; Ujurak frowned as he gazed at them, deep in thought.

"I think flat-faces made them," he announced at last. "When I was with Sally, I saw her holding a stick that left a blue trail on something flat and white."

"What did she do that for?" Lusa asked.

Ujurak shrugged. "They obviously mean something to flat-faces."

Lusa had padded closer to the lines and blotches, gazing at them with a puzzled look. "I think I see . . ." she murmured after a few moments. "Look, those shapes there, and that curved line . . . They look like a caribou."

"You're right!" Ujurak exclaimed. "And there's another, and another!"

At first Toklo was doubtful, but after a moment he had to admit that the marks did seem to take the shape of caribou. "And these others," he pointed out. "They look like flat-faces hunting. One of them has a spear, or maybe it's a firestick."

"And there's a caribou they've killed." Kallik pointed to the cave wall with one paw. "There's the spear sticking out of its side. They've even put red blobs for the blood coming out."

Toklo didn't see why flat-faces would come here to make marks on the walls, but he marveled at the different scenes that he could see. There were flat-face dens made out of brown pelts, and flat-faces of all different sizes milling around them.

"Look at those streaks," Ujurak said, pointing to marks above the flat-faces. "I think they must be the spirits in the sky, the Iqniq, the ancestors of all the creatures."

"And look over here!" Lusa called out, nodding toward a different section of the wall. "There are white bears! I wonder if one of them is Aga?"

Kallik and Toklo padded over to look; Kallik let out a rumble of pleasure at seeing her own kind pictured on the wall.

Toklo leaned forward and gave the markings a good sniff. "There's no scent," he said. "They must have been here a long time." *Longer than even Aga has been alive,* he thought with an inward shiver.

"Come here! Come and look!" Ujurak called from a distant corner of the cave.

Toklo thought Ujurak's voice sounded tense and strange,

and he quickened his pace as he went to join him. "What have you found now?" he asked.

Ujurak pointed in silence at the cave wall. Toklo gaped in astonishment as he saw four tiny bear shapes: two brown, one black, and one white. Above their heads were white markings that looked like stars in the shape of Ursa.

"It's us," Ujurak whispered, as Lusa and Kallik padded up behind. "All the time we have been here, in this cave. This is where we're meant to be."

Toklo's belly lurched; he felt strange and prickly under his fur. *Flat-faces left an image of me, here in this cave! Possibly even before I was born!*

He grew dizzy, and the cave swirled around him. "We have reached the end of our journey," he choked out. "So what happens now?"

"We have to save the island," Ujurak muttered, his gaze still fixed on the tiny bear shapes. "If the oil drilling destroys this cave, everything is lost. This island has been waiting for us; it must know that we can help it."

Lusa moved away abruptly, her shoulders hunched; Toklo thought that something about finding the bear shapes there had upset her. When she spoke, her voice was sharp. "How?" she demanded. "I've done what I was supposed to do, figuring out that the seals were sick, and moving them. What else can we do? We're just bears!"

To Toklo's amazement Ujurak rounded on her. The fire in his eyes made Toklo take a pace back, and when he looked more closely, he realized it was as if the brown bear's eyes were filled with stars.

"It must be a trick of the light," he mumbled to himself. "The way it filters through the snow. It must be!"

"No!" Ujurak's voice was low and intense. "We're more than just bears! We've come so far, without even knowing where we were going. Ursa brought us to this place—Ursa and the white bears who chased us and Tulugaq the raven. He only stayed alive long enough to show us the cave. We cannot give up!"

CHAPTER TWENTY-ONE

Lusa

Ujurak's words echoed in Lusa's mind as she stared at the little black bear on the cave wall. *Is this it?* she asked herself. *The reason I came so far, across ice and lakes and oceans—to look at a tiny image of myself?*

This didn't feel like the end of her journey. It didn't feel like the end of *anything*. She was tired and hungry, and tired of being hungry. Deep longing woke inside her to go *home*—not to the Bear Bowl, but to a place where she would truly belong, with trees and sunlight and berries and grubs, and *other black bears*.

"Toklo has Ujurak, and Kallik has Kissimi," she sighed softly. "But I have no one. And now that the journey is over, we'll be separating soon, and then what will I do?"

"It's not over yet." Ujurak's voice jerked Lusa out of her thoughts.

He and Kallik and Toklo were talking together a couple of bearlengths away. Lusa cast a last look at the four bear images and shuffled reluctantly over to join them.

"Tulugaq showed me the flat-face structure up at the top

226

of the valley," Ujurak went on. "There are fences and a tall tower made out of sticks—that's the only part we can see from here—and a lot of flat-face machines. That's where the oil is coming from."

"So?" Toklo asked.

"Remember when you came to rescue me from the flat-face hospital?" Ujurak went on. "The oil structures there had spread, and the flat-faces had built a whole denning place around them. Maybe if we can destroy this rig here, while it's still small, the flat-faces will think it's not worth the trouble, and go away."

"Destroy it?" Kallik asked, disbelief in her voice. "We can't do that. We're just bears! The no-claws would hurt us with their firesticks." She bent her head and nuzzled Kissimi, as if she was most afraid for him.

"Then we need help," Ujurak declared.

Kallik's head snapped up again as she glared at him. "We won't get help from the white bears."

"And the flat-faces—Tulugaq's people—can't do anything, either," Toklo added. "Or they would have acted before now."

"Unless they're just waiting for us to sort it out," Kallik argued.

Lusa couldn't think of anything to add. Outside, the wind had risen again; she closed her eyes and listened to it raging around the mountainside. It sounded like rumbling hooves . . . like a storm of caribou pouring down a narrow gully, churning the snow under their feet.

"Caribou!" she exclaimed, sitting upright. Her three friends stared at her. "Remember the caribou charging up the gorge near the new bay? They could knock down the flat-face structure if there were enough of them. They could knock down *anything*!"

Ujurak and Kallik exchanged a doubtful glance, and Kallik began to shake her head.

"I think I see . . ." Toklo began slowly. "If we could make the caribou stampede from the top of the valley, they would trample the fences and the tall sticks and the machines."

"But they might get hurt," Kallik objected.

Ujurak's eyes clouded. "It will be dangerous for all of us," he whispered.

The four bears looked at one another in silence; Lusa could see the doubt in their faces fading into determination.

Oh, Arcturus! What have I started?

Toklo was the first to break the silence. "Okay," he said briskly. "We need a plan. The cave is here"—he made a mark on the gritty floor of the cave with one claw—"and the valley slopes up this way. Ujurak, the flat-face structure is here, right? And we've seen the caribou tracks . . . so I guess their grazing area must be about here."

Lusa watched carefully as Toklo drew the plan, admiring how strong and capable he was. *We can trust him,* she thought, reflecting on the angry, hurt cub she had found in the forest, and how Toklo's experience had changed him into the confident bear he was now.

"That's right," Ujurak confirmed, looking down at the lines Toklo had drawn. "That's where we'll find the caribou. I saw them when I was flying over the island."

"It's a long way from the oil rig," Kallik muttered, staring at Toklo's plan. "Can we move them that far?"

"We can if we get them good and scared," Toklo replied confidently.

Ujurak murmured agreement. "We need to chase them this way," he added, indicating a route over the shoulder of the hill on Toklo's plan.

"Good." Toklo gave a satisfied nod. "That sounds straight-forward enough."

Lusa wondered if he was right. Even though this was her idea, she felt as though thousands of butterflies were swarming in her belly. *Can we really chase the caribou so far?*

"I don't know what I'm going to do about Kissimi," Kallik fretted, giving the little cub another gentle nuzzle. "I'm not taking him anywhere near a herd of caribou."

Toklo gazed straight into her eyes. "Then you'll have to leave him here."

Kallik hesitated, then nodded reluctantly. "You're right. It's the only way to keep him safe."

Nudging the little cub to his paws, she guided him over to the heap of snow in the middle of the cave. Here she dug out a den and tucked Kissimi into it, almost burying him in snow so that only his snout poked out.

"You have to stay here," she explained. "I promise I'll be back soon. And whatever you hear outside, *you must not leave the cave*. Do you understand?"

The tiny cub nodded, flicking flakes of snow from his ears.

With Toklo in the lead, the four bears headed out of the cave. As she entered the tunnel, Lusa cast a glance back at the image of caribou being hunted by flat-faces.

Now a whole herd of caribou is going to be chased by just four bears. There is no image of that. Will it work?

Although the wind had risen, whirling the snow up from the ground, Lusa was relieved to see that no more of it was falling from the sky. Ujurak took the lead, trekking fast across the island.

"We'll cut right across the center," he explained. "I remember the way from when I was a raven."

Lusa panted in the rear as they climbed a hill and halted at the top to look down on a gently sloping plain. A herd of caribou—so many that they looked like a shoal of fish clustered together—was moving slowly through the snow. The air was full of the bellows of the full-grown animals and the higher-pitched calls of calves left behind. Lusa could hear the clicking of their feet, and she remembered how strange she had found it when they'd first heard it in the Last Great Wilderness. Her belly rumbled as she breathed in the scent of the huge creatures.

"Now, listen." Toklo turned to face the others, fixing them with a serious gaze. "We need to flank the caribou. It will only take one bear to get them moving. The tricky part will be to keep them together and heading in the right direction.

"I'll take that side," he went on, angling his ears toward the farthest edge of the valley. "Lusa and Ujurak, you take the other. Kallik, you go over there," he ordered, pointing, "and scare them from behind. They'll already be familiar with white bears as their enemy. Any questions?"

"What do you think they'll do?" Lusa asked nervously.

Toklo bared his teeth. "What would you do if you were a caribou? They'll run." He paused and added, "We'll need to keep them bunched together, and moving steadily but not too fast until they're close to the oil rig. Otherwise they'll be too tired to break anything. Then, once we're near the oil place, we'll let them spread out and run as fast as they can."

Kallik nodded. "That should work."

"Keep out of the way of their hooves." Toklo raked his companions with a hard glance. "Don't risk your own safety."

"I bet you'll risk yours," Lusa said, aware once again of how deeply she trusted this bear.

"That's what I'm here for," Toklo retorted. "Any more questions?"

When no bear spoke, Toklo gave a brisk nod. "Then the spirits be with us all."

Lusa watched as he turned and headed down the hill at an angle that would take him to the far side of the herd of caribou. Kallik followed, on her way to the rear; both bears crouched low behind snow ridges to stay out of sight of the caribou.

"We'll go this way," Ujurak said, striking off down the hill in the opposite direction, crouching down like Toklo and Kallik and keeping as far away from the herd as possible, so as not to spook them too soon.

Lusa hurried after him. "Should we roll in the snow to

make our fur white?" she suggested.

"Good idea," Ujurak agreed.

Lusa almost wished she had kept quiet; the bitter cold thrust icy claws into her fur as she wallowed in the snow. She scrambled to her paws again; snow was clinging to her pelt in sticky lumps instead of making a smooth covering.

Ujurak was looking just as uncomfortable. "It's better than nothing," he said, craning his neck to get a good look at his snow-dappled pelt. "It will help us get closer without being spotted."

Lusa imagined herself getting near the pounding hooves of the caribou and remembered the force of their stampede that day in the gorge.

"I'm scared," she confessed, her throat dry.

Ujurak nodded. "So am I."

He looked suddenly vulnerable, which for some reason made Lusa feel better. "Don't worry. I'll look after you," she promised him.

Together they crept alongside the caribou herd, until they came to a dip in the ground. "Let's hide here," Lusa whispered. "Then the caribou won't see us while we're waiting for Kallik's signal."

Ujurak nodded, slipping into the hollow beside her. Lusa poked her snout over the edge, staring at the peacefully grazing herd, a whole forest of caribou legs. The moments seemed to stretch out until each one was a whole suncircle.

"What's keeping Kallik?" she whispered.

She had hardly finished speaking when she heard the

powerful roar of a white bear coming from the rear of the herd. Lusa felt Ujurak tense beside her.

A few caribou skittered aside, and Lusa spotted Kallik, poised in a threatening stance with her jaws wide as she let out another drawn-out bellow. Lusa felt a shiver run through her.

She's scaring me, and I'm her friend!

But only a few caribou moved, pressing themselves into the center of the herd, while the rest went on grazing unconcernedly. Kallik took a menacing pace forward, and to Lusa's horror a bold male caribou stepped out of the herd and faced her.

Snarling, Kallik struck at him with one paw, and the caribou shied away, but more of the herd came to join him, giving out a rumbling call of defiance as they advanced on the white bear.

Oh, no! Lusa's heart sank as she imagined the sharp hooves trampling Kallik. *They're fighting back!*

Then she spotted Toklo charging around the end of the herd to join Kallik. He rose to his hind legs and let out a full-throated roar, turning all his fury on the caribou that threatened Kallik. They tossed their antlered heads, skittering backward, away from Toklo's claws.

Movement rippled through the caribou. Lusa could sense their fear as the whole herd started to head in her direction. She got ready to leap out of the hollow, but Ujurak stopped her with a paw on her shoulder.

"Wait. We have to give Toklo time to get back to the other side."

Lusa nodded, though her belly lurched with terror as she saw the herd of caribou bearing down on her like an ocean wave ready to crash on the beach. The whole world seemed to be filled with the trampling, pointed hooves.

The caribou were almost on top of them before Ujurak whispered, "Now!"

Side by side, the two bears leaped out of the hollow and roared. The caribou reared backward in a wave of gray-brown fur and spindly legs, heading at last in the right direction. They were moving fast, their hooves thudding against the ground in a deafening rumble, their heels click-click-clicking.

Lusa and Ujurak ran alongside, their muscles bunching and stretching as they strove to keep up with the panicked herd. In a swift glance backward Lusa spotted Kallik dropping back.

"They're going too fast!" she gasped. "Remember what Toklo said! They'll be too tired to break down the oil rig if they keep up this pace."

She and Ujurak slowed down to let the caribou slacken their speed, and for a moment Lusa thought that their plan was working. But then the pace dropped again; some of the caribou halted completely, putting down their heads to graze, while others pushed their way to the sides of the herd, letting out threatening bellows at the bears.

They're so brave! Lusa marveled.

Shoulder to shoulder, she and Ujurak charged at the caribou again, pushing them back into the mass of animals. Kallik reappeared, harrying the animals from behind, while Toklo's distant roaring broke out on the far side. The caribou picked up speed again.

But instead of heading in the way the bears wanted them to go, the herd started to break up, fleeing in smaller groups toward the edges of the valley.

"It's not working!" Lusa cried in frustration.

Then from above a volley of caws broke out, and the air was filled with the flutter of dark wings. A crowd of ravens swooped low over the bears' heads and dove down close as the caribou scattered across the valley. They flapped their wings and jabbed with their beaks until the caribou skittered and lurched back, the herd forming up again.

"Tulugaq's ravens!" Ujurak called out, his eyes shining. "They've come to help!"

Hope flooded back into Lusa's heart as the caribou started to move up the valley, their pace steadier this time, kept in place by the bears flanking them and the ravens flying overhead. She had to stay alert, ready to chivvy any of the hulking beasts who tried to slow down or escape, but now the herd had settled into a steady, drumming rhythm.

This is how it should be, Lusa thought, exchanging an exultant glance with Ujurak. *Bears, birds, and caribou working together to save the island. All our ancestors are in the stars, after all.*

Snow began to fall again as the herd reached the crest of the hill. Lusa paused to survey the mountain range ahead of them. For the first time she saw all the way to the top of the narrow valley where the cave was, and spotted the flat-face structure raking the sky like a leafless tree.

But there are no bear spirits living in that tree.

All around them the wind had risen, and falling snow mingled with flakes whirled up from the ground. The sky grew dark and threatening, and from somewhere in the distance came a rumble of thunder.

A storm is rising, Lusa thought, feeling new power coursing through her from ears to paws. *The wild has come to destroy the oil rig.*

CHAPTER TWENTY-TWO

Kallik

Through a flurry of driving snow that almost blinded her, Kallik saw Toklo rear up on his hind legs and roar, flailing his fore-paws in the air.

"Now! Charge!" he bellowed.

This is it! Kallik realized. *This is our only chance to save the island.*

She plunged forward, fire burning in her blood; she felt as strong as the storm, as fierce as all the bears in the sky.

Panic seized the caribou, and they fled along the valley, heading for the no-claw structure. Now that they were gal-loping, it was even more of a battle to keep them going in the right direction. The pace picked up as bears and ravens worked together; Kallik snapped at the hooves of a caribou calf that tried to turn back, and it reared away, mingling with the herd again. A huge male broke away next, and Kallik stumbled in the snow as she pursued it. She looked up to see a raven flap-ping its wings and clawing at the beast's face until it veered away and rejoined the rest of the caribou.

"Get back!" Toklo's throaty roar came from the other side

of the herd, and though Kallik couldn't see him, she could picture him driving another of the huge animals in the right direction.

She wondered what had happened to Lusa and Ujurak, but a moment later she heard Lusa's high-pitched squeal, warning Ujurak to watch out.

They're all safe—for now.

The no-claw structure loomed closer. Kallik gazed upward and spotted pale-faced no-claws running out of it, yelping in alarm.

Too late, she thought with satisfaction. *There's nothing you can do. The herd is unstoppable.*

The caribou plowed on up the valley, running blindly in their panic. An old male stumbled and fell, and Kallik, who was hard on its hooves, almost tripped over it. She leaped across its flailing legs and left it bleating on the ground.

No time for prey.

A moment later a calf broke out of the herd, its spindly legs teetering in the fresh snow. Kallik swerved around it and let it go.

The strongest, fittest caribou are the ones we need.

The caribou bore down on the no-claw dens like an arching wave. Kallik heard a splintering sound as the first of them trampled the outer fence. She saw one of the wooden dens topple and crash down, then another and another, covering sticky pools of oil with the wreckage. Too panic-stricken to swerve, the caribou pushed firebeasts over and stamped on them in an ear-splitting screech of hooves and metal.

Kallik felt power pulsing through her: the power of the wild united against the destruction of the no-claws, who ran away, shouting. She galloped in the wake of the herd, spotting her friends again close by as they leaped over splintered wood and wire and wove their way around the broken bodies of firebeasts.

Ujurak swerved up to her, his eyes distraught. "The caribou are heading away from the rig," he panted. "We have to turn them back!"

Looking up, Kallik saw that the tall sticklike structure in the middle of the denning area was still standing; the herd parted and thundered around it like a foaming river around a rock. They were moving too fast for the bears and ravens to catch them and chase them back in the right direction.

"Maybe we've destroyed enough," Kallik suggested.

Ujurak shook his head. "No, the rig has to go. Or the flatfaces will just come back and rebuild."

Lusa and Toklo ran up to join them, in time to hear Ujurak's last words.

"What can we do?" Lusa asked.

"I'll have to lead the caribou that way myself," Ujurak said.

Kallik stared at him, not understanding at first. Then she saw his legs start to lengthen and grow spindly, and his shaggy brown bear fur changed into the smoother pelt of a caribou.

"No!" she cried. "It's too dangerous! You might get crushed."

Ujurak gazed at Kallik, his eyes filled with immense sadness. "This is the end of my journey," he told her. "We're going to save the wild, but I am going to die. I have to do this."

Kallik stared, stunned with horror as the last of the change came over him: A powerful male caribou, he bounded away on sticklike legs.

"No!" Lusa wailed, gazing after him. "Ujurak! He can't die!"

"No one's going to die if there's anything I can do about it," Toklo said tersely. "Let's help him move these caribou."

Lusa and Toklo raced away to their original places flanking the herd. Kallik thought her paws would never move again after hearing Ujurak prophesy his own death, but she managed to shake off her paralysis and dropped back again to the rear.

Snapping at the caribou's heels, Kallik was aware of the Ujurak-caribou forcing his way through the herd, bellowing above the noise. His strength and size made him stand out, his head rising above the surging mass. For a moment the herd milled around uncertainly; then it began to turn.

He must be telling them to follow him, Kallik thought. *Please, Ujurak, don't die here!*

She had to force herself to keep chasing the caribou. She could see the Ujurak-caribou's head raised above the rest of the herd, and she was terrified that it would vanish and he would be crushed by the stampede.

A mighty screech split the air as the herd hit the rig. The top of the structure swung from side to side, then seemed to hover in midair as the terrible shrieking of metal went on and on.

Kallik let out a scream that rose above the wind, above the bellowing of the caribou, above the death throes of the no-claw structure. "Watch out!"

The caribou scattered like a shoal of frightened fish, plunging past the pursuing bears. Kallik cowered down, terrified of being struck by the flying pointed hooves. As the last of them fled past her, she rose and raced after them, Lusa and Toklo by her side, bundling down the valley behind the herd.

Kallik dared to halt and look back, in time to see the structure tilt over and begin to fall, slowly at first and then faster and faster, until it hit the ground with a crash that seemed to split the whole world.

For a moment all was still. Even the wind seemed to drop as Kallik and her friends gazed at the destruction. Then the no-claws began to stir, shouting and clambering among the wreckage or heading for the few firebeasts that still remained on their round black paws.

The caribou herd was vanishing down the valley. One large male separated from them and circled back toward the bears, changing into Ujurak as he ran. "We did it!" he yelled.

"You're alive!" Lusa squealed, bounding down to meet him and flanking him closely as he joined the others.

Kallik pressed close to Ujurak, rejoicing in his safe return, while Toklo let out a pleased rumble. Then in the midst of their delight Kallik heard a low chopping noise coming from the top of the valley. She raised her head to listen.

Is it the rig disintegrating? Or thunder?

The noise got louder and louder, until to Kallik's dismay

a silver bird appeared over the horizon behind the destroyed oil rig, its metal wings thrashing the air. Horror turned her muscles to ice.

"Look!" she shrieked. "They'll catch us in a mesh and take us away! Run!"

As one, the bears took off racing down the valley, slipping and stumbling in the churned-up snow, but the silver bird followed them. Its vicious wings sliced through the sky, screeching against the buffeting wind.

No matter how fast they ran, the bird was faster. It hovered over them, but instead of the silver mesh Kallik expected, something spattered into the snowy ground beside her, sending up a spray of snow.

"Firesticks!" Lusa exclaimed.

Kallik realized the terrible truth. The silver bird didn't want to take them away. Instead there were no-claws inside it, trying to hurt them. They were leaning out of the bird, and their shouts reached Kallik on the gusts of wind.

They're angry because we destroyed the oil rig, she thought with a pang of guilt. *Oil is important to no-claws. But they can't take the oil from here,* she added to herself, pushing the guilt away. *This island is more important than oil.*

"Head for the cave!" Toklo bellowed.

The bears ran faster than ever, fleeing for their lives in front of the silver bird. They swerved and ducked to dodge the balls of fire that spat down around their heads; Kallik felt one whistle past her fur. Lusa tumbled over her own paws and rolled several bearlengths down the slope before Toklo hauled her to her paws and pushed her on.

As the mouth of the cave came in sight, Kallik looked around frantically for Kissimi. He was nowhere to be seen, and she hoped he had done as he was told and stayed safely within the cave.

We're going to make it! she thought.

But before they could reach the shelter of the cave, the silver bird swooped even lower. Kallik could see one of the no-claws leaning out of it, his firestick aimed straight at Ujurak. She heard the crack of the weapon, but at the same moment Lusa shoved Ujurak out of the way. The fiery ball struck her, and she fell to the ground. A trickle of blood came out of her hind leg, staining the snow scarlet.

Above their heads the silver bird mounted higher and whirled away.

CHAPTER TWENTY-THREE

Toklo

Toklo stared dumbfounded as Lusa dropped to the ground in front of him. For a moment he could scarcely understand what had happened.

"No!" Kallik shrieked, bending over Lusa and desperately nudging her.

Ujurak was staring at the little black bear with horrified eyes. "Not Lusa! Me!" he whispered.

Toklo bent over Lusa, sniffing at her wound. Blood was still oozing from it, but when he looked closer, he could see it was only a graze. Relief washed over him as he realized that she was still breathing.

"She's alive!" he exclaimed.

Lusa began to stir, raising her head and looking around groggily. "Is Ujurak okay?" she asked.

"He's fine," Kallik said soothingly. "Let's get you into the cave."

But before they could start to move her, Toklo heard a gigantic rumbling sound; it was much louder than the silver bird, making the ground shudder.

"What's happening?" he asked, looking up. "That can't be thunder!"

Kallik was staring up the valley, her eyes wide with fear. "Avalanche!" she gasped.

Following her gaze, Toklo saw the silver bird just vanishing over the top of the hill. The wind whipped up by its blades had loosened the snow on the slopes, sending it sliding slowly, slowly down. Toklo stared in horror as the massive chunks of snow built up speed, like white bears sliding on their bellies.

"Get to the cave!" he roared.

"There's no time!" Kallik whispered.

Frozen with fear, the four bears watched the wall of snow bearing down on them, churning like a wave, swallowing the valley with a deafening roar. It was faster than a firebeast, faster than the silver bird, and more unstoppable than the herd of caribou.

I can't believe this is how it ends, Toklo thought. *After everything I've done to keep us all alive, after trekking all this way from our homes, we're going to die in a wall of snow!*

Rage flooded through Toklo. He reared up on his hind legs, ready to battle with the snow with his forepaws splayed out. But his roar of defiance was lost in the growing thunder from the avalanche.

Then he heard a bellow from Ujurak. Glancing around, he saw that the smaller bear had vanished. In his place was a gigantic musk ox with a shaggy pelt and broad, curving horns.

"Ujurak?" he said uncertainly.

The musk ox stumbled forward and shoved at a lump of snow. As the snow fell away, a massive boulder appeared, its dark surface stippled with snow and lichen. Slowly the Ujurak-ox broke it free from where it sat, then thrust at it with his shoulders so that it rolled toward the bears.

What are you doing? Toklo wondered, baffled.

The avalanche thundered on until it seemed to hover over their heads, filling the air with an icy snow-fog. Toklo knew it would sweep over them at any moment, yet somehow he felt as if there were all the time in the world for the Ujurak-ox to move the boulder.

Scarcely visible in the foggy air, the Ujurak-ox put his mighty shoulder against the rock again and heaved it into position above Lusa, who still lay wounded on the ground, jamming it against another, smaller rock.

Suddenly Toklo understood. "Kallik, here!"

Together they cowered down over Lusa. The Ujurak-ox let out a tremendous bellow as the leading edge of the avalanche hit them and the world was filled with the deluge of snow.

Toklo closed his eyes and crouched low, pressed against Kallik and Lusa. The boulder juddered, but it held still, while snow poured around and over them in a hideous, thunderous, jagged noise. Toklo thought that it would go on forever.

This is the end of the world.

At last the crashing and thunder and the cascade of snow died away. Everything was still and silent. Toklo opened his eyes and felt snow all around him; hot panic rushed through his fur. He could see faint light filtering through above his head, and he thrashed wildly until his head broke through the surface. Thanks to the boulder, the snow around him wasn't too deep; he was able to spring out into the open.

Kallik's head popped up close by, and while she was heaving herself out, Toklo raked the snow vigorously until he found Lusa and could drag her clear. He was thankful to see that her wound still wasn't bleeding badly, and she was able to sit up.

Drawing long, panting breaths, Toklo stared down into the valley. The landscape was hardly recognizable. The avalanche had filled up the valley with debris and chunks of ice and earth that had been ripped up from beneath the snow.

Behind him Lusa let out a squeal. "Ujurak!"

Fear clawed at Toklo as he and Kallik sprang up and started to search, floundering around in the fresh snow. Then Toklo spotted a lump of shaggy fur poking out of a heap just beyond the boulder.

Bounding over to it, he began scraping off the snow, gently at first and then more vigorously as the body of the musk ox was revealed.

"Wake up, Ujurak!" he begged. "It's all over. You saved our lives!"

The ox's eyes were closed, and Toklo couldn't detect the slightest movement of its chest to show that it was breathing. "Ujurak!" Then the shape of the musk ox seemed to blur in front of his eyes. It shifted and became the shape of a small brown bear, lying limply in the snow. His eyes were still closed, and he didn't move.

Kallik and Lusa joined Toklo and stared down at their friend.

"He's dead!" Kallik whispered.

"No!" Lusa squealed. "He can't be!" She bent over Ujurak's body, sniffing him and nudging him frantically. "Ujurak, wake up!"

Kallik stood still for a moment, deep shudders running through her body. Then she reached out a paw to draw Lusa back. "It's no use. He's gone."

Toklo stood silently over the body of his friend, too stunned to speak or move. Even though Ujurak had warned them of his coming death, Toklo had never believed that it would really happen. Now belief was being forced on him. His whole world had shrunk to this moment of cold understanding.

I failed. I should have protected Ujurak, and I failed.

"He knew he was going to die," Lusa protested, her dark eyes full of grief. "Why didn't he do something to keep himself safe?"

Kallik nuzzled Lusa's shoulder, almost as if she were comforting a cub. "He gave his life to save us. He knew what he was doing. Now his journey is truly over."

"But he was my friend!" Lusa wailed, raising her muzzle to the sky.

"He was a friend to all of us," Kallik said. "We will—" Her voice started to shake, and she had to pause, swallowing, before starting again. "We will never forget him, and as long as we have his memory in our hearts, we will never be without him."

"He was the best friend a bear could have," Toklo murmured.

But even as he spoke the words, as he watched Kallik still trying to comfort Lusa, Toklo felt that his heart was breaking. *I can't believe this is where it ends.*

He had always known that one day he would say good-bye to his friends, that once their journey was over, he would live alone in the forest as a brown bear. But he had imagined that the time would come when they were all safe.

No, Toklo thought, looking down at Ujurak's small broken body, so helpless amid the snow.

He let out a bellow of rage and pain. As it echoed around the peaks, the snow shifted ominously, as if another avalanche was about to begin. Toklo couldn't make himself care. *Did he know from the beginning?* he wondered. *What was the point of all that fighting, all that hunting, learning to survive on the ice, if this was going to happen? We came all this way, and Ujurak died.*

A trickle of snow fell onto Ujurak's limp body, dusting his brown fur with white. Thankful to have something to do, Toklo turned and began kicking more snow over his friend's body with powerful scoops of his hindpaws.

"I'm sorry, Ujurak," he whispered. "I can't cover you with stones and earth and sticks, as I would if we were in a forest. This snow will have to do."

He dug into the snow more and more viciously, casting huge swaths of it over Ujurak's body. "We should never have come here," he muttered. "I should have refused to follow Ujurak on his bee-brained journey. We should have stayed in the trees, where we belonged." Pain surged through him, so sharp that he could scarcely get his breath. "If I'd been brave enough, we could have marked out a territory for ourselves, with plenty of food. . . ."

A voice murmured behind him. "Oh, Toklo, you *were* brave enough!"

Toklo felt as though his pounding heart had slammed into his throat. He spun around. "Ujurak?"

A brown bear was padding toward him through the snow, coming from the direction of the cave. Everything else—the mound of snow covering Ujurak's body, the figures of Lusa and Kallik huddled together a couple of bearlengths away—had grown blurry and indistinct.

Toklo focused his gaze on the approaching bear. Incredulously he recognized her powerful shoulders and claws, and the scars on her muzzle.

"Mother!" he exclaimed.

Oka halted on the other side of Ujurak's body and gazed at Toklo, with all the love in her eyes he had longed to see when he was a cub. "I am so very proud of you," she said. "You are the reason that Ujurak made it this far. He fulfilled his destiny because of *you*."

Toklo couldn't accept his mother's comfort. "His destiny wasn't to be squashed under the snow," he growled.

"His destiny was to save this island," Oka told him. "And he has achieved that, thanks to you. All those times you fought to save him, caught food for him, kept him out of danger? *You* brought him here, just as you were always destined to."

Rage surged up inside Toklo. "But it wasn't enough! If I

could bring him here, why couldn't I take him home again?"

Blinking sadly, Oka looked down at the mound of snow that concealed Ujurak's body. "We can't save everyone," she whispered. "Not all of the time."

She's remembering what happened to Tobi, Toklo thought, regret sweeping over him that nothing he or his mother could do had kept his little brother alive.

"I tried so hard." His voice was hoarse with grief. "I wanted Tobi to live."

"I know you did," Oka replied, raising her head to meet his gaze once more. "And I let you down when I left you to fend for yourself. You will never know how sorry I am for that."

"Now I think I do," Toklo replied. He understood his mother's rage and her sense of failure after Tobi died, because his own heart was shattered. "I just feel so . . . empty."

Oka's eyes shone with the fire of stars. "You are not empty!" she insisted. "You have the spirit of the wild inside you. Ujurak taught you so much. Now you owe it to him to take that spirit back to the forests where you were born, to be a truly wild brown bear, with your own territory and your own cubs."

"I don't think I want to," Toklo replied. "Without Ujurak it just doesn't seem worth it."

The fire in Oka's eyes died away, leaving a gentle warmth. "Once you thought you'd lost me and Tobi forever, didn't you? And yet you carry us with you always, you still speak to us, and we are always here when you need us. It will be the same with Ujurak."

Wishing that what his mother said might be true, Toklo

didn't know how to respond. While he was still searching for words, a smaller bear, unseen until now, slipped out from behind Oka. At first Toklo didn't know who he was. Then his jaws gaped in astonishment as he recognized Tobi: not the scrawny, sickly cub he had been, but strong and healthy, his eyes glimmering with amusement at his brother's surprise.

"I'm very proud of you, too, Toklo," Tobi said. "Ujurak was very lucky to have you as his big brother on his journey."

"Remember your BirthDen," Oka went on. "The trees, the waterfall, the open meadows rich with flowers and prey, where you and Tobi played together. All that is waiting for you." She paused, and when she continued, her voice had grown deeper and more serious. "You have done what you needed to do for Ujurak. Now go and find your home."

She stretched out her neck to Toklo, and he leaned toward her. Above the snowy mound that concealed Ujurak's body, their muzzles touched.

"I will," Toklo said. "I promise."

CHAPTER TWENTY-FOUR

Ujurak

Ujurak's eyes fluttered open. Around him everything was dark and silent. The terror and pain when the avalanche hit him in his musk-ox shape, the rush of power he had felt as he moved the boulder to save his friends, had all ebbed away. His body didn't hurt anymore; instead he was filled with a great calm.

Blinking, Ujurak tried to work out where he was. The darkness was too thick for him to make out any scenery around him; he couldn't even feel solid ground underneath him.

Then a burst of starlight dazzled his eyes. When his vision cleared, he saw Ursa looming over him, her fur glowing with the light of many stars. She lowered her nose to touch Ujurak's. "You have done well, little one," she murmured.

Ujurak's gladness at seeing his mother warred inside him with his sense of failure. "No, you're wrong," he responded. "I haven't saved the wild. I don't even understand what that means—not really."

"Look into my eyes," Ursa told him.

Ujurak gazed up and felt as if he were falling into those

starry depths like a leaping salmon falling back into a pool. The darkness rippled away, and he found himself traveling: He saw brown bears in a lush forest, rearing on their hind-paws as they challenged one another; a family of black bears digging for grubs under a bush that was heavy with bright berries; a white bear resting on an iceberg, with the body of a plump seal lying beside her paws.

As he watched, he began to understand; he could sense a new wildness and determination entering the hearts of all the bears. By saving the island and the cave of the Selamiut, he had kept open the door between living bears and their ances-tors. He had preserved the free spirit that was so important to every bear. If the cave had been destroyed, the spark at the heart of every bear would have died.

Ursa's voice spoke close to him, taking on a warm affection. "And see what has happened to your friends."

Now Ujurak found that he could see the companions of his wanderings from the distance of death, as if he were looking down on them from the sky. "I wish I hadn't needed to leave them," he said sadly. "They're going to think I'm dead, and I'm not, am I?"

"No, you're not," Ursa responded, touching his shoulder with her muzzle. "And they will come to understand that. Look closely now."

Ujurak focused once more on his three friends. He realized that each of them had been transformed by their journey. He knew them as closely as if he could walk in their skins: Toklo, who had become a steadfast champion, strong and brave and willing to protect any bear weaker than himself; Lusa, who had embraced the wild in her journey to find Oka's lost cub; Kallik, who was ready to nurture future generations of white bears.

"They are truly wild bears now," Ursa said, "and they will show others whose paths they cross what wild bears can be."

Ujurak's visions faded, and he returned to the place of darkness, lit by the starlight of his mother's fur. Ursa beckoned to him, and he rose to his paws at her side.

"Now you are home," she said. "I have been waiting for you for such a long time, my precious cub. Come, walk in the sky with me, and know that I am very proud of you."

CHAPTER TWENTY-FIVE

Lusa

Lusa stood in snow that reached almost to her belly fur, but the grief inside her was colder still. The day was drawing to an end, shadows shrouding the peaks as the last traces of sunlight faded from the sky.

"Ujurak is dead!" Lusa whispered to herself, gazing down at his limp body, where gently falling snowflakes were already beginning to cover the few scraps of brown fur still visible after Toklo had buried him. She couldn't make her mind move away from that terrible truth.

"Lusa." Toklo gave her a gentle nudge. "We have to go into the cave now."

Lusa scarcely heard him, and she couldn't make her paws move until Toklo gave her a harder nudge.

"Come on," he urged her. "We can't do any more for Ujurak now."

Slowly Lusa began to move, one pawstep at a time, stumbling through the snow with Toklo a solid, reassuring presence at her side.

"I'm going to check on Kissimi," Kallik said, hurrying on ahead.

Lusa couldn't bring herself to care about the cub, or anything else. *How will we get home without Ujurak?* she asked herself. *He brought us to this place; he can't abandon us now!*

"He knew he might die, so he should have been more careful," she growled to Toklo.

"Ujurak couldn't escape his own destiny," Toklo responded gruffly, "any more than we can. He wouldn't have brought us here if we were all going to die."

Lusa wished she believed Toklo was convinced by what he said. She trudged after him into the cave, limping on her grazed hind leg, wishing that the pain of her wound would blot out the pain in her heart.

They padded along the entrance tunnel and reached the big cavern, where Kallik was bending over Kissimi, covering him with loving licks. "You see, I came back," she assured him. "I won't leave you again."

Kissimi looked around, blinking bright eyes. "Where Uj'rak?" he asked.

Kallik hesitated, glancing at the others. For a moment Lusa thought she wouldn't be able to reply. "It's okay," she murmured at last. "He had to go away."

It's not *okay,* Lusa thought mutinously. *Nothing will ever be okay again. Ujurak is* dead.

She padded over to the far corner of the cave where the pictures of the four bears were on the wall, vaguely feeling that she wanted to see all four of them together again. But when she reached it, she stared in disbelief. Instead of four bears there were only three: one black, one white, one brown.

"No!" she screamed. "Toklo, come and look at this!"

Toklo padded over to her and stared at the picture, his jaws gaping as he realized that one brown bear was missing. Then he looked more closely and pointed with his snout at the stars in the sky above the bear images.

"Look," he said hoarsely. "They're different."

Lusa stared where he pointed and saw that more stars had appeared. The shape of Ursa was still there, but now she had a smaller white-dotted shape at her heels.

"Do you think—?" Lusa whispered.

She broke off, blinking. The white star markings had started to hurt her eyes, and she realized with a gasp of amazement that they had begun to glow, brighter and brighter until they blazed with the white radiance of real stars.

They weren't markings on the wall anymore. They swelled to fill the whole cave, and two star-bears stood there, one gigantic, one smaller, with starlit fur and the wisdom of oceans swimming in their eyes.

"Ursa and Ujurak!" Toklo choked out the words.

Kallik had joined her friends, and all three bears watched openmouthed as the star-bears dipped their heads and padded silently toward the mouth of the cave.

Lusa was the first to speak, out of surging joy and excitement. "Come on! We *have* to follow them."

Outside, darkness had fallen, and starlight glimmered on the debris-strewn valley. While Lusa and the others watched from the cave entrance, the two star-bears padded forward into the snow.

"Look!" Lusa whispered. "They aren't leaving any paw-prints!"

Suddenly the starry bears began to run, skimming faster and faster over the snow, then soaring into the air. As they rose higher, their fur and the details of their legs, paws, and muzzles faded, until only their starry outlines were left. Gracefully they galloped higher and higher, until they merged with the rest of the stars and became the familiar constellations that had guided the bears throughout their journey.

"Ujurak has gone home," Kallik whispered.

CHAPTER TWENTY-SIX

Kallik

As Kallik gazed up at the stars, they seemed to glow more brightly. Then she noticed a strange wispy light rising from the horizon at the top of the valley. At first it was the pale pink of approaching sunrise, rapidly deepening to the crimson of ripe berries.

"What's happening?" she muttered. "Is that no-claw place on fire?"

But then the brilliantly colored wisps grew thicker and began to billow upward into the sky. Rivers of color cascaded down to meet them: streams of gold and forest green and the icy blue of the sky above the Endless Ice.

"It's the spirits!" Lusa's voice was awestruck. "The spirits have come back!"

Kallik's breath came faster, and her heart thumped in her chest like a captive bird. She felt she could stand there forever, watching the swaths of color spread until the whole sky vibrated with them.

The spirits are dancing again. They haven't abandoned us. We saved the wild and brought them back to us.

A dazzling tongue of fire swooped down from the sky and lapped around Kallik's neck and shoulders. She flinched away, expecting to feel the searing pain of burning, but the touch was a gentle caress.

Nisa's voice spoke softly in her ear. "You have done well, little one. I am so proud of you."

And while Kallik blinked in wonder at her mother's words, another shining coil of light encircled her, and another voice spoke.

"My name is Sura. You saved the life of my cub, and I can never thank you enough. And you have saved his home, too." The voice fell silent, then began again. "I trust you to know what to do now."

Kallik gazed down at Kissimi, who had tottered out behind them and was staring openmouthed at the torrents of colored fire that flowed across the sky. He raised his head to meet her gaze.

"Wow!" he squeaked.

"These are your ancestors, Kissimi," Kallik told him, dipping her head to touch his shoulder with the tip of her snout. "They will be here forever, watching over you, guarding your home, keeping you safe. Don't ever forget them."

Straightening up, she took a deep breath and turned to the others. "Tomorrow I must take Kissimi home," she announced.

Lusa cocked her head to one side. "To the Frozen Sea?"

"No." Kallik found the words hard to say, but she knew that

she had no choice. "His home is here, on this island."

Toklo gave her a long, solemn look. "You're doing the right thing," he said, his voice unusually gentle.

"I hope so," Kallik responded.

The bears spent the night huddled together in a corner of the cave. Kallik woke as the pale snow-light began to filter down through the hole in the roof. Her companions were stirring beside her: Toklo heaved himself up and gave his pelt a good scratch, while Lusa parted her jaws in an enormous yawn and stared around blearily as if she wasn't sure where she was.

Kallik woke Kissimi with a gentle prod in his flank; the tiny cub's eyes blinked open, and he gazed up at her with such love in his eyes that Kallik's heart almost failed her.

Can I really do this?

"Come on, little one," she murmured. "There are some bears that you must meet."

"Brown bears?" Kissimi asked, with a glance at Toklo.

"No, white bears, just like you."

Kallik felt as if a splinter of ice were wedged inside her heart. But she knew that Kissimi belonged here on the island, with his kin. Crouching down, she nudged the little cub onto her shoulders and led the way out of the cave for the last time.

Outside, the wind had dropped, and everything was still. The sun shone in a pale sky, its light gleaming on the tumbled surface of the snow. The mound Toklo had built to cover Ujurak's body had gone, and the body itself had vanished, too; there was nothing left of it, not even a tuft of fur.

The bears halted a moment, heads bowed. Kallik

remembered the wonder she had felt as she'd seen Ujurak's transformation into stars; it still wasn't enough to blot out her sadness that her friend would never travel with them again.

After a few moments in silent reflection the bears headed for the top of the valley, stumbling over the remains of the avalanche. When they reached the crest, Toklo took the lead, making a wide circle around the wreckage of the oil rig. The no-claw structure was in ruins, and no-claws were picking their way among the wreckage. Kallik glanced sideways to watch as they hauled away splintered wood and twisted metal and dumped them into the back of huge firebeasts.

Good, Kallik thought. *Take it away and don't ever come back. The island does not want you here.*

Leaving the destruction behind them, the bears trekked across the snowy whiteness in dazzling sunlight. It seemed the journey back passed more quickly, perhaps because she knew that every pawstep was leading her to her final parting with Kissimi. Of course time felt as if it were going too fast.

They stopped on the hillside above the no-claw denning area and shared an Arctic hare that Lusa and Toklo caught together. It had been so long since they had eaten that Kallik's belly was flapping like a fish tail, but it was hard to choke down the mouthfuls. She chewed up some of the meat for Kissimi and gently stroked his flank with one paw while he ate.

Oh, my little cub! I'm going to miss you more than I can say.

Kallik wanted her paws to move more and more slowly as the bears approached the new hunting ground in the bay. As they headed down the hill toward the frozen river, two white bears came running to meet them. Kallik recognized Tunerq and Illa.

They halted in front of Kallik and the others; their manner was reserved, and she could tell from the wary expressions in their eyes that they could quickly turn hostile.

Kallik braced herself for the confrontation. She knew that Yakone had seen her carrying Kissimi away while Toklo was fighting with Unalaq.

Did Yakone tell the other bears? she wondered. *Do all of them know what I did?*

Tunerq was the first to speak, his voice curt and unfriendly. "Is it true what Unalaq said?" he demanded.

Kallik swallowed nervously. *This is it.*

"That you fought him on our hunting ground?" Illa added, looking straight at Toklo. "You shouldn't have done that. Those are our seals."

Kallik blinked, puzzled. *So this isn't about Kissimi . . . ?*

Toklo took a pace forward to face the island bears. "That didn't give Unalaq the right to treat us like trespassers," he grunted. "We saved those seals from the poisoned water!"

"That's right," Lusa put in, coming to stand beside Toklo. "Aga was expecting me, remember?"

Tunerq and Illa glanced at each other, shuffling their paws in embarrassment. Kallik realized that they were much more open to reason than Unalaq.

"So why have you come back?" Illa asked.

Toklo glanced at Kallik, who realized that the moment had

come. Kissimi had been hidden in the fur on her shoulders; now Kallik nudged him gently down to stand on tottery legs and blink up at the two white bears.

Illa and Tunerq gazed in disbelief at the little cub, their jaws gaping in astonishment.

"Is . . . is that Sura's cub?" Illa whispered.

"Yes," Kallik replied, forcing herself to raise her head and meet the other she-bear's gaze. "I . . . I called him Kissimi." She hesitated, bracing herself for an attack, wondering how to tell the story of how she had taken Kissimi from his dead mother and hidden him from the other white bears.

"We found him on the cliffs," Toklo said, before Kallik could begin. "We don't know how he survived."

"But we looked everywhere for him!" Tunerq exclaimed.

Kallik shrugged, trying to look unconcerned, though her heart was pounding. "I guess we got lucky."

"So did he," Illa responded.

While the adult bears were speaking, Kissimi was looking up at the two island bears, blinking in wonder. "Are you my family?" he asked.

"Sura was my sister," Illa replied, bending her head to look the little cub in the eye. "So yes, I am."

Kallik felt as though the pain in her heart was tearing at her like the jaws of an orca. She gave Illa a long look. "Take care of him for me, please," she murmured.

"I will," Illa promised. "Another of our bears lost a cub, just before you came to the island. She will have milk to give

Kissimi." She paused, then added, "Thank you for bringing him back."

There was a look in Illa's eyes that suggested to Kallik that the island bear knew they were not telling the whole truth. But along with it was deep relief that Kissimi was back where he belonged. Kallik said nothing more, only gave a tiny head-shake before reaching her head down to nuzzle Kissimi and nudge him to her side.

"You should come and speak to Aga," Tunerq said. "Last night we heard terrible storms coming from the no-claw structure. And then we saw the Iqniq dancing in the sky, brighter than ever. What happened? And where is the other brown bear who was traveling with you?"

"Take us to Aga," Toklo replied, "and we'll tell you."

Tunerq led the way down the hill; Illa paced just behind him with Kissimi on her shoulders, and the rest of the bears followed. As they approached the frozen river, Kallik spotted Yakone bounding over to her. She halted and waited for him, letting her friends go on without her.

"You came back!" Yakone exclaimed as he reached her.

Kallik studied her paws, wishing that the snow would open and swallow her up. She knew that Yakone must hate her now, because she had stolen Sura's cub.

"You . . . you didn't tell the other bears about the cub," she whispered.

She was aware of Yakone's gaze upon her. "What was the point?" he asked. "The white bears on this island have suffered enough. What you did was wrong, but I trusted you to look after him."

He paused, but Kallik's heart was too full for her to speak.

"I'm glad you're here now," Yakone went on. "You did the right thing."

"Kallik!" Toklo's voice came from farther down the hillside. Kallik looked up to see that he and the others had almost reached the riverbank, where she spotted Aga with more of the white bears. "Come on; Aga's waiting!"

Kallik gave Yakone a hasty nod and ran down the hill, her paws throwing up showers of snow. She realized that Yakone was following at a distance; she could feel her fur prickling.

I wish everything had been different, she thought. *I would have liked a chance to get to know him better.*

Kallik caught up with the others close to the riverbank, but before they reached Aga and the bears around her, they heard a furious bellow. Glancing around, Kallik saw Unalaq charging up to them.

"What are you doing here?" he roared. "You're not welcome. Haven't you realized that by now?"

Aga shouldered her way through the group of bears and stepped forward to confront him. "Stop blustering," she snapped at Unalaq. "These bears have come in peace—haven't you?"

Kallik and Lusa nodded earnestly, though Toklo was glaring at Unalaq as if for two fish tails he would have leaped on him again with teeth and claws bared. Lusa gave him a shove, and he nodded hastily, though his eyes were still hostile.

"Go away, Unalaq," Aga told him. "Take your temper

somewhere else."

Unalaq let out an angry snort and stomped away in the direction of the beach.

"He is an unhappy storm, that bear," Aga muttered, watching him go. "But he's a good hunter, and loyal to us." She gave her head a shake, as if she were dismissing Unalaq from her mind. "But there are only three of you," she went on. "Where is the small brown bear—Ujurak?"

"He died saving us from an avalanche," Kallik explained, forcing her voice not to shake.

"Yes, and the no-claw structure is gone," Lusa added eagerly.

Aga looked puzzled. "What structure?"

Kallik realized that some of the white bears might never have seen what the no-claws were doing in that part of the island. "The no-claws built a tower to take oil from the ground," she explained. "If we hadn't stopped them, they would have destroyed the whole island."

"Ujurak led the caribou to break down the tower," Lusa went on. "The flat-faces are taking all the wreckage away, so the island will be safe from now on."

I hope so, Kallik thought, unable to share Lusa's certainty. *Who knows what the no-claws will do in the future? But for now it is safe, and the spirits have returned.*

Aga nodded slowly. "Thank you. Last night I saw the spirits dancing, and I rejoiced that our ancestors have returned to us." For a moment she was silent; then she went on more briskly, "Illa and Tunerq, you may leave us. I wish to talk to our guests alone."

Illa and Tunerq dipped their heads respectfully and with-drew, to be surrounded by a cluster of excited white bears, all exclaiming over Kissimi. Illa nudged him over to another young she-bear, who bent her head and licked his ears lovingly. A pang of pain pierced Kallik's heart, even as she rejoiced that Kissimi would have a mother.

Aga watched them for a moment. "I can see there are many stories to be told. But for now . . . did you find the cave of stars, with the marks on the wall?" she asked quietly.

"Yes," Lusa replied.

"The other white bears don't know about it," Aga went on. "My mother showed me, and her mother before that, and so on for all the time there have been bears on this island. It is a secret known only to one bear at a time. I will tell Illa when my turn comes to join the Iqniq."

"The stars are—" Lusa began, only to fall silent as Toklo gave her a nudge.

Kallik realized that Lusa wanted to tell Aga about the way the stars in the cave had changed. *But there's no need for that,* she thought. *Perhaps Aga will discover it for herself one day.*

"Everything is safe," Toklo said solemnly, with a long look at Aga.

Aga nodded. "What will you do now?" she asked.

Kallik, Toklo, and Lusa exchanged glances; then Toklo shrugged. "Go home, I suppose," he said.

"That's right," Lusa agreed. "We don't belong here, on the ice. We need to find rivers and trees and sunshine."

"And what about you?" Aga turned to Kallik. "You don't need trees and rivers. You could stay here, if you like."

"That's a great idea!" Yakone put in; the red-pelted bear had padded up to listen without Kallik being aware of him.

Kallik took a deep breath. Aga's offer had surprised her, and Yakone's enthusiastic agreement sent a warm glow through her from snout to paws. She liked the way that these bears lived together, instead of roaming solitarily on the ice. The thought of staying tempted her like the scent of fresh-caught prey. But she knew what her answer had to be.

"Thank you, Aga, but this is not my home. My home is on the Frozen Sea, where the bears are in even greater trouble. And I must try to find my brother, Taqqiq, again. I cannot live without knowing that he is safe and well fed."

Aga nodded. "I understand. Travel well, all of you. I shall think of you each night when I look at the stars."

Kallik wondered whether the wise old bear knew where Ujurak had gone. *Perhaps she'll find out for sure when she next visits the cave of stars. I hope so.*

While Kallik stood in thought, Toklo had turned away. "Come on," he said. "We should get going while the weather is good."

"Feel free to hunt from our seals," Aga invited them.

But Kallik's paws were itching to be gone, and she guessed that her friends felt the same. They would be able to hunt some prey on their way.

"Plants for me!" Lusa exclaimed, making a face. "I've eaten enough seal to last me the rest of my life."

As they headed toward the shore, Kallik spotted Kissimi as he broke away from Illa and the other she-bear and scampered toward her. Tunerq padded after him.

Please, no, Kallik thought, anguished. *Don't ask to come with me, little one. Don't make our parting harder than it need be.*

But Kissimi seemed quite cheerful as he bounced up to her and butted her leg with his head, letting out an excited squeak.

"He'll be fine with us," Tunerq assured Kallik. "I'm going to teach him to hunt seals when he's bigger."

Kissimi puffed out his chest. "Big now!" he announced.

"You'll be a great hunter, little one," Kallik murmured. "Be good and listen to your elders and . . ." Her voice choked, and she bent to nuzzle his head.

"Come on." Toklo gave her a nudge, gruffly sympathetic.

"Good-bye, Kissimi." Kallik felt as though her heart had been trampled by caribou.

"Bye, K'lik." Kissimi touched his nose to hers.

Kallik drew in his scent for the last time and gave the top of his head one final lick. "There. Go to your family," she murmured.

Tunerq dipped his head to her and nudged Kissimi away, back to the other white bears.

Kallik was turning to follow Toklo and Lusa when Yakone stepped up to her and planted himself in front of her. "I don't want you to leave," he said bluntly.

"I'm sorry," Kallik said, a new pain invading her heart. "I wish things could have been different. . . ."

"They can be," Yakone responded. "Let me come with you."

Kallik stared at him, not knowing how to reply. "But this is your home . . ." she began.

"My home is wherever I want it to be," Yakone countered.

Kallik gazed into his eyes. She yearned to say yes, but she shrank from allowing him to make such a momentous decision, to leave his home and his family and everything he had ever known. *He would do that for me?*

"You could be making a terrible mistake," she faltered.

"Maybe. But at least let me be free to make it." Incredibly, Yakone's eyes held a mischievous glint. "Are you going to tell me that you do even worse things than steal cubs?"

Kallik felt a rumble of pleasure rising from deep inside her. "You'll have to wait and find out!"

As she finished speaking, Toklo padded up with Lusa behind him. "What's going on?" he asked, glancing from Kallik to Yakone and back again.

"Yakone wants to travel with us," Kallik explained.

Toklo narrowed his eyes, sizing up the young red-pelted bear. "Well, I guess extra paws for hunting won't hurt," he grunted. "What do you think, Lusa?"

The black bear hesitated, while Kallik waited anxiously for her reply. She knew that Lusa had been hurt by how much time she had spent with Kissimi, and she didn't want her friend to be jealous of Yakone.

There's no need. Lusa will always be my friend. Kallik stretched out a paw, gazing at Lusa as if her eyes could reassure the black she-bear of all her affection and trust.

Finally, to Kallik's relief, Lusa nodded. "We came here as

four," she pronounced. "We should still be four. Ujurak would like that. Let's go."

While Yakone turned back to say good-bye to the other white bears, Kallik gazed up at the sky. She knew that somewhere beyond the blue, Ujurak was watching them. His scent whisked around her, and she heard him whisper.

"I will be with you every step of the way home."

"Thank you," Kallik whispered back.

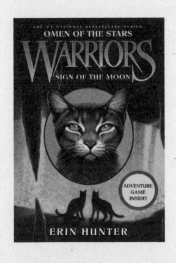

PROLOGUE

Water thundered down from the mountaintop, screening the entrance to the cave with a shimmering cascade. Gray light filtered through it and shadows gathered in the corners of the cavern like soft black wings. Near the sheet of falling water, two kits were scuffling over a bunch of feathers, batting it back and forth and letting out shrill squeals of excitement. The pale tabby fur of the little she-cat and the tom's brown pelt almost blended into the dark stone floor.

At the back of the cave, an old brown tabby tom was crouching in the mouth of a tunnel. His eyes were narrowed, and his amber gaze never left the kits. He was motionless, except for the occasional twitch of his ears.

The tabby kit leaped high into the air, clawing at the feathers; as she landed with the bunch in her paws her brother flung himself on top of her, rolling over and snapping at the feathers with teeth like tiny white thorns.

"That's enough." A gentle voice came from close by as a graceful brown tabby she-cat rose to her paws and padded across to the kits. "Mind you don't get too close to the water.

And Pine, why don't you try jumping high like Lark? You need to practice for when you're a prey-hunter."

"I'd rather be a cave-guard," Pine mewed. "I'd fight every cat that tried to trespass on our territory."

"Well, you can't, because I will," Lark retorted. "I'm going to be a cave-guard *and* hunt prey, so there!"

"That's not how we do things," their mother began; a swift glance over her shoulder showed that she was aware of the old cat watching from the shadows. "Every Tribe kit has to—"

She broke off at the sound of pawsteps coming from the narrow path that led behind the waterfall and into the cave. A broad-shouldered gray-furred cat appeared, followed by the rest of his patrol. Instantly the kits let out squeals of welcome and hurled themselves at him.

"Careful!" Their mother followed and gathered the kits in with her tail. "Your father has been on border patrol. He must be tired."

"I'm fine, Brook." The gray tom blinked at her affectionately and gave her ear a quick lick. "It was an easy trip today."

"Stormfur, I don't know how you can say that!" a black tom put in, shaking water from his pelt as he left the cliff path. "We waste our time and wear out our paws patrolling that border, and for what?"

"Peace and quiet," Stormfur replied, his voice even. "We aren't going to get rid of those cats, even though we do think they're intruders. The best we can hope for is to protect our own territory."

"The whole of the mountains should be our territory!"

the black tom spat.

"Give it a rest, Screech," a dark ginger she-cat meowed, with an irritable twitch of her tail. "Stormfur's right. Things aren't like that anymore."

"But are we safe?" asked Brook. She glanced at the kits who were now tussling over a morsel of rabbit fur.

"The borders are holding, mostly," Stormfur told Brook, a worried look in his amber eyes. "But we did pick up the scent of other cats in a couple of places. And there were eagle feathers scattered on the rock. They've been stealing prey again."

The ginger she-cat shrugged. "There's nothing we can do about that."

"We can't just let it go, Swoop," Stormfur murmured. "Otherwise they'll think they can do exactly what they like, and there was no point in setting the borders in the first place. I think we should increase the patrols and be ready to fight."

"More patrols?" Screech lashed his tail angrily.

"It makes sense to—"

"No!"

Stormfur jumped as a voice rasped out from the shadows and he saw the old tabby cat standing a tail-length away.

"Stoneteller!" he exclaimed. "I didn't see you there."

"Evidently." The old cat's neck fur was bristling and there was a trace of anger in his eyes. "There will be no more patrols," he went on. "The Tribe has enough to eat, and with the thaw approaching, there will soon be more prey: eggs and young birds stolen from nests."

Stormfur looked as if he wanted to argue, but he picked up

a flickering glance from Brook and a tiny shake of her head. Reluctantly he dipped his head to Stoneteller. "Very well."

The old cat stalked away. Making an effort to flatten the ruffled fur on his neck, Stormfur turned to his kits. "Have you behaved yourselves today?"

"They've been very good," Brook told him, her eyes warm. "Lark is growing so strong and sturdy, and Pine jumps really well."

"We've been hunting," Lark announced, pointing with her tail toward the bedraggled lump of feathers. "I caught three eagles!"

"Didn't," Pine contradicted her. "I killed one, or it would have flown away with you!"

Brook met Stormfur's eyes. "I can't seem to make them understand that they'll have separate duties when they're to-bes."

"They shouldn't have to decide now," Stormfur began, only to break off as Brook flicked her tail toward Stoneteller, who was still in earshot. He let out a sigh. "They'll learn," he murmured, a trace of regret in his tone. "Is there any fresh-kill left? I'm starving!"

As Brook led Stormfur over to the fresh-kill pile, to-bes and their mentors headed back into the cave, and Stormfur's kits shot across the cavern floor to intercept them.

"Tell us about outside!" Lark squeaked. "Did you catch any prey?"

"I want to go out," Pine added.

One of the to-bes butted his shoulder gently with his head. "You're too small. An eagle would eat you in one bite."

"No it wouldn't! I'd *fight* it," Pine declared, fluffing up his brown fur.

The to-be let out a *mrrow* of laughter. "I'd like to see that! But you still have to wait until you're eight moons old."

"Mouse dung!"

Stoneteller stood watching the to-bes and kits romping together for a few heartbeats before he headed back toward his tunnel. As he approached it, a gray-brown she-cat rose to her paws and padded up to him.

"Stoneteller, I must talk to you."

The old tabby glared at her. "I've said all I have to say. You know that, Bird."

Bird did not reply, merely stood there waiting, until the old cat let out a long sigh. "Come, then. But don't expect any different answers."

Stoneteller led the way into the second tunnel, and Bird followed. The sounds of the young cats died away behind them, replaced by the steady drip of water.

The tunnel led into a cave much smaller than the one the cats had left. Pointed stones rose up from the floor and hung down from the roof. Some of them had joined in the middle, as if the cats were threading their way through a stone forest. Water trickled down the stones and the cave walls to make pools on the floor; their surface reflected a faint gray light from a jagged crack in the roof. All was silent except for the drip of water and the distant roaring of the falls, now sunk to a whisper.

Stoneteller turned to face Bird. "Well?"

"We've spoken about this before. You know you should have chosen your successor long ago."

The old cat let out a snort of disgust. "There's time yet."

"Don't tell that to me," Bird retorted. "My mother was your littermate. I know exactly how old you are. You were chosen from that litter by the Tribe's previous Healer, the last Teller of the Pointed Stones. You have served the Tribe well, but you can't expect to stay here forever. Sooner or later you will be summoned to the Tribe of Endless Hunting. You *must* choose the next Stoneteller!"

"Why?" Bird flinched at the harshness of the old cat's retort but Stoneteller continued. "So that the Tribe can go on, generation after generation, scrabbling their lives from these uncaring stones?"

Bird's voice quivered with shock when she replied. "This is our *home*! We have earned the right to live here many times over! We fought off the trespassers, remember?" She padded closer to Stoneteller and held out one paw appealingly. "How can you think of betraying our ancestors by not preserving what they began?"

Stoneteller turned his head away; there was a flash of something in his eyes that warned Bird he was not telling her everything.

At that moment a thin claw-scratch of new moon appeared from behind a cloud; its light sliced down through the hole in the cave roof and struck one of the pools of water, turning its surface to silver. Stoneteller gazed at it.

"It is the night of the new moon," he murmured. "The

night when the Tribe of Endless Hunting speaks to me from the sky, through reflections in the water. Very well, Bird That Rides the Wind. I promise you I will look for signs tonight."

"Thank you," Bird whispered. Touching Stoneteller affectionately on the shoulder with her tail-tip, she padded quietly out of the cave. "Good luck," she mewed as she disappeared into the tunnel.

When she had gone, Stoneteller approached the edge of the pool and looked into the water. Then he raised one paw and brought it down with force on the surface, shattering the reflection into shards of light that flickered and died.

"I will never listen to you again!" Each word was forced out through bared teeth. "We trusted the Tribe of Endless Hunting, but you deserted us when we most needed your help."

Turning his back on the pool, he paced among the pointed stones, his claws scraping against the rough cave floor. "I hate what the Tribe has become!" he snarled. "I hate how we have taken on Clan ways. Why could we not survive alone?" Halting beneath the rift in the roof, he raised his head with a burning gaze that challenged the moon. "Why did you bring us here if we were doomed to fail?"

CHAPTER 1

Dovepaw slid out through the thorn tunnel and stood waiting in the forest for her sister, Ivypaw, and their mentors to join her. A hard frost had turned every blade of grass into a sharp spike under her paws, and from the bare branches of the trees, icicles glimmered in the gray dawn light. Dovepaw shivered as claws of cold probed deeply into her fur. Newleaf was still a long way off.

Dovepaw's belly was churning with anxiety, and her tail drooped.

This is your warrior assessment, she told herself. *It's the best thing that can happen to an apprentice. So why don't you feel excited?*

She knew the answer to her question. Too much had happened during the moons of her apprenticeship: important events beside which even the thrill of becoming a warrior paled into insignificance. Taking a deep breath, Dovepaw lifted her tail as she heard the pawsteps of cats coming through the tunnel. She couldn't let the cats who were assessing her see how uneasy she was. She needed to do her best to show them that she was ready to be a warrior.

Dovepaw's mentor, Lionblaze, was the first cat to emerge, fluffing his golden tabby pelt against the early morning chill. Spiderleg followed him closely; Dovepaw gave the skinny black warrior a dubious glance, wondering what it would be like to have him assessing her as well as Lionblaze. Spiderleg looked very stern.

I wish it was just Lionblaze, Dovepaw thought. *Too bad Firestar decided that we should have two judges.*

Cinderheart appeared next, followed closely by her apprentice, Ivypaw, and last of all Millie, who was to be Ivypaw's second assessor. Dovepaw's whiskers quivered as she looked at her sister. Ivypaw looked small and scared, and her dark blue eyes were shadowed with exhaustion.

Padding closer, Dovepaw gave Ivypaw's ear an affectionate lick. "Hey, you'll be fine," she murmured.

Ivypaw turned her head away.

She doesn't even talk to me anymore, Dovepaw thought wretchedly. *She's always busy somewhere else when I try to get close to her. And she cries out in her dreams.* Dovepaw pictured how her sister twitched and batted her paws when they were sleeping side by side in the apprentices' den. She knew that Ivypaw was visiting the Dark Forest, spying on behalf of ThunderClan because Jayfeather and Lionblaze had asked her to, but when she tried to ask her sister what happened there, Ivypaw only replied that there was nothing new to report.

"I suggest we head for the abandoned Twoleg nest," Spiderleg announced. "It's sheltered, so there's a good chance of prey."

Lionblaze blinked as if he was surprised that Spiderleg was trying to take over the assessment, but then nodded and led the way through the trees in the direction of the old Twoleg path. Dovepaw quickened her pace to pad beside him, and the other cats followed.

"Are you ready?" Lionblaze asked.

Dovepaw jumped, startled out of her worries about her sister. "Sorry," she mewed. "I was thinking about Ivypaw. She looks so tired."

Lionblaze glanced back at the silver-and-white she-cat, then at Dovepaw, shock and anxiety mingling in his amber eyes. "I guess the Dark Forest training is taking its toll," he muttered.

"And whose fault is that?" Dovepaw flashed back at him. However urgent it was to find out what the cats of the Dark Forest were plotting, it wasn't fair of Lionblaze and Jayfeather to put the whole burden on her sister's shoulders.

Ivypaw isn't even a warrior yet!

Lionblaze let out a sigh that told Dovepaw he agreed with her privately, but wasn't prepared to say so. "I'm not going to talk about that now," he meowed. "It's time for you to concentrate on your assessment."

Dovepaw gave an irritable shrug.

Lionblaze halted as the old Twoleg nest came into sight. Dovepaw picked up traces of herb scent from Jayfeather's garden, though most of the stems and leaves were blackened by frost. She could hear the faint scutterings of prey in the grass and in the debris under the trees. Spiderleg was right: This would be a good spot to hunt.

"Okay," Lionblaze began. "First we want to assess your tracking skills. Cinderheart, what do you want Ivypaw to catch?"

"We'll go for mice. Okay, Ivypaw?"

The silver tabby gave a tense nod.

"But not inside the old Twoleg nest," Millie added. "That would be too easy."

"I know." Dovepaw thought her sister sounded too weary to put one paw in front of another, let alone catch mice. But she headed off into the trees without hesitating; Cinderheart and Millie followed at a distance.

Dovepaw watched until the frostbitten bracken hid Ivypaw from her sight, then sent out her extended senses to track her as she padded behind the abandoned nest toward the group of pine trees. Mice were squeaking and scuffling among the fallen needles; Dovepaw hoped that her sister would scent them and make a good catch.

She was concentrating so hard on following Ivypaw that she forgot about her own assessment until Spiderleg flicked his tail-tip over her ear.

"Hey!" she meowed, spinning around to face the black warrior.

"Lionblaze *said* he'd like you to try for a squirrel," Spiderleg meowed. "If you're sure you want to become a warrior, that is."

"I'm sure," Dovepaw growled. "Sorry, Lionblaze."

Lionblaze was standing just behind Spiderleg, looking annoyed. Dovepaw was angry with herself for missing his order, but even more with Spiderleg for being so obnoxious about it.

It's mouse-brained to have two judges, she grumbled to herself. *Mentors have been assessing their own apprentices for more seasons than there are leaves on the trees!*

Raising her head, she tasted the air and brightened when she picked up a nearby scent of squirrel. It was coming from the other side of a clump of bramble; setting her paws down lightly, Dovepaw skirted the thorns until she came out into a small clearing and spotted the squirrel nibbling a nut at the foot of an ivy-covered oak tree.

A wind was rising, rattling the bare branches. Dovepaw slid around the edge of the clearing, using the bracken for cover, until she was downwind of her prey. Its scent flooded strongly over her, making her jaws water.

Dropping into her best hunter's crouch, Dovepaw began to creep up on the squirrel. But she couldn't resist sending out her senses just once more to check on Ivypaw, and she jumped as she picked up the tiny shriek, quickly cut off, of a mouse under her sister's claws.

Her uncontrolled movement rustled a dead leaf, and instantly the squirrel fled up the tree, its bushy tail flowing out behind it. Dovepaw bounded across the grass and hurled herself up the trunk, but the squirrel had vanished into the branches. She clung to an ivy stem, trying to listen for movement beyond the wind and the creaking of the tree, but it was no use.

"Mouse dung!" she spat, letting herself drop to the ground again.

Spiderleg stalked up to her. "For StarClan's sake, what do you think you're doing?" he demanded. "A kit just out of the nursery could have caught that squirrel! It's a good thing none of the other Clans saw you, or they'd think ThunderClan doesn't know how to train its apprentices."

Dovepaw's neck fur bristled. "Have you never missed a catch?" she muttered under her breath.

"Well?" the black warrior demanded. "Let's hear what you did wrong."

"It wasn't all bad," Lionblaze put in before Dovepaw could answer. "That was good stalking work, when you moved downwind of the squirrel."

Dovepaw flashed him a grateful look. "I guess I got distracted for a heartbeat," she admitted. "I moved a leaf, and the squirrel heard me."

"And you could have been faster chasing it," Spiderleg told her. "You might have caught it if you'd put on a bit more speed."

Dovepaw nodded glumly. *We haven't all got legs as long as yours!* "Does this mean I've failed my assessment?"

Spiderleg flicked his ears but didn't answer. "I'm going to see how Millie is getting on with Ivypaw," he announced, darting off toward the abandoned nest.

Dovepaw gazed at her mentor. "Sorry," she meowed.

"I guess you must be nervous," Lionblaze responded. "You're much better than that on an ordinary hunting patrol."

Now that she was facing failure, Dovepaw realized just how much she wanted to be a warrior. *Being a warrior is way better than being part of the prophecy with my so-called special powers.* She tensed as another thought struck her. *What if Ivypaw is made a warrior and I'm not?*

Her sister deserved it, Dovepaw knew. She didn't have any special powers of her own, but every night she put herself in danger to spy for Lionblaze and Jayfeather in the Dark Forest.

Ivypaw's better than me. I can't even catch a stupid squirrel!

"Cheer up," Lionblaze meowed. "Your assessment isn't over yet. But for StarClan's sake, *concentrate!*"

"I'll do my best," Dovepaw promised. "What's next?"

In answer, Lionblaze angled his ears in the direction they had come from. Dovepaw turned to see Icecloud picking her way across the frosty grass.

"Hi," the white she-cat mewed. "Brambleclaw sent me to help you."

"You're just in time." Lionblaze dipped his head. "The next part of the assessment is hunting with a partner," he explained to Dovepaw.

Dovepaw brightened up; she enjoyed hunting as part of a team, and Icecloud would be easy to work with. But she was disconcerted when Icecloud looked at her with her head cocked to one side and asked, "What do you want me to do?"

"I . . . er . . ." Dovepaw wasn't used to giving orders to a warrior. *Come on, mouse-brain! Shape up!*

"Let's try for a blackbird," she suggested. "Icecloud, your white pelt is going to be a problem, though."

"Tell me about it," the white she-cat mewed ruefully.

"So we'll have to find somewhere you can stay in cover until the last moment. When we find a bird, I'll stalk it and try to drive it toward you."

"You'll need to make sure it doesn't fly off, or—"

Lionblaze interrupted Icecloud's warning with a meaningful cough.

"Oops, sorry," Icecloud mewed. "I forgot. Go on, Dovepaw."

"Blackbirds often nest just beyond the old Twoleg den," Dovepaw went on after a moment's thought. "I know it's too early for them to be nesting, but it might be worth scouting there for good places."

Lionblaze nodded encouragingly. "Then what?"

"Well . . . the ground slopes away there. Icecloud could take cover down the slope."

"Okay, let's see you do it," Lionblaze meowed.

Dovepaw had only taken a few pawsteps when Spiderleg reappeared, shouldering his way through the bracken. He said nothing; Dovepaw's paws itched with curiosity to find out how her sister was getting on, but there was no time to ask. It felt weird to be padding a pace or two ahead of Icecloud, as if she was leading a patrol, and weirder still to be the one who was making the decisions. Panic pricked at Dovepaw, like ants crawling through her pelt. Her head felt as empty as an echoing cave, as if everything she had ever learned had flown away like birds from a branch.

I've spent more time eavesdropping on other Clans than training to be a warrior!

Dovepaw wanted to finish her assessment without using her special powers. *Ivypaw doesn't have them, so it's only fair.* But it was hard to switch her senses off when she was constantly wondering what her sister was up to. Besides, when she tried to focus on the sounds that were closest to her, she felt trapped and smothered by the trees.

How do the other cats cope? she wondered. *I can hardly catch my breath!*

Dovepaw led the way up the old Thunderpath, then struck off into the trees where the blackbirds nested. Icecloud followed her closely, while Lionblaze and Spiderleg hung back, observing. Sliding into a hazel thicket, Dovepaw raised her tail to warn Icecloud to keep back, where her white pelt wouldn't alert any possible prey. Her paws tingled with satisfaction when she spotted a blackbird, pecking at the ground underneath a hazel bush.

Dovepaw drew back. "Go that way, down the slope," she whispered to Icecloud, signaling with her tail. "I'll scare the bird and send it in your direction."

Icecloud nodded and crept away, silent as a wisp of white mist. Dovepaw watched her until she was out of sight; without meaning to, she extended her senses to track the white she-cat even after she disappeared. Puzzled, she realized that Icecloud's paws sounded different on the ground.

Something isn't right.